Spitfire

By J.R. Zimmer
Book Four
Fisher/Lafayette Saga

Badlanders Press

Spitfire

©2020 by Janette Walker

Model image Credit:

(c) lofilolo www.fotosearch.com

Cover design by Janette Walker

ISBN 9781737626916

Fisher/Lafayette Saga

If There Hadn't Been You

Now and Forever

Someone Like You

Spitfire

Something Magical

The Dreamer

Eagle's Wolf

Coming Home (Free Ebook when signing up for my newsletter at www.jrzimmer.com. Not available anywhere else.)

You can find J.R. Zimmer at:

Web site: www.jrzimmer.com

Email: jrzimmer17@yahoo.com)

For

My parents

JoAnn and Albert (Al) Schrenk

Thank you for everything you did for me.

(I miss you dad, every day.)

Spitfire

by J.R. Zimmer

Prelude

May 1981

Was he going to kill her?

Amanda Anderson quivered with fear and apprehension as his ice-blue eyes continued their intense stare. Once she thought his eyes were breathtaking; now they were angry and hateful.

And definitely full of rage.

She supposed she could not blame him for what he was so obviously feeling as he stood there, glaring. And she admitted she had brought this hatred upon herself. But she would not apologize for what she'd done.

Hadn't she warned him? It was a pity he hadn't taken her seriously when she told him what she could make happen if he kept refusing to give her what she wanted from him.

Still wanted from him, but now that he experienced her wrath, she doubted he was any more willing to comply with her wishes.

"Why?" he hissed, causing Amanda to jerk with surprise. He had been standing there, in the middle of her living room, for well over two minutes, not saying anything. Only holding her captive with those fury filled eyes.

She hadn't anticipated he might somehow escape from prison.

Her eyes left his for a moment, taking in the change in his appearance. He had been thinner when he first came to work

1

at the ranch, a little over a year ago. Now he was more muscular in all the right places. His dark brown hair, once cropped short, hung to his shoulders, kept back by a blue bandana tied around his forehead.

The past six months had enhanced his handsomeness and sexual allure. The only physical difference since his time in prison was a fading red mark located directly under his chin. As though someone had thought to slice his throat but missed.

He was positively yummy to look at, even in his rage. Regardless of thinking her life might be in danger, Amanda's body tingled with sexual tension.

She forced herself to relax. Perhaps he learned his lesson and was here to, finally, comply with her desire, though she would obviously have to calm him down.

In a purr, she said, "Now, Jake, darling...."

"Why!?" his outburst caused her to jerk back.

He advanced, grabbed her shoulders, and shook her until her teeth rattled. "God damn it, why?!"

For one moment, her lust was forgotten as she wondered, once again, if he were here to kill her and she could do nothing if that was his intent.

Nor was there anyone here to prevent Jake from following through with his intent, whatever it might be. She was alone at the ranch tonight. Her husband left a few hours ago, traveling to New York on some business trip she could not care less about. The few hired hands were gone for the evening, doing whatever they did for entertainment, and the housekeeper had the night off.

For one fleeting second, she wondered how long it would be before anyone found her body.

Abruptly he released her. She fell back. The air rushed from her lungs as she landed hard on the couch.

He loomed over her, and the image that brought to mind had her heart pounding with the thought, the anticipation, that he was going to take advantage of her.

She positively hoped that was what he was here to do. She would have hated having died without knowing what it was like to have him between her legs as he pounded into her.

She had spent the first three months of his employment to this ranch desperately trying to seduce him, without results and much to the chagrin of her vanity. She was a woman who could have any man she chose at the snap of her fingers.

But not him. Oh no, he was the one man who had rejected her time and again. It enraged her and motivated her to fabricate the lie that resulted in his incarceration.

She found witnesses to confirm her accusations. All male, of course. What she had had to do for each of them, for their claims to have observed the alleged theft of her husband's prized Appaloosa stallion, had been immensely satisfying for each of them.

She was, admittedly, a slut.

Breathlessly she asked, "Are you going to rape me?"

His face contorted as though a foul odor rapidly entered the room. "I don't fuck old ladies," he snapped.

Her face flamed hot. "How dare you!"

"How dare I!?" his explosion vibrated throughout the entire twenty-seven room mansion. "You accused me of stealin'

3

Thomas's purebred stallion! You got me thrown into prison! And all because I wouldn't screw you, and you have the fuckin' gall to be angry with me?!"

Amanda pushed herself up from the couch and stood before him as though ready to battle. "What did you come here for, Jake?" she shouted back, placing her fists on her slim hips. Evidently, she was wrong on both of her assumptions.

He was not here to kill her, and he was not going to take his pants off.

"I want to know why you made up that lie about me! I was never anywhere near Thomas' appaloosa that night, and you know it!"

"Of course, I do! But I warned you that last time you refused to take me to bed. I get what I want, or there are consequences."

"So, you sent the law after me?!" Hearing her admit the truth almost rendered him speechless.

How was it that throughout his entire life, he kept winding up running into spiteful women who only wanted one thing from him?

But this one was absolutely the worst of them all.

When he came to this ranch to work cattle, and everything else required concerning the operation of the place, this woman threw herself at him repeatedly. He did not deny the fact she was pretty for a woman her age. He suspected she might be around fifty or fifty-five, but she did not appeal to him.

Never had.

But out of all those women he'd encountered over the years, this one had been vindictive enough to accomplish having him thrown in jail because he said no to her invitations to bed her.

Not that the jury sitting in that kangaroo court heard that reason. They convicted him of stealing a horse he hadn't, anyway.

It was too unbelievable.

He should have hightailed it out of there the first time she came on to him. But he had not expected she was malicious enough to manipulate a tale that would convince the judge to send him to prison.

Amanda, he discovered, had the majority of men in the area at her beck and call.

Perhaps if he had swallowed his pride and contacted his father, the trumped-up charges would have been stopped instantly. But he had not believed anyone would believe that ridiculous accusation of hers. By the time he realized they actually were going to lock him up, it had been too late.

Would he have called his old man had he known what the outcome of that joke of a trial was going to be? Hard to say, although he hated his parents enough to consider the answer would have been, no.

Amanda shrugged.

She moved away from him, her slim figure settling gracefully into the plush recliner next to the couch. Once comfortable, she studied him openly. He was the most handsome man she had ever encountered, and young, about twenty-five or twenty-six, if her memory served. His muscled arms,

showcased by the torn-off sleeves of his dull gray T-shirt, instantly revived her fantasy of having him in her bed.

She sighed inwardly. How dare Jake Harper refuse her?

"Why, Amanda?" his voice was not as loud as before, but the fury was still there. "Just because I wouldn't...."

"Exactly!" she screeched. "I have never been refused!"

He stared at her. This whole situation would be laughable if it had not honestly happened. No one in their right mind would believe his story if he told it, and he was not about to tell anyone this ludicrous tale.

Six months elapsed before the investigation into Jake's case could start, spanning the time between the appointment of the new sheriff and the pending election. The investigation was delayed because the former, corrupt sheriff, who'd been Amanda's pawn, intentionally sabotaged the office, leaving records and operations in such disarray that an immediate start was rendered impossible.

Jake would always be grateful the new officer was law-abiding enough to investigate his case. The work revealed the central lie: Jake was in prison for stealing a horse that was still grazing on the Anderson ranch. Had Jake actually taken the appaloosa, the animal would undoubtedly be missing.

Maybe he should have stayed in Texas. He had gone from one boiling pot into another, and he would like to know how he'd managed that.

Well, this bad dream was about to take care of itself. As long as Jake played his part and did not give in to the urge to strangle Amanda, she would take his place in a prison cell.

SPITFIRE

Jake had never been a man who would hit a woman. Nor had he ever desired to kill one, but he wanted to kill this one. He itched to wrap his hands around her neck and squeeze the life out of her.

But he was not going back to jail. He would avoid that like the plague. But it would satisfy him to know Amanda would no longer be free to cause some other unsuspecting guy hardship. And it elated him, knowing he would have a clean slate once this drama played out.

Man, oh man, had he definitely learned that hell hath no fury as a woman scorned.

"I have a hard time understandin' why," Jake told her, "the wife of a prominent rancher, would sink so low as to destroy someone else's life merely because their advances were turned down."

Amanda reminded him so much of his mother it made him sick.

The mention of her aging husband brought contempt to her voice. She married Thomas Anderson five years ago only because he was rich, and she liked beautiful things.

"I detest my husband!" she shouted, the veins in her neck standing out. "He is an old man and hasn't a clue how to make love to a woman. He should have died years ago! He is eighty-five years old, for Christ's sake. But no, the old buzzard keeps ongoing. I'm hoping one of the men around here will want me enough to get rid of him for me since Tomas doesn't seem capable of dropping dead on his own!"

Footsteps echoed from within the outer hallway.

Amanda froze. Her eyes were wide as she turned toward the sound. Jake's face remained impassive when he saw the two people entering the room. He knew they were in the house, staying out of Amanda's sight until the right moment to reveal themselves came along.

Amanda's eyes bulged when she saw not only her husband but the new sheriff with him.

She had tried to get that new lawman into her bed. Not because she found him attractive, but men were easily enough controlled if given the right motivation. In Amanda's experience, the right motivation had always been sex.

Obviously, she was losing her touch.

It took the conniving woman three seconds to recover from her shock. She hoped Thomas's hearing was worse than his lovemaking.

She leaped from the chair and rushed to the elderly man's side. "Darling!" she cried, "Oh, thank heavens you're here! He came here to kill me!" She threw her arms around Thomas as though her life depended upon it.

"Kill you, dear wife?" Thomas Anderson questioned tonelessly, feeling as though his advanced years had sped up on him. It was hard to admit to making mistakes and having married Amanda was the biggest mistake of his life.

No. He knew that was not true. His biggest mistake had been allowing Amanda to convince him Jake Harper had stolen from him when the kid was a hard worker and an honest man. However, Thomas's eyes were wide open now, and he saw the gold-digger for what she was: a calculating bitch. But he was not the one to have suffered Amanda's vindictiveness.

SPITFIRE

Jake Harper had been on the receiving end, and Thomas wondered how one made amends to someone who had been allowed to lose six months of their life because of his weakness? If Harper never forgave him, he would understand.

Thomas answered his soon to be ex-wife by saying, "I don't believe he will kill you, but if the Sheriff weren't here, I would be pleased to do so myself."

Sheriff Watts sighed, "Sorry, Thomas. I wish these were the old days, and I could simply turn my back. I wouldn't blame you a bit if you wrung her scrawny neck."

Amanda noticeably stiffened. "Thomas, what is this all about?" She pushed tears past her lashes as she tried to look innocent in the performance she was about to give. If someone were to give out awards in the real world for falsifying emotion, Amanda would have owned several of them by now.

She reached out, tentatively running her hand down the sleeve of his arm, confused when her touch did not take away the hate she saw for her in his eyes. The old buzzard should be assuring her he had not meant to imply he wanted her dead. Never mind the fact she daily hoped he would keel over; this ranch would then be hers, and she would gladly sell it off to the first bidder. But Thomas was not embracing her. Was, in fact, looking at her with so much hate and anger, she had a terrifying moment to consider that she was about to lose everything she had worked so hard for.

"Thomas!" she exclaimed in fear, and it wasn't an act now.

Thomas pushed his wife away from him and shoved her toward the sheriff. "Get her out of my house."

Sheriff Watts wasted no time handcuffing the fifty-five-year-old aging beauty.

"Thomas!" Amanda screamed as she tried to resist arrest. How dare they do this to her!

She cursed her husband, the Sheriff, Jake, and God almighty to hell and back as the sheriff forcefully pulled her from the room.

Jake watched as the Sheriff and Amanda disappeared from sight and marveled as the woman continued to insist she did nothing wrong. Evidently, the woman believed she was the victim this night.

Jake hoped Amanda would rot in jail for a good long time. But he was honest enough with himself to know she would probably seduce all the guards in the place to make her stay behind bars enjoyable, and not a punishment.

Thomas Anderson stepped forward, extending an over-stuffed envelope toward Jake. "I can only say I'm sorry, kid," Thomas said, sighing and shaking his head. "I should have known all those months ago you were innocent. I've suspected Amanda of infidelity for years, but I kept turning my back on the truth, desperate to believe she loved me. But what she did to you..." Thomas trailed off, unable to finish the thought. There were no words sufficient to give the younger man. Nothing he could say would return the months robbed from Jake because Thomas had been such a fool.

Debating whether to accept Thomas's offering, Jake eyed the envelope which, he knew, was a blatant payment for a guilty conscience.

After a moment he took the packet, justifying it as back pay
for the six months of life he'd lost. The money was meaning-
less to him; he planned to donate it to charity. He didn't utter
a word to the man who held the power to have shut down that
entire mockery of a trial before it began.

As Jake turned away, Tomas said, "There's enough cash in
there," Thomas indicated the envelope he held in his hand,
"to get you started wherever you wind up." He sighed, adding, "There's also a letter of recommendation- " Thomas
looked at him, moisture in his eyes. "I don't know what else
to say. Thanks for your help lacks in its intent. You've paid a
high price for my turning my back on Amanda's selfish
ways." He offered his hand for a parting shake but did not
take offense when the younger man did not accept it.

Jake clutched the envelope in his fist as he made his way
to the front door. He was so completely finished with the
whole ordeal that he didn't even spare the old man the cour-
tesy of telling him to fuck off. Walking straight through the
door, Jake headed directly to the brand-new, jacked-up Ford
pickup truck. The truck was yet another payoff from Thomas
Anderson, a replacement for Jake's vehicle, which the man
had sold while Jake was in prison.

That probably pissed him off more than anything else. He
loved that truck. It was custom painted with wild horses on
either side.

This truck was plain ol' black.

Yuck.

Well, he supposed he could get this one painted but did not
know if he wanted to bother. Custom paint jobs took time,

and Jake was not planning to stay around here longer than necessary.

Jake tossed the envelope into the glove compartment without looking at its contents. He knew the sizable amount of hundred-dollar bills it contained.

Gazing out the windshield of the truck, he almost laughed as he thought of that money. If Anderson knew how much Jake was worth, he probably would not have been as generous with his guilty conscious payoff.

Looking at the road leading from this ranch, Jake had no idea where he wanted to go next.

He did know he would not go back home to Texas.

Turning the ignition key, Jake sat back in the seat and almost broke out in hysterical laughter. It struck him funny, in a cynical way, that when he had left Texas to be rid of his mother, he had found her clone in a little nothing of a town north of Casper, Wyoming.

Chapter One

The child stood in the doorway of his parent's room watching as his mother, sitting in front of the vanity mirror, applied cosmetics to her already impossibly beautiful face. The child, although only five years old, knew his mother was lovely.

He could not remember a time when he had not known this fact. And, if for some unforeseen reason he would think differently, there were countless people in this Texas community to remind him. Whenever he was with his mother in town, people they passed would whisper among themselves, "Oh, there goes Clair Harper. I declare she is the most beautiful creature in this state."

Men would whistle in a way that disturbed the child but caused the recipient to smile coyly over her shoulder at them and wink in such a way the boy would frown. It did not seem right that his mother would look at other men like that when she never gave the same affection to her husband.

His father was not at home. Gone for the weekend, attending a horse sale in Dallas. Gregory Harper's one true passion seemed to be horses. The man built an Appaloosa horse empire from the ground up, and today that ranch was world-famous for the trophy-winning mounts produced each year.

Young Jake had gained his love of horses from his father. Above anything, he would rather be with his father in the corrals, working the horses, then sitting with his nanny reading books. Or learning some silly nonsense Clair thought he should be educated on. Such as the violin, which was her latest idea to add culture to her only child. Jake shuddered with

the thought. He hated the squawking instrument more than the piano she gifted him last year for his fourth birthday.

Clair wanted, for reasons known only to herself, her son to be musically inclined when there was not any talent. Jake grew to hate the sight of the grand piano with each passing lesson.

The grand piano now sat in the ballroom, alone and forgotten. Thank God the instructor had finally dared to inform Clair her son did not have any talent for the ivory keyed instrument.

The woman's honesty had gotten her fired. But Jake felt liberated when the woman's bags were packed, and she was gone. He was free to enjoy his toy trucks in the sandbox in the backyard whenever he wasn't working horses with his father. He may have recently turned five, but it was clear to anyone who cared to notice that the child was born for the saddle. That was his natural talent, and one his mother refused to acknowledge. It was her belief that anything resembling Gregory Harper must be crushed. One month later, she handed Jake the violin, insisted he learn it, and refused his pleads to ride the ranch with his father.

Jake vowed to find some way to break that new instrument of torture, and didn't care one whit that Clair would become enraged by the act of rebellion. Fortunately, it never came to that. His father, seizing a rare moment of backbone, took a stand against his wife and told Clair to stop trying to make his son a sissy.

For the time being, Jake was free from cursed musical instruction. If Clair knew precisely how much her son relished

SPITFIRE

that fact, she would have instantly found some other device to push into his hands. But Jake was smart enough to keep his joy to himself. It was that or have Clair in an angry rage.

The boy realized his mother was no longer focused on her self-pampering when he caught her looking at his image in the mirror's reflection. Their gazes locked: hers filled with disapproval, his with sadness and loneliness.

If only she would love him. Even a little. Better still if he would not desire her attention. But he was only a child, and she was his mother. He longed for the affection she held back from him.

Clair sighed and turned eloquently towards him. The carefully waxed brows that normally arched gracefully over her almond-shaped blue eyes lowered in an unattractive manner as she regarded him for several moments before speaking. "Why are you not in bed?"

The tone he knew well enough. It told him his mother wished he were anywhere but where she was.

He had interrupted her, and she was not happy about it.

"I," he hesitated. "I cannot sleep. Would you read me a story?"

Her laugh was dismissive. "Go find Alice. You have a nanny. She will be more than happy to read to you." Clair turned back to the mirror, picked up one of her cosmetic brushes, and began stroking her face with it, dismissing him with, "It is what she gets paid for, for heaven's sake."

Although he was aware she would respond in such a manner, it didn't stop him from asking. He had predicted her reaction, and it only fueled his rebellious spirit. "Papa would

read to me!" he declared bravely, standing tall with his head held high, challenging her to refute his statement.

"Well," Clair sneered, "he is not here now, is he?"

The boy hung his head, refusing to give in to the urge to cry. Clair would like it if she knew she had struck his heart, but he learned early enough not to show her the power she had to hurt him.

He swallowed a few times, trying to find a voice that would not betray him when a loud buzzing sound seemed to come from somewhere distant. It was faint at first, then louder as the room before him faded to mist, and his eyes snapped open to the here and now.

Jake ripped the alarm clock from the nightstand and threw it against the wall.

He fell back heavily onto the bed as his foggy brain reminded him, he was no longer a little boy. He was a grown man, in a hotel room, and the alarm clock he had broken did not belong to him.

"Fuck," he groaned as he reached for the spare pillow and covered his face with it. He hated those memories, those intrusive dreams. He needed no reminders as to why he was not in Texas anymore.

As far as he was concerned, his parents were dead to him.

At least the dream had not been one of Clair after he turned seventeen. That's when she began giving him the attention no son wanted from their mother.

It made his skin crawl.

He viciously shook his head, wanting to shake the past away.

SPITFIRE

Sitting up, he reached for the television controller. Flipping the TV on, he placed his feet on the floor and headed for the bathroom. He might as well shower and checkout. The sooner he was out of Wyoming, the better. He would have made it across the border last night if it had not been so late in the evening when all that business with Amanda took place. But once he hit the highway, and the miles rolled away, he felt the tension in him wearing him down. By the time he reached Gillette, he decided to spend the night here before moving on to he did not know where.

After the shower, he wiped the fogged-up mirror with a single swipe of the towel he used to dry off with.

He finished shaving and regarded his reflection. While women swooned over his looks, he cursed them. The mirror showed his blue eyes, but it failed to reflect the deep-seated anger and hardness that had formed him over the years. He wondered what he had done to deserve a life marked with nothing but ill fate when it came to women.

He sighed heavily and pushed the question down. He needed time to regroup from the last few months, and he wanted to be someplace where there wasn't some damn deceitful female hanging around.

For a moment, he considered cutting his hair back to a more conservative style but knowing the longer locks would piss Clair off had him forgetting the notion. There was nothing more enjoyable than going against mommy dearest to give him a fresh start to the day.

He dressed in a pair of faded jeans and a short-sleeved T-shirt and tied a blue bandana around his forehead to keep the

hair from his eyes. After that, he packed up the meager items he bothered to bring inside with him last night and headed out of the room to the main lobby.

He ignored the flirtatious blonde behind the counter as much as he could during the checkout process. She was not holding her interest in him at bay, but he was not in the mood for anything other than breakfast.

When he asked her where he could get a decent stack of pancakes, her answering frown told him she was not used to being ignored in such a manner.

Too bad for her, he thought as he picked up his duffle bag from where he dropped it on the lobby floor and headed out the door.

He did not give her another thought for the rest of his life.

He found the little café the girl directed him to without a hitch. Hell, if a person got lost in Gillette, Wyoming, they did not have the brains of an apple peel.

A waitress showed him to a corner booth. He placed his order immediately, without glancing at a menu, and then asked if there was a newspaper he could read while he waited.

"Sure, Sugar," the middle-aged woman drawled, snapped the gum she was chewing, and winked at him. "I can find yah one." And she did, in record time. "There you go, Sugar." She winked again. "Anything else I can do for you?"

Inwardly Jake shuddered. Couldn't women leave him alone?

"No," he answered, "thanks," and he snapped the paper open in a dismissive gesture. He felt, rather than saw, the

woman's disappointed frown before she left him to move onto another table and leaving him blissfully alone.

He scanned the news and found nothing of interest.

He turned to the help-wanted section on a whim. It wasn't that he needed employment, as he was, in fact, quite wealthy, having inherited a substantial trust fund from his grandparents when he was ten. However, having cut all ties to his parents, he preferred not to touch that account. His primary motivation was to maintain secrecy about his location and proving to his mother; correction, his parents, that he was perfectly capable of succeeding without relying on the Harper family fortune.

He knew, with absolute certainty, that if he touched his account, the bank manager, Mr. Todd, would run straight to Clair and reveal where the money had been sent. Jake was determined to prevent that from happening. Maintaining his secrecy was also why he contacted absolutely no one at the ranch following his arrest on the bogus charge. The thought of reaching out for help never once formed in his mind, not even after he was imprisoned.

As far as anyone knew, he was not related to the rich Texas Harpers, and he intended it to remain that way for possibly the rest of his life.

As he scanned the paper, his eyes fell on a notice that seemed to leap off the page at him. The lengthy size of the ad would draw eyes, but its contents spoke to Jake in such a way he could not resist rereading it:

Wanted: Full-time working Foreman.

*F & L Ranch is a family-owned establishment located 20
miles South of Medora, ND.
We are seeking a single, mature, honest, hard-working man
between the ages of 25-30, who would be a full-time assistant Foreman. Expected to help maintain headquarters,
string fences, organize guided tours, and oversee part-time
summer employees. Must have excellent communication
skills and enjoy being around children. Experienced horseman required, able to start young horses, maintain equipment, weld, trim, and shoe. Help with hunting tours during
the winter season and anything else needed by the head of
family. The F & L Ranch believes that ranching is far more
than a job and is more than a career. It's a lifestyle. Excellent pay and benefits to include private efficiency apartment
with own kitchen and bath.
Prefer application done in person, otherwise, send resume
to F & L Ranch.
C/O Colten Fisher.*

Jake leaned back, smiling. The job sounded made to order, and the fact it was in North Dakota- Well hell, Clair would not think to look for him there if she was looking at all when the woman still believed wild Indian's roamed the plains. Clair's opinion of the Dakota's had always been they were a godforsaken place. But right now, to Jake's way of thinking, it could prove to be his saving grace.

He glanced up at the date on the paper, noting today's date. It was the middle of May. Hopefully, the job had not been filled yet.

SPITFIRE

If his geography was correct, which it had better be considering the sum of money Clair spent on private tutors for him, he was not that far from the South Dakota border.

He would check the map in his truck to be sure. If he was not mistaken, the location of this F&L Ranch wasn't much farther once he passed through the edge of South Dakota and crossed the border into North Dakota.

With a plan in mind, Jake folded the paper precisely as his breakfast order arrived. No, he did not need the job. The money Thomas Anderson handed him in that envelope last night would serve him for a while if he chose to spend it instead of donating it.

He shoved the half-eaten breakfast away. Time to hit the road. With any luck, once he reached North Dakota, the only women he would have to deal with would be little old ladies, far past their prime, who wanted nothing more than a horse guided tour into the Badlands.

Chapter Two

Jacqueline Fisher watched as her husband paced the length of their bedroom and thought she knew, without asking, what might be on his mind. Several things were possibly bothering him, perhaps starting with the fact this was their last night together for a few weeks, as she would soon be in France visiting family. He never liked it when she traveled outside of the state, especially not out of the country. Not because he was possessive, but because he worried her stepbrother, an evil son-of-a-bitch, would discover the hitman he hired years ago to kill her had not done the job and would come after her himself. Although Jacqueline wore a disguise while in France and was accompanied by Colten's former boss, a close family friend who acted as a bodyguard, there was always the risk of discovery.

Another reason for his moving restlessly about could be because he wanted to hire a foreman and had not yet found the right person for the job. Their eldest son, Clinton, now twenty-six, was an amazing asset to the ranch, and his knowledge of horses was valuable, but he could not run the property. He had autism, and although high-functioning, he wasn't capable of fully managing the entire business side of the estate. This property, along with daily responsibilities, allowed tourists to take guided horseback tours and overnight campouts through the rugged Badlands; the campouts having been added five years ago as another option for tourists. Although Clinton helped with those events, he could not organize them.

SPITFIRE

Their eldest daughter Donna, now nineteen, loved this ranch as much as her father did and would be capable of running it one day. Currently, however, she wasn't interested in learning the bookwork that went along with the daily operations. Besides, her interests lay in starting her own business: a horseback program for children with disabilities, which she began working on last year by integrating horses with children who have mobility limitations.

Their third oldest child, sixteen-year-old Hunter, had no desire to run the ranch. His focus had always been a career in the military, and he was determined to join the Navy as soon as possible, already pestering his parents to sign him up when he turned seventeen. Eleven-year-old Melissa and the five-year-old twins, Wyatt and Rebecca, were simply too young to consider taking over the ranch if Colten ever took sick. Although Colten was in perfect health, he was always thinking of the future. So, he had been hoping to find someone who could help run this place if something happened to him. Colten would not want his wife to have the burden of overseeing the entire operation by herself in an emergency.

However, Jacqueline doubted any of those reasons were causing her husband's sleeplessness tonight. Something else was on his mind, and it had more to do with young love than the ranch.

"Colten," Jacqueline told him gently. "Come to bed. It is after one in the morning, and I leave right after breakfast if Cadman and Kasey arrive as scheduled."

Colten stopped his relentless pacing long enough to say, "I don't like him, Jacqueline." And for what seemed like the

millionth time, he moved the curtain aside and looked out the window.

Sighing, Jacqueline tossed the covers off the bed. She knew she wouldn't be falling asleep anytime soon if he kept this up; she would obviously have to nap tomorrow once she was aboard Cadman's plane. She moved to join her husband by the window. "We have only scarcely met the young man."

Their oldest daughter had invited her new boyfriend to the ranch for the weekend. He did not impress Jacqueline either, but she gave her daughter enough credit to figure out that this boy was not her type. Jacqueline knew that sometimes you had to kiss a few frogs along the way before you found your prince. Not that she herself had to kiss many toads before Colten swept her off her feet. Her Prince had come into her life right when she needed a hero, and, after nineteen years of marriage, he still caused her heart to flutter.

Colten turned from the window where he'd been watching the young couple sitting on the porch of the guest cabin. He would make damn sure his little girl did not get any ideas about spending the night over there. It was late, and as far as he was concerned, Donna should be over here, in the main house, in her bed, not over there with that… that jock. But since it did not look as though they were ready to call it a night, he was not about to give up his vigilance quite yet. Not that he didn't trust his daughter; he simply didn't trust that boy. Colten had been twenty once, and he certainly hadn't been an angel. His gut told him the kid out there probably wasn't one either.

He felt his wife's hand caress his face. It distracted him from his vigil enough for him to wrap his arms around her, lean forward, kiss her cheek, and then her lips before saying, "Doesn't matter, I still don't like him."

Gentle laughter escaped her. "Darling, I do not think you have liked anyone your daughter has brought home to meet us."

"Now, that's not true—"

"Poof," she snorted, "Name one boy she has brought home that you have liked."

Colten's brows drew together as he concentrated. When no one came to mind, he ignored his wife's observation and repeated, "Well, I don't like this one."

Jacqueline almost laughed. He was more of a mother hen than she was.

"It won't last," Colten said out loud, more to convince himself than his wife. "She might think she's in love, but it won't last."

Jacqueline shrugged. "Then it will not last. It is not as though she has a ring on her finger."

Colten would not let that happen.

"Maybe I should have Cadman do a background check on him," Colten speculated, making a note to himself to ask his former boss to do precisely that.

His wife gasped, swatted his arm. "You will do no such thing!"

He looked at her. "I've run background checks before, and you haven't objected."

"That's different! You do that for potential employees, not guests, and, like it or not, Donna's boyfriend is a guest."

Colten opened his mouth to argue his point, but the pointed look she shot him shut it real fast. He did not want to be in the doghouse with her. No sir. Throughout the years, Jacqueline had only kicked him out of the bedroom a handful of times, and he wasn't about to make it more if he could help it. He loved his wife too much to quarrel over this, but he vowed to keep a watchful eye on that kid.

Maybe, with any luck, the right guy would answer the foreman ad he'd taken out, and "jock boy" would soon be history. Not that Colten had intended for the ad to attract the right guy for his daughter, but hey, if it worked, what the hell. So far, the guys Donna was attracting didn't suit her. None of them shared her passion for special needs children, and "jock boy" over there seemed more interested in football, cars, and parties than anything else.

Jacqueline's hand pushed past the buttons of Colten's shirt, gaining his full attention as nothing else could. "It is time to come to bed," her husky voice, coaxed.

He looked down at her, watched as her hands roamed his chest. "I think you do that on purpose," he told her.

Tilting her head up, she kept her face blank as she told him, "I have no idea what you are talking about."

His hand came up to cover the one she held against him. "Yes, you do. It's your way of distracting me."

Now she smiled. "Is it working?" she whispered throatily, making Colten groan.

SPITFIRE

Colten let the curtain drop from the hand he'd been using to keep the cloth from obstructing his view. "You know it does," he admitted. He leaned forward, taking her mouth with his and putting all he felt for her into that touch of lips. It was her turn to moan.

He smiled against her mouth. "I'll allow you this win because you're leaving tomorrow, and it will be a long three weeks without you. I guess I can trust Donny enough not to do anything stupid. At least for now." He led his wife to the bed, nudged her onto the mattress, and settled his weight down on her.

Nuzzling and kissing her slender neck, he whispered, "But don't be surprised if that kid isn't around by the time you come back."

Laughing, knowing he was teasing, she unzipped his fly. "I think you need to concentrate more on giving me a reason to want to come back to you."

His eye twinkled as he met her gaze. "These kids of yours aren't enough to bring you back?"

"Oh, they are. But, once I return, you might have to find somewhere else to sleep. I need some reason to continue to put up with your snoring."

His eye widened. "I don't snore! You're making that up. You've said nothing about it in all these years together."

"You snore like a freight train coming through the house."

He sat up. "I do not!"

She grinned. "Yes, you do. But sex with you is worth having to listen to all the snorts."

"How come you've never told me this before?"

"Now you're only fishing for compliments. I've told you before you're good in bed."

"You know what I meant."

She laughed. "Colten, are you going to make love to me?"

He saw it then, the twinkle in her eyes. She had been teasing him.

He reached out, cupping and kneading her breasts while he nuzzled her neck again. "I'm going to curl your toes," he promised. And did exactly that.

* * * *

In the morning, Colten drove Jacqueline to the small airstrip located a little north of the house as Cadman's plane circled the ranch before descending onto the runway. The Fishers arrived as the plane touched down and taxied to a stop.

Once the engine was cut and the propeller ceased rotating, Cadman alighted from the cockpit and helped his wife disembark. Their five-year-old German shepherd promptly leaped out and peed on one of the aircraft's tires.

"Mutt!" Cadman exclaimed, scolding the dog. "You could have done that somewhere else."

Cadman's wife, Kasey, chuckled. "Leave him alone and be happy he didn't do that inside the plane."

"I would have tossed him out," Cadman claimed.

Kasey shook her head, knowing it for the lie it was, Cadman loved that dog.

Glancing around, Cadman saw Colten and Jacqueline walking toward the plane, suitcases in tow, but he missed the

SPITFIRE

old days when the Fisher children would have been there to greet him.

"Couldn't you have brought the twins and Melissa with you?" he asked Colten as he reached out to take one of the bags he carried to place into the plane.

"I'm sorry," Jacqueline told him. "Hunter took them to Bismarck yesterday for cousin playtime, and to visit Colten's parents. They'll be there for at least a week." She kissed him on the cheek. "I promise they will be here when you bring me home."

"You know I would have brought you home, even without the bribe," Cadman told her, smiling. He had never had children of his own, which was by choice. But he loved the Fisher children as much as he would have had they been biologically his.

Colten helped Cadman load Jacqueline's luggage into the plane while the two women chatted nearby. Leaning in, Colten whispered, "If I give you a name, could you check the guy out for me without telling my wife?"

Cadman looked at him and cocked a brow. "And how do you suppose I do that while I'm in the air? This isn't a short flight. We're heading to New York to catch a commercial flight, then on to France."

Colten sighed, realizing he should have considered the logistics.

"You know you can always call my secretary for background checks," Cadman offered. "He knows I do it for you for a new hire."

"It's for Donna's new boyfriend."

Laughing, Cadman asked, "Don't you think you're going overboard with the whole protective dad thing?"

Colten shrugged. "If they are still hanging out together by the time you bring my wife back in three weeks, you'll have the pleasure of meeting him."

"He can't be all that bad."

"My wife tells me I have to give him a chance, but I know he isn't the one for my little girl."

Cadman chuckled and patted him on the back. "We both know no one will ever be good enough for her."

Colten couldn't' respond because Jacqueline and Kasey had decided it was time to go and were now too close to risk discussing Travis Carlson.

As the three people boarded the single-engine Cessna, Colten kissed his wife. "You had better come back to me safe and sound," he told her.

"And you had better be here waiting for me when I get back," she replied.

They smiled at each other and said in unison, "Promise." And sealed it with a kiss.

Chapter Three

Once the single-engine plane was airborne, Colten headed back toward the house. While he drove, he made a mental list of things he needed to accomplish today before attending a meeting in Medora later that afternoon.

He was barely stepping onto the porch when a jacked-up black pickup drove into the yard. Colten waited as the driver pulled up to the house, turned off the motor, and stepped out from the truck. Colten scrutinized the young man as he grew closer; for someone so young, his eyes suggested he had matured quickly.

"I'm lookin' for Colten Fisher," the stranger said. "I saw his ad in the paper for a foreman. I'm here to interview for the job if the position is still open."

Colten stared at him for a moment, considered, then shrugged. The young man might be worth the interview. "Come on in," Colten said. "You found me. I have a meeting in Medora, but I won't have to leave for a few hours, so I've got plenty of time to talk."

He led the way through the house to his office. "Have a seat," he indicated the chair on the opposite side of the oak-carved desk as he took a seat behind it. "So, where are you from?" Colten asked.

Jake, more than anything, wanted to lie. But lies had a way of catching up to you, so he decided to give only as much of the truth as he deemed necessary. "Texas."

Colten cocked a brow. He could have practically figured that out from the accent the kid had. "And that's such a small state. Want to elaborate?"

"West of Houston."

"So's California. If you want the job, it would be in your best interest to give me a reason to hire you. For all I know, you don't know the difference between a horse and a cow."

Without a flicker of emotion, and looking Colten straight in the eye, Jake deadpanned, "A horse says neigh, and a cow says moo."

Colten blinked. For two seconds, he stared, then he threw his head back and guffawed. He found the answer hilarious. People usually took job interviews a tad more seriously. And yet, he gave the best response Colten had ever heard.

He liked the young man's humor.

It took a while for Colten's laughter to subside. Once his chuckling was under control, he said, "How about you tell me about your qualifications, where you've worked in the past, and we'll go from there."

Jake stood up. From his back pocket, he pulled out the letter of recommendation he'd gotten from Thomas Anderson. Handing it to his potential employer, he sat back down. As Colten scanned the paper, Jake told him highlights of jobs he'd had over the past few years.

He did not mention the 300,000 acres of the Harper Appaloosa Ranch his father owned.

Colten listened to Jake's list of qualifications as he scanned through the letter. If what the kid was saying was true, and

the letter implied it was, he was more than qualified for the job.

Glancing out the window, Colten watched his daughter walking hand-in-hand with jock-boy.

Ugh. Why couldn't his daughter find a man who knew horse ranching like the back of his hand and-

Colten's eye moved to Jake. Jacqueline would have chastised him if she were here and knew what he was thinking, but he thought it anyway.

He grinned.

"I'll tell you what," Colten said, standing up abruptly. "If you wouldn't mind hanging out in the kitchen with our housekeeper, Sara, for a bit, I'll call Mr. Anderson and verify your previous employment with him."

Jake knew verifying his employment claim was standard practice. He only hoped Anderson wouldn't go into details; Jake preferred no one knew he had been in prison, especially why he'd been there. And Anderson hadn't inquired about his past when he hired him, so he didn't know Jake's family history.

"Sure," Jake told him, "Not a problem." Except, Jake did not, under any circumstances, want to be alone in the kitchen with the woman named Sara. Nope. Not with his track record with women. It didn't matter that he hadn't met her yet. For all he knew she could be older than dirt and blind as a bat, but he wasn't taking the chance of losing this job before it began. "Actually," Jake quickly corrected himself, "I could kill some time in Medora, then come back here."

Colten shook his head. "Nonsense. No point in your going twenty miles, only to come back here. Besides, at this time of year, there's not much to do there."

"Honestly," Jake told him as he stood up, "I would enjoy the drive. Besides, I wouldn't want to inconvenience your housekeeper."

"Sara won't mind."

Colten went to the door of the study; bellowed Sara's name.

Jake felt as though he was trapped. If he insisted upon driving someplace, and did not take the offer of hospitality, it would raise suspicion. But he knew, absolutely knew, that somehow, he would get accused of something and he'd be out of a job before he had it.

Colten looked at Jake; wondered why the guy seemed to look ill. "She's a great gal. She runs the kitchen efficiently and is a wonderful help to my wife. You'll meet my wife in a few weeks. She's on her way to visit relatives." He waved that away. This man did not need to know anything more than that.

Sara entered the study. "Mr. Fisher, what can I do for you?"

Nodding toward Jake, Colten told the woman, "Could you take Jake into the kitchen, give him some coffee or something? I have to make a phone call, and if all goes well, he might get the job as the foreman."

Sara glanced at Jake. Smiled. "Aren't you a handsome one?"

Jake felt ill. The woman might look to be in her late sixties, but he'd had plenty of older women throw themselves at him.

"I don't want to be a bother," he tried.

"Don't be silly. It's no bother at all."

Feeling as though he were heading to the hangman's noose, Jake followed Sara to the kitchen. She indicated for him to sit at the counter, poured him a mug of coffee then went back to doing whatever chore she'd been doing before Colten interrupted her.

Jake silently sat there, waiting to see how long it would be before she made known her interest in him. Time passed. She seemed to ignore him as she went about her daily chores, only occasionally asking him a question, but mostly letting him sit there as though he didn't exist. He was torn between being insulted and relieved.

"Would you like a cookie?" Sara unexpectedly asked, sliding a plate full of cookies before him, jerking him out of his thoughts.

"If he doesn't want them, I wouldn't say no."

Sara looked up at the woman who had spoken and smiled. "I thought you were on your way to Dickinson by now, Beth."

The woman, who seemed to be around the same age as Sara, walked to the housekeeper and kissed her on the lips. "I'm heading that way now. I'll see you next weekend, honey."

Jake blinked, shook his head, and couldn't prevent his laughter from escaping his lips. He had worried about her throwing herself at him, but she apparently preferred women.

Sara looked at him inquisitively. "Did you find something funny? Do you have a problem with our kiss?"

Jake shook his head and put his hand on his heart. "Not at all." He grinned, feeling relieved and carefree. "Kiss away. You have no idea how extremely happy that made me."

Beth's eyes widened. "Oh! Are you gay?" she gushed. "Were you afraid to let anyone know? This family isn't like...."

Holding his hands up, palms out, Jake stopped her. "Whoa, whoa." He shook his head. "I'm straight as an arrow, but I have absolutely no problem with your relationship."

That was the gospel truth. Each to their own was Jake's motto, as long as both parties were interested.

After Beth walked out the door to drive back to her home in Dickinson, Sara took a break in her work to sit with Jake for conversation. It was a surprise to Jake when he noticed an hour and a half had passed before Colten Fisher walked into the kitchen and announced, "Well, Jake Harper. If you want the job, I'll put you on a six-month trial period. You can put your things in the bunkhouse. There is a small apartment attached to the building, it opens into the wider room where the summer help stays. The apartment is all yours."

Colten glanced at his watch and saw it was almost time for him to leave for the meeting in Medora. Through the kitchen window, he caught sight of that yellow Trans Am belonging to "jock-boy" driving away, and watched his daughter slowly making her way to the house. Colten grinned, thinking, perfect timing.

He looked at Jake. "Put your things away and then head over to the corral. I'll have Donny meet you there. Best

SPITFIRE

person I know to give you a tour of the place, since I've got that meeting to attend."

As far as Colten was concerned, having received an education from Thomas Anderson about the wrong done to the boy, Jake could certainly use this fresh start. Besides, it wouldn't be the first time Colten had seen potential in a person who'd had trouble with the law. He'd given an ex-pickpocket from New York City a job years ago, and the ranch had gained the best cook for miles around because of it—Sara excluded.

Colten learned, after speaking with Cadman's secretary, who performed a background check on young Harper while Colten waited on the phone, that Jake was more than qualified for this job. He had grown up on the famous Harper Appaloosa horse ranch and had graduated from Utah State University with a master's degree in Farming and Ranch Management. However, it appeared there had been a severe falling out with his family, nor did they know where he was. It was apparent by his long absence that he was not looking for a family reunion.

For now, Colten decided he would not inform them of the kid's whereabouts. Jake Harper was legally an adult, and what he did with his life was up to him, although Colten was not opposed to doing some quiet investigating.

Coincidentally, Colten's oldest son, Clinton, had decided a few months ago he wanted an Appaloosa. For weeks Clinton had obsessed over the idea and recently talked his youngest uncle into driving him on a cross-country search for precisely the right one. One of the planned stops was the Harper Appaloosa horse ranch where Jake was from. The idea of Clinton

wanting an Appaloosa grated on Colten's convictions; Colten always thought the boy shared his passion for Quarter Horses, which was what was mostly on this ranch. But, Colten supposed, Clinton had gotten the idea that if his mother could have her favorite horse breed here, so could he.

Sigh.

Regardless. Colten vowed that when his youngest brother called the next time, for his progress report, he would have TJ do a little digging when they arrived at the Harper ranch. Colten couldn't help but wonder why the sole heir of a spread that size would want to work on one that was not quite so grand.

SPITFIRE

Chapter Four

Nineteen-year-old Donna Fisher stared at her father. She was almost speechless. "Dad, you cannot be serious!" For one fleeting moment, she was positive he had lost his mind, regardless of the fact he was only forty-nine years old. He was too young for a mental breakdown, but he kept himself busy enough to wear out a younger man, so perhaps his mind finally snapped.

Colten stood up from behind his desk, chuckling to himself. It was easy for him to guess Donna's thoughts; she was looking at him as though he had a screw loose, but he knew what he was doing. "Now, Donny," he drawled softly, "You know well enough, it's time to hire a year-round hand. I've mentioned it several times this past year. And Hunter…"

Donna's sigh was full of exasperation. "I know, I know." She held her hands up, palms out. "He'll be seventeen soon and headed for the nearest Navy Recruiter." She gazed upward at the ceiling, seeking, she supposed, guidance for what she could say. Her sixteen-year-old brother had dreamt of joining the Navy and becoming one of their elite SEALs for as long as she could remember. She loved him to pieces and was proud of his desire to protect America, but it seemed to her he was overeager to face death. Servicemen and women put their lives on the line each day; she was not looking forward to the day her brother's life would be in jeopardy.

"And that's precisely why we need the extra help now," Colten told her. "With all the courses Hunter's cramming,

along with his Martial Arts and ballet training, he doesn't have time to help out often enough."

Colten walked around his desk to stand in front of his daughter. "And with all you've got going on with your Adventure camp, you won't have time for guiding tours, and doing the books for the ranch, either."

Donna walked to the window, looked out, and saw the man her father had only moments ago hired. He was unloading a few duffel bags from the back of his black Ford pickup. No doubt his next destination would be the bunkhouse where the temporary summer help lived. Having him that far away from the main house should have eased her nerves, but it didn't. There was simply something about him that screamed trouble. What on earth could her father be thinking, hiring a man like that?

"Donny, he comes highly recommended from the Circle C in Wyoming." Colten's face showed his decision was final. Colten would not share Jake's history with anyone other than his wife when she returned; his daughter did not need to know the sorted details. He wanted her to judge Harper on his abilities and personality, not out of pity.

Donna threw her hands in the air. "Dad, he's… he's…!" This still had to be a bad joke. The man looked like a hood, a gang member, or an ex-convict and probably was all three.

"He's perfect for the job," Colten finished, abruptly stopping his daughter's argument.

"What if he's reckless?" she thought to point out.

Her father had the gall to grin, much to Donna's chagrin. He would find this funny. It was not the first time she recognized where Hunter had gotten his humorous nature from.

"Well, then he and Hunter will have something in common."

Donna's jaw dropped. Hunter was one of the orneriest people she knew, though he was gentle with the children she worked with.

But she wasn't about to give up her misgivings quite yet as she watched Jake Harper light a cigarette when he reached the bunkhouse. He dropped his bags on the ground instead of going inside. Shouldering himself up against the building's doorframe, he began a conversation with one of the newly arrived temporary summer help.

"He smokes," Donna said, trying to come up with any excuse that would change her father's mind. Deep down, she hoped it would be a strike against Harper; her dad rarely liked his employees smoking anything.

Her father nodded, and his tone took on a conspiratorial whisper as he said, "Yep, and he told me he occasionally has a beer." He chuckled. "I don't approve of smoking, Donny, you know that, but don't worry. I've spelled out the rules to him. If he gets drunk on my land, causes a fire with a carelessly tossed cigarette, or uses profanity around your young charges, he's out. No second chance."

Colten walked to her, dropped his arm around her shoulder, and looked out the window with her, watching Harper crush out his finished smoke, pick up the butt, and toss it in the

nearby garbage can. After that, Jake hefted his bags over his shoulder and headed into the bunkhouse.

"See," Colten's voice was full of amusement, "the boy's taken my advice to heart." He kissed the top of his daughter's head. "Yep, I believe he will work out perfectly."

"But dad…"

Now Colten's smile faded, and she knew what was coming. This was, after all, her father she was talking to. "Donna Athenais Fisher," she cringed at the use of her full name. He never used it unless he had reached his boiling point. "I said I checked him out. No one is in danger." He turned her to face him. "How can you believe I would allow anyone to work here if I thought for one minute they were dangerous?"

He was right, but still, "Dad…"

He cut her off, his voice becoming heated. "And do not forget who has been living here for almost a year! Not to mention the fact his parents will be here in July to collect him. We are always careful when we hire because we want this place to continue to be a sanctuary for the Lafayette's, not be overrun by the paparazzi. Every employee signs legal papers stating they will not divulge information on any guests who visit this ranch."

Colten stared at his daughter. "Do you honestly believe I would jeopardize the Lafayette's, or anyone's, safety?"

Donna felt properly chastised because no, her father would always keep the fact the Lafayette's visited here once a year a secret. But that didn't mean she didn't still have misgivings. She opened her mouth to protest once more, but his glare caused her to shut it right quick. It was disconcerting how a

man with only one eye, and who wore a black patch over his missing one, had perfected a glare that caused shivers to go down one's spine.

"He deserves a chance," Colten told her. "Keep that in mind while you're going over the trails with him."

Donna's eyes widened. "Dad, you cannot be serious!"

And darn it all, that stupid smile was back on his face.

"Well," he drawled, "since your mother has flown the coup, and Clinton is with your uncle T.J., neither one of them are available to show him around the place. Hunter took Melissa and the twins to Bismarck and won't be back until next week, so that leaves him out too."

Donna opened her mouth to make a suggestion as to who could show the new hire around, but Colten cut her off: "And as for Mason, he's learned a lot since he's been here, but I don't believe he would be the best choice, even if I hadn't sent him into Dickinson for a few things I needed. I would do it myself, but I've got that meeting in Medora," he glanced at his watch, "in forty-five minutes."

"But dad! Travis only left for a little while! He's coming back…"

Donna did not know it, but Colten cringed upon hearing that bit of news.

But this was business, and so he said, "Your boyfriend can wait, Donny. If he arrives before you get back, Sara can tell him where you are. If the guy is as wonderful as you think he is, he shouldn't mind having to wait a while longer to see you." He turned and walked to his desk, picking up some

papers. "Oh, and show Jake that fence that came down. I want it fixed in the morning."

"But..." she had to give it one more try. However, one look at her father convinced her this conversation was over, or there would be hell to pay. Without doubt, he would instruct Sara to send Travis home before he stepped out of that cute yellow sports car of his if she argued her case farther.

Gritting her teeth, but without another word, Donna walked away from her father and marched straight to the kitchen where she knew Sara would be. She had to make sure the woman did not chase Travis away.

Her father's laughter caused her shoulders to stiffen. Why had she been blessed with such a humor-filled father and hellish brother?

It simply wasn't fair!

SPITFIRE

Chapter Five

Jake shifted his weight, pushed away from the door frame, and crushed the cigarette under his boot. He picked up the butt and tossed it into the trash container next to the building. His new boss made it clear: if he was going to smoke, he had to pick up the butts and make damn sure they were out before they were thrown away.

Glancing at his watch, he noted he had half an hour before meeting the guide who would show him around. Shouldering the duffel bags holding his belongings and nodding a see ya later to the guy he'd been talking to, he walked into the bunkhouse.

His quarters were easy enough to find. Mr. Fisher had given him the space reserved for the Head Guide; the only private area in the place. Because he would be here year-round if things worked out, he was entitled to a space of his own. He reached the door, which bore a plaque reading Private Room—Keep Out, opened it, and walked in.

Tossing his bags onto the single bed, he gave the room the once-over. It was larger than he expected, reminding him of an efficiency apartment. There was a small fridge, stove, and microwave, along with a table and two chairs, a sofa, and a television occupying the space. Best of all, he had his own private bathroom.

"Nice," he whistled low. These people knew how to take care of their employees. He would never have dreamt of getting something like this, not that he couldn't have afforded a

nice apartment. A job that provided room and board, along with a salary, was definitely worth hanging onto.

He had six months to decide if he wanted to stay or convince Colten he was the man for the job. So far, he liked this setup and would hang onto this position if it killed him; provided there wasn't any woman who would cause him to high-tail it to the Canadian border.

Jake looked out the only window in the room, taking in the main entrance to the ranch. The sizeable, arched iron sign above the gate, carved with silhouettes of horses and a cow-boy roping one, proclaimed this to be the F&L Ranch and re-flected the sunshine on this bright, cloudless day. He hoped it was an omen that he had finally found his place in the world.

As he stood there, he witnessed a blue pickup leaving the ranch, presumably his boss, Colten, heading to his meeting. In the back of his mind, Jake wondered what F&L stood for, but didn't care enough to figure out the answer. For better or worse, here he was. At least it was far enough away from Wy-oming that people wouldn't know him. Regardless of his ex-oneration, people tended to remember only the bad.

He thought of his new boss. He secretly liked the man, but he was still wary. His recent experiences hadn't left him easily accepting everyone he met.

Colten seemed good-natured and easy-going, with a strange sense of humor Jake wasn't sure how to read. Why the man chuckled after mentioning some guy named Donny would show him around was beyond him, unless it was be-cause grown men ordinarily dropped a childhood endearment

after a certain age. Jake shrugged; it didn't matter to him what Donny preferred to be called.

He quickly put away his meager belongings, checked his watch, and headed out the door straight for the corral Colten had pointed out where he would have Donny meet him. Two horses were already saddled and waiting, but he didn't see anyone around at the moment.

Putting a foot up on one of the corral's wooden posts, he admired the Quarter Horses in the pen. They complimented the rest of this ranch. All around him were the Badlands, a maze of rugged hills, ridges, and buttes; some barren, scarred, and repelling, resembling nothing else on earth. He was accustomed to the rugged beauty; the ranch in Wyoming might be in another state, but it was surrounded by a different section of this unyielding terrain. For some reason, this area was more appealing to him. It definitely wasn't Texas, which he considered the first prison he lived in until he endured the actual thing, all because of Amanda Anderson.

He felt the bitterness rise up, but before it could take root and sour his good mood, he saw the girl coming out from the barn.

The surrounding splendor paled; resentment was momentarily forgotten.

She was loaded down with two saddlebags and canteens and was headed his way. But what held his attention were the tight-fitting jeans and red cotton shirt covering her slender body. He had wanted nothing to do with women for a long time, especially after Amanda's scheming. But that didn't mean he didn't like to look, and he liked what he saw.

He watched her walk toward him. Her brows were thin and arched precisely enough to highlight her oval face. She had sapphire eyes, made more prominent by thick black lashes. She had high cheekbones, complimenting a slim nose and delicate chin.

He felt pulled toward her as though someone had thrown a rope around him and tugged him forward. He resisted the pull with sheer determination, reminding himself he needed to tread easily around unpredictable females. At least until he no longer feared a repeat of the nightmare caused by one.

Until proven otherwise, this woman, beautiful creature that she was, was at the top of the watch-your-back list.

"Jake," she said, her voice held a no-nonsense tone. "I'm Donna. Are you ready for your tour of the land?"

She extended one canteen and a saddlebag toward him. Donna knew the tour would take well over four hours to show him the trails and highlights the tourists enjoyed seeing. They would need the canteens of water, and to be safe, she'd thought to bring along some jerky in the saddlebags in case either of them needed a nibble.

It still upset her that her father was making her do this, but she was professional enough to keep that fact to herself. It wasn't this man's fault her dad forced this on her. But when she turned the corner of the barn and gotten her first close-up look at Jake Harper, she had been taken aback. She hadn't had a clear view of him through the window of her dad's study, having focused on that long hair and blue bandana around his forehead. But up close, she could see he was beyond handsome.

SPITFIRE

She felt an immediate, inexplicable pull toward him, which was unacceptable; she had a boyfriend. Jake Harper was attractive, even dangerous, but that was no excuse for her legs turning to jelly. Though her boyfriend Travis wasn't as tall, he was broad-shouldered. When an inner voice compelled her to look at his arms, she did, then promptly told her mind to shut down the reaction, especially after she found herself salivating at the defined muscles. She had to believe this man was wanted by the law for something. The fact that Travis had never made her feel this way only intensified her annoyance.

"Sure," Jake answered. And before he realized he was doing it, his eyes raked Donna from the top of her straw cowboy hat, past her long, wavy dark brown hair with golden highlights, down her slim hips, to her boots and back up again.

He had done it in such a way that it sent Donna blushing, causing her to push the canteen and saddlebag into his chest with enough force to move him back a step.

"I hope you know what to do with these," she gritted abruptly and turned toward her horse. She hung her own canteen over the saddle horn and secured the saddlebag. Glancing over her shoulder, pinning Jake with a heated stare, she asked, "You do know how to ride, don't you?"

The sarcasm wasn't hard to miss.

Jake had no idea why he said and did what came next; it was a total contrast to the reminder he had given himself a moment before to tread easy around females. Of their own accord, his eyes raked her figure one more time, and out of his mouth popped, "Oh, yeah," he drawled, "I can ride." God

save him. He couldn't believe he actually said that. Why was he courting trouble? One would have to be a dimwit not to understand the suggestive tone he used.

Donna gasped.

Jake cringed.

Fricken A. He hadn't consciously intended to be crude, and he had no idea who this person was or if she was capable of the same deception as Amanda. And yet, he'd egged her on with an answer that could certainly be taken one of two ways. Well, he might as well find out right off the bat if she was friend or foe, angel or demon.

Donna was fully aware of what his tone implied, but she refused to give him the satisfaction of acknowledging it. She opened her mouth to say, mount up, but knew well enough what lewd response he would probably give. Instead, she gritted, "My father told me to go over the trails with you. You want to keep this job before it's begun, you'd best sit your ass in that saddle and keep your snide remarks to yourself."

That statement brought up red flags in his mind, warning him he might have taken things a bit too far. Wait a minute. Did she say her dad told her to show him the layout of this spread? Cautiously, he said, "The boss told me I'd be meetin' Donny here."

It was Donna's turn to stare. Was he dense, or what? "That's me," she bristled. "My dad has called me that for as long as I can remember."

The boss's daughter. The knowledge made him feel ill. And he'd been stupid enough to make sexual innuendos. Smooth move, Harper, he thought to himself. Obviously, you

SPITFIRE

were born a dumb shit. No wonder his mother had always been disappointed with him; until he turned seventeen, and that was a whole other story.

Donna would probably run straight to Daddy and tell tales. But yet, the boss himself was allowing her to go into the Badlands alone with him. Jake knew he was either being punished or tested. Every fiber of his being objected to this whole scenario.

"Perhaps we should wait until your father returns." He turned to leave, taking two steps before she stopped him with a question that sounded too much like a dare.

"Afraid I might jump your bones?"

He spun back around to face her. "What?!" He could not believe his ears. Had she really said that?

Donna couldn't help herself; she laughed hysterically. "Oh, come on! I was kidding!" He was either paranoid or thought himself so alluring that women threw themselves at him. "Mount up, Harper. My dad told me to show you the trails, so let's get it over with."

She swung herself into the saddle, then looked down at him with eyes that twinkled with laughter. "You can hide in the bunkhouse when we get back." Amazing. Donna thought. She'd never realized she could sound like her father and Hunter in one of their buffooneries.

Jake was gritting his teeth. It was either get in that saddle or run like some virgin schoolgirl. The latter was not an option. And she was sitting there, daring him with her eyes. Stubborn courage and male vanity got him mounted onto the horse, and cynicism made him say, "All right, Donny, lead

the way. I'm sure a youn' thin' like you wouldn't know what to do with me, anyway."

Oh. My. God, Jake thought to himself, unable to believe he said that. Was he purposely trying to get locked back up?

Donna gasped. Of all the—No, no. She asked for that. Her father and Hunter were naturals at using humor to taunt people. She was not, so she would not reprimand him for having retaliated. But she took exception to his using her nickname, and she would clear that up here and now before he thought he was welcome to use it.

"Donna," she corrected him frostily.

He managed to wipe that smugness from her face, which did wonders for his ego. He admitted to himself he liked the sound of her voice; it had a North Dakota drawl, but there was some other accent mixed with it that gave it a uniqueness all its own.

"Sure thin', Spitfire," he drawled, wondering what in the world was possessing him to push his luck.

Donna gave him a warning look. "It's Donna," she emphasized once more, "and before we head out into the mauvais terres, I suggest you get it right."

The foreign words took Jake off guard. "Into the what?" he asked.

"The mauvais terres," she repeated, glad to have something neutral to discuss with him. "French explorers called it les mauvais terres pour traverse, meaning: bad lands to travel through."

Jake glanced around. He knew the Badlands well enough, but not this area; yet. What he knew for certain was, before

SPITFIRE

this year's tourist season was over, he would know every hill, valley, plateau, and prairie dog hole better than he knew his own name.

"Lead the way, Spit—" The warning glare her sapphire eyes cast his way was enough to detour him from repeating his pet name for her. He didn't figure it was a bright idea to ruffle her feathers any more than he already had, intentionally or not.

Chapter Six

"And over there," Donna said, shifting her weight in the saddle and motioning toward a mass of rock with a red tint, "is the Maiden of the Badlands."

From their current position, they could clearly see a grouping of rocks that, from a distance, looked like the head, face, and bust of a woman. "The tourists love to hear folklore, so you'll want to point it out when you're on this trail."

Jake nodded, taking stock of his immediate surroundings. "And the legend is…?" he asked after it appeared she would say nothing more. He wasn't sure what to make of the boss's daughter. She was a wound-up ball of conflicting emotions. Earlier she'd been hostile, but once the tour began, she transformed into a friendly companion, even if she kept her conversation to an unadorned minimum. He wished she would talk more; he liked the sound of her voice, the way it drifted on the air like a song.

They reached a steep embankment and allowed the horses to pick their way cautiously down the rocky incline. Once safely at the bottom of the butte, Donna answered his question.

With a casual shrug, she said, "According to the lore, she's an Indian maiden. The daughter of the spirit of storm, whose dwelling place is in the mountains." Her chin jerked toward the west, indicating the direction she meant, even though the Rockies weren't visible from their location. North Dakota was almost as flat as a pancake with nothing resembling any looming mountain ranges.

SPITFIRE

"Supposedly," Donna told him, "the woman became fascinated with a brave from the Crow Nation, and she left her mountain home to become his wife." She reined her horse in, and Jake did the same. "Because of that, the story goes, in his wrath, her father changed her to rock, destroyed the country, and played havoc with the young man's tribe. She has stood here ever since, gazing toward the mountains, pleading with her unmoving father for restoration to her former self."

Jake regarded the formation once again, almost feeling sorry for the fictitious woman. He knew firsthand what it was like to suffer someone's vengeance. "Doesn't seem fair to me," he declared softly, still looking at the rocks.

Donna used her legs to get her horse moving forward again and wondered at the regret she heard in his tone. Unwittingly, it tugged at her heart.

"So, where are you from, Jake?" she asked. Although she suspected she knew the answer. His southern drawl was a dead giveaway, and she found it sexy as hell even though she knew it shouldn't have that effect on her.

He eased his horse beside hers. "Texas."

It amazed Jake he was telling her anything about himself, and he wondered how she managed to get him to answer that question honestly when he usually refused to talk about himself. A truce seemed to have formed between them, and it felt pleasant to ride next to her as they followed the trail, though he remained leery. He wasn't ready to relax his guard; in his experience, women could change their spots in the blink of an eye. And yet, the moment he met Donna Fisher, that promise to himself seemed to have gone out the window.

"And you?" he asked.

"North Dakota born and raised," she told him with a grin. "Although my mother was born in France."

"Ah, that explains it."

She looked at Jake, confused. "Explains what?"

"That accent of yours."

Her eyes widened with disbelief. "I don't have an accent!" She burst out laughing at the idea. If anyone had a twang in their speech, it was the man riding beside her.

Despite his resolve, he found himself smiling lazily as he said, "Yes, you do, Spitfire. It's faint, but it's there, nevertheless. You probably picked it up from your mom."

Donna thought about that for a moment. Her mother did have a trace of a French inflection in her speech, though not as remarkable as Mason's. That was likely due to the fact her mother had been living in America for several years and had picked up the local dialect. "I'll give you that point," Donna told him. "Perhaps I have her speech pattern."

Jake grinned. It brought forth a dimple on his left cheek and showed a row of teeth which, for someone who smoked, were not yellow. Yet. He had one crooked tooth, slightly askew from the rest of his straight teeth, and for some odd reason, she found it adorable. Gad, how ridiculous! There was nothing attractive about a damn crooked tooth!

They fell silent again, lost in their own thoughts. It was Jake who broke the quiet with a question: "So, what else should I know about the F&L Ranch?" He glanced at her. "What does F&L stand for?"

Donna was more than happy to explain, so that she would have something else to think about other than that cute tooth of his.

Eyeroll, please.

"F&L," she told him, "stands for Fisher, my family, and the Lafayette's." She doubted he would realize precisely who these Lafayette's were until he met them, but elaborated a little by adding, "They are special friends of ours. You'll meet them in July. We always have an annual reunion here the week of July 4th."

They rode up a narrow incline, down another, before she continued. "Their son, Mason, is staying with us for a while. My dad sent him into Dickinson for supplies, so you'll probably meet him when we get back to the yard."

Their horses ambled over the terrain, the solid thud of their hoofs the only sound other than an occasional bird call breaking the quiet.

In the near distance, Jake spotted a small cabin. "Is that place part of one of the overnights offered?"

Donna's eyes shifted toward the cabin, taking in its rustic charm, and she felt a blush creep up her face. Why on earth she felt embarrassed explaining the little homestead now, when it never bothered her before, was baffling. Luckily, Jake was still regarding the cabin and didn't notice the rosy hue, but knowing all about that cabin, combined with the unwanted attraction she was feeling toward this man she suspected was a hood, brought out the heightened color in her cheeks.

When she glanced back at him, he was clearly expecting her to enlighten him. She shook her head to clear it and told him, "That's not open to the public. My great-grandfather built it in the 1880s. It was their homestead. We lived there the summer after I was born while the main house was built, but I don't remember it." She hurried on, "But, occasionally, my folks go there for a weekend or two. To be alone…" Dang it. She could feel her face heating up again. She was used to her parents' open affection, but discussing it with a total stranger, especially this one, was a different matter. "They like to get away once in a while by themselves," she finished in a rush, and she saw a twinkle of understanding leap into his blue eyes, and that dimple was back.

Donna set her horse into a trot, moving away from him until she could rid herself of the embarrassment. She wasn't a prude. She liked the fact her parents were attentive to each other and hoped she would find someone one day she could have that same openness with. For crying out loud, she still hadn't been interested enough in any of the guys she'd met to want to experiment with sex. With a frown, she wondered what that said for Travis. She liked him well enough and enjoyed it when he kissed her, but she had yet to experience desire for him. He had tried several times to convince her to sleep with him, but she held her ground; she wanted her first time to mean something, not simply be done out of curiosity.

By the time Jake was back at her side, her discomposure had disappeared. Bless him, he didn't mention the subject again. For that, he earned her thanks, and she figured her

father was right: he deserved a chance to see if he could run this ranch alongside her dad.

For another hour and a half, she showed him more trails and explained the ranch's other services. Not only did tourists have the choice between a half-hour ride, or one- or two-hour guided tours, but all-day ones which lasted five to six hours, or two-day rides, which included camping out on the trail. "As I'm sure you know, my dad and brothers will take care of those." She didn't add that he would probably inherit that job, too, if he stayed on, especially since Hunter would leave this winter for a four-month stay in Korea to advance his martial arts training.

Jake could see the F&L Ranch coming into view, spread out in the valley below. This place was on a grander scale than the Circle C, resembling a small village. Not only was there the impressive three-story, eight-bedroom, stone-faced chateau where the Fishers lived, but also the almost equally grand bunkhouse. It wasn't as elaborate as the one on the Harper ranch in Texas, but it was remarkable nonetheless.

The property included twelve guest cabins, freshly painted stables, a barn with a tack room, and a mess hall with a small general store attached where tourists could purchase forgotten items or pick up souvenirs. Farther away was a shop housing the ranch's machinery. Corrals, fences, and pastures spread out for as far as Jake could see from his vantage point.

Jake wondered if his father would have been impressed; his mother would likely pretend not to care.

When Jake glanced up at the clear blue sky, Donna couldn't help but notice the strange scar under his chin. It pricked her

curiosity, but she was too polite to question him about it. Perhaps one day she might ask, but today was certainly not that day.

Chapter Seven

They were laughing as they rode into the yard, amused over some joke Jake made. But when Donna saw the yellow Trans Am parked in front of the guest cabins, she sobered, having completely forgotten about Travis. The fact that she had dismissed him from her mind bothered her immensely, especially since she'd been excited to spend the rest of the day with him only four hours ago.

She spotted Travis sitting on the porch of the cabin he was staying in, a drink in hand, which Donna assumed was Sara's famous lemonade. Travis stood up as they neared, and he looked angry.

Donna supposed she couldn't blame him, as she didn't know how long he had been waiting. However, like it or not, this was a working ranch, and that meant she had responsibilities—even if she hadn't wanted to give Jake Harper the tour.

Travis set his glass down on the small table next to his chair, stepped off the porch, and headed toward them.

"Where have you been?" It was a whip-like demand, causing Donna to jump and her horse to sidestep. She'd never heard him use that tone before. It irritated her that he would be so vocal in his upset; she had done nothing wrong.

Donna reined in her horse, and Jake immediately did the same. He would have kept riding toward the corral, but she had mentioned she needed to show him a fence that needed mending, so he waited and wondered what the guy's problem was. Turning her attention to Travis, Donna tried to ignore his

angry stance, asking as calmly as she could, "Have you been here long?"

"Long enough," he snapped, shooting Jake a glare.

Jake returned the withering look with an unwavering stare of his own, instantly disliking this apparent jock with his get-a-load-of-me strut. "Not my circus," he thought, deciding to ignore the loud jerk and wait silently for the drama to conclude.

Donna's spine stiffened. Travis had never acted like this before, and she was not appreciating his current behavior. It bordered on possessive, and although he was her boyfriend, he did not own her.

"Didn't Sara tell you where I was?" she asked.

That brought Travis's attention back to her. "The old lady said you were giving a private tour."

Donna almost choked at that. Private tour indeed. Obviously, Sara had taken a dislike to Travis and had stretched the truth.

"This is Jake Harper," Donna said, nodding toward Jake before continuing, "He's our new foreman." She gave Travis a tight smile, daring him to argue. Jake would be around all the time; Travis needed to deal with it. To Jake, she said, "This is Travis. My boyfriend," she glared back at Travis and added a no-nonsense, "for now." He'd gotten jealous over nothing, and she wanted him to know she did not appreciate it one iota.

The moments ticked by as Travis digested that revelation, and once he realized what she was implying, his whole

demeanor changed. "Sorry, baby." He managed a sheepish look. "I shouldn't have..."

"Oh, you've got that right, buster." Donna's upset did not ease. No one talked to her like that. "So, while you're cooling off, I'll show Jake a fence that my dad wants him to fix." With that, she used her heels to get her horse moving again, ignoring Travis standing there with a look of pure shock, as if he couldn't believe she dared reprimand him like that in front of someone.

Jake couldn't resist giving Travis a look that clearly said, better luck next time, pal, before nudging his own mount to follow Donna's retreating form. His little Spitfire was not one to be walked over, that was for sure. The sight of Travis's face turning red with seething anger had him stifling a laugh as the jock watched Donna ride away.

Jake forced his attention to the pleasing sight before him, liking the sway of Donna's dainty heart-shaped derrière in those well-worn, tight-fitting jeans as it moved with the motion of the horse. When he realized his thoughts were straying toward the provocative, he mentally shook himself. He snapped his eyes up, riveting his gaze to the top of Donna's hat. It simply wasn't right. He was drawn to her when he didn't want to be. Especially since he had only recently met her boyfriend, jerk that he was, and that meant hands-off, even if he didn't like the guy. Besides, it wasn't as though he wanted to pursue her, though why that bothered him, he couldn't discern.

Ignoring his body's response, he concentrated on the task at hand. They reached the gap in the barbed-wire fence, and

Jake looked at the section, knowing it wouldn't take long to fix it. Something to be grateful for, he thought. Fixing fence wasn't his favorite thing to do, but he had the knowledge and know-how.

Donna, still fuming over Travis's behavior, snapped, "There; think you can manage to fix it?!"

Her hostility caused Jake's mood to sour. Great. She was mad at her boyfriend, and who was getting the brunt of it? He was, damn her. Typical of the women he knew, he thought bitterly.

"O golly miss Donna. I shuah think I can," he answered in a hillbilly drawl, unable to keep the sarcasm out of his voice.

Her eyes snapped to his, eyebrows lowered in a frown. "What's that supposed to mean?"

He wouldn't get into an argument with her. He even reminded himself to tread lightly around unpredictable females.

"What in the dadgum hell do you think?!" So much for good intentions. She took them right out of him.

"Hey, it was a simple question…"

"A demeanin' one, and I resent it. I'm not your jock boyfriend. He may deserve your pissy mood, but I do not." With that, Jake abruptly turned his horse around and headed back toward the ranch. She needed to cool off. He did too, for that matter.

She would probably go running to Daddy with some fabricated tale, and he would be repacking his bags before sunset. Fine. He gritted his teeth, wondering how he managed to, once again, have another female problem he didn't want nor

deserve. He was beginning to hate the opposite sex, fickle creatures that they were.

He rode straight to the barn, unsaddled the horse, rubbed it down, and turned it loose in the corral. He heard Donna's own mount racing into the yard, but he didn't look her way as he walked toward the employee lodging and his apartment. He slammed the door in his wake.

Donna's eyes followed Jake as he walked to the bunk-house. When she heard the door slam behind him, she cringed and felt guilty for having taken her upset at Travis out on him. It wasn't characteristic of her to be such a shrew, but when Travis had laid into her over such a trivial misunderstand-ing—

Travis was being ridiculous and insecure. He had no reason to be jealous of Jake Harper, and she would make sure he knew that. However, she didn't owe Travis any reassurance after the way he treated her for following her father's orders.

It took her a few moments to realize she was still staring after Jake well after he entered the bunkhouse and wishing she had the courage to go and apologize. She knew he was right: she shouldn't have taken out her frustrations on him be-cause of Travis's behavior. It was what she should do, needed to do, but there was another reason she didn't want to go near Jake right now.

She liked him. Over these past hours, she had found herself utterly drawn to him, and that stinking lopsided crooked tooth grin of his caused her heart to flutter in ways Travis never had.

Her eyes widened. She'd done it again! Forgotten about Travis! Good god, what was wrong with her?

A quick survey of the yard showed her that her father was back, and Travis's Trans Am was still where he had left it. Where Travis was now she didn't know, but at least he was still here, so that eased her mind somewhat.

Donna finished taking care of her horse quickly, then walked to the cabin Travis was staying in and knocked on the door. When there was no answer, she hoped he was already in the main house. She needed to find him, then look for her father.

Sure enough, Travis was in the main house, in the basement, shooting a game of pool with her dad. She hesitated for a moment, trying to compose herself before approaching them. She didn't want to let her frustration show in front of her father, who, she knew, wasn't fond of her boyfriend, and she didn't want to give him any more reasons to dislike Travis. It was unexpected to see her dad spending time with Travis, though, and she wondered if he was trying to get to know him better.

That thought put a smile on her face and helped ease her tension. As she watched him move around the billiard table, she knew she couldn't stay angry with him. Travis was all hard muscle and good-looking to boot, a typical College Football jock, and all the girls back in Bismarck would die to have him for their boyfriend. She decided to give him some leeway because he didn't fully understand the demands of ranch life, and his reaction may have stemmed from his own insecurities.

SPITFIRE

Her father noticed her first. "Hey, Donny," his smile was warm. "Did you give Jake the grand tour like I asked?"

She didn't need her father to bring that up, not when she wanted to forget Travis's jealous streak. "Yes, and the fence, too," she confirmed.

"Splendid!" Colten exclaimed with gusto. After placing his cue stick in the rack, he walked past Travis and gave him such a hearty, manly pat on the back that it staggered Travis forward. "Good game. We must do it again sometime."

Colten was not interested in doing this again with the boy, but he was attempting to like the kid. So far, the effort had not been worth it; he still didn't like him. Colten headed up the stairs, leaving them alone despite his misgivings. He wanted to check in on Jake, see how the tour went, and give him the checklist of responsibilities he expected him to take on starting tomorrow.

Travis recovered his balance, silently cursing the older man's strength. Somehow he earned that man's dislike, but couldn't figure out why when he knew he was a cool dude. Travis's eyes found Donna, and he strolled toward her at a lazy gait as his eyes raked her, pleased again with himself for having won this beauty. He hadn't doubted for a moment when he'd seen her across the room at that house party in Bismarck that she would be his; she had been the best-looking chick there. It bugged the hell out of him she hadn't slept with him yet, but that would happen soon, he was sure of it. He was irresistible, and he knew it.

"Hey, baby. I'm sorry about earlier." He reached for her, pulled her into his arms, and gave her a kiss.

His apology helped to soothe her remaining anger towards him. Yet, as he leaned in for a kiss, it felt different from earlier. She couldn't quite pinpoint why, so she brushed the thought aside. She placed her arms around his neck and said, "Me too." She smiled. "Did Sara invite you to eat with us? Because if not, I'm doing it now."

In a low voice, Travis grumbled, "She did, but she probably plans to put strychnine in whatever she serves me."

Donna couldn't help the humor from showing in her laugh. "She wouldn't do that!"

Travis was not assured. The housekeeper scrutinized his every move, especially after he met Mason Lafayette. The woman displayed a protective nature toward the teenager, but Travis couldn't guess the reason, even though the kid's name kept ringing a bell in his head because he thought he should know it.

Lifting an arm and draping it around Donna's shoulder, Travis moved her toward a nearby couch. This was the first time he set foot in this section of the Fisher's home. He admitted this basement was grander than any he had ever been in, reminding him that Donna Fisher's family was wealthy.

This side of the basement had a pool table with a bar, stools, and a couple of couches. The far side of the room looked like a weight room and ballet studio, complete with a wall full of mirrors, exercise mats, and punching bags.

"Your dad into bodybuilding?" Travis asked as they sat down and would be unsurprised if the answer were yes, given the older man's strength.

SPITFIRE

Donna snuggled close. "Na. That's my brother Hunter's domain. He practices his ballet and martial arts there when he's home. I can't wait for you to meet him and the rest of my family."

Travis couldn't prevent his laugh. "Your brother takes ballet?" God, he must be a sissy.

"Along with his martial arts," she emphasized, having a feeling she knew what Travis was thinking. Hunter was no pushover; he took ballet in conjunction with martial arts because its choreography kept his muscles loose and allowed him better agility, making him faster and better honed. Many opponents he met in the ring suffered the consequences of his rigorous training.

Travis kept his snide comment to himself and didn't care if he ever met her "sissy" of a brother.

His eyes roamed the rest of the room, scanning a wall of photos, dismissing them momentarily as unimportant...until something in his mind told him to look again.

His eyes snapped back to a particular photo, and his heart thumped with astonishment when he realized exactly who was in that photo with Donna. His mind kicked into overdrive as he understood that by dating Donna, he had stumbled upon an opportunity of a lifetime. The knowledge almost made him jump up and celebrate.

Donna had told him special guests were arriving in July, but she hadn't elaborated on whom they were expecting. He had dismissed the information, thinking it might be the governor or some other official. But seeing that photo helped jog

his memory as to why the name Mason Lafayette had sounded familiar.

It was mind-boggling to realize that out here, in the middle of nowhere, was a goldmine. If the people coming were the ones in that photo, and since their son, correction: her son, was here, wouldn't that mean she would come for him?

Travis was so giddy he almost giggled. This relationship offered far more potential than he'd considered. He could become a rich man whether or not he stuck with Donna. If he could get the one photo of Rosalinda Lafayette that had eluded the paparazzi for years, he could sell it for millions. His own uncle had been trying for the past ten years to get that shot, having been arrested countless times for trespassing on the starlet's property in California or New York City, and even spent two weeks in jail in France trying for the picture.

Well, there was no restraining order against him, and Travis planned to use his relationship with Donna to pump up his bank account.

Chapter Eight

As Donna and Travis entered the dining room and took seats at the long table that easily sat twelve people, Colten entered from the kitchen. Donna didn't find that unusual; her dad always liked to steal a sample or two of the evening's fare merely to ruffle Sara's feathers. But when he glanced her way, her guilty conscience made her assume the look on his face was one of displeasure, rather than the deep concentration it actually was. Maybe Jake had told him how she snapped at him when she'd shown him that fence. Regret had her sinking into the chair as she wondered if her father would reprimand her for it.

But when Sara entered from the kitchen, potholders on her hands and carrying a steaming dish, Donna chose to ignore whatever caused his upset.

"Lasagna! My favorite," Donna exclaimed when Sara placed the dish onto the center of the table. "Hope you're not too hungry," she told Travis, "'cause this is…"

Sara scooped a fourth of it into a food-to-go container. "…mine," Donna trailed off, wondering what the older woman was up to. Her gaze moved up from the container, and she gave Sara a questioning look.

"Not to worry, dear. There is enough for you. But this is for Mr. Harper. Your father invited him to join us for tonight's meal, but I was told he declined."

"I think he has a headache," Colten spoke to no one in particular, though the statement seemed, at least to Donna's ears,

to be directed at her. Whether or not her father was truly upset with her didn't matter; her shame instantly returned.

"Oh, too bad," Travis said, not sorry in the least. He hadn't liked the fact Donna had been alone with the guy, and he was not at all happy to know Harper was a new hire. The man would be here with Donna all the time when he couldn't be. He sensed the man's hostility, but Donna was his, and no one else better be looking at her.

Sara closed the lid on the food box and headed toward the patio door, intent on taking the meal out to Jake while it was still hot.

"Forget it, Sara," Colten sighed. "I gave him the evening off. He left for Dickinson. Told me he wanted to purchase a few items for his place." Colten began loading his plate with his own serving of lasagna. "Perhaps if someone would have been a little more hospitable, he would have waited until after he had eaten to go into town."

Donna bristled. Obviously, Jake had blabbed to her father about her snapping at him.

And to think she'd been feeling guilty over her behavior and contemplating apologizing to the man. Well, not anymore, by golly. When Jake got back, she would have a chat with him. How dare he turn her father and Sara against her!

"Hey, baby, would you pass the salt?"

Donna's eyes snapped up, wide. Good god, she'd forgotten Travis was there, again!—and he was sitting not more than five feet away, digging into the lasagna like a starved man. One more strike against Jake Harper. She couldn't wait for him to come back to the ranch.

SPITFIRE

Mason entered the dining room at that moment, saving Donna temporarily from being singled out. He didn't take a seat at the table. Instead, he asked Colten for permission to attend some gathering in Medora that evening.

"I suppose I'll let you," Colten told him. "Since you did that errand for me without complaining."

With a grin, the sixteen-year-old told him, "When have I ever refuzed you?" His French accent was thick.

"Don't push it," Colten told him. "Be back before one in the morning, or you'll be cleaning out the barn."

Mason grimaced, hating that chore. "Not to worry, I will be here." And he was gone in a flash, with Travis's gaze following him as he calculated if photos of the kid would be worth something.

Donna didn't notice Travis's distraction. She was fuming because she knew Mason was going out tomcatting, and surely her father knew that, too, since Mason was known to enjoy the opposite sex. But did he get reprimanded? Of course not.

* * * *

It was nearly midnight when Donna caught sight of Jake's pickup coming into the yard. She had said goodbye to Travis a little over two hours ago. He'd surprised her by telling her he couldn't stay the weekend as planned. Something came up, he said, and he needed to drive to Bismarck to help his dad with a roofing job in the morning. He wasn't sure when he

could come back to visit, but he would call her whenever he could.

The fact she wouldn't see him for a while should bother her, and yet, it did not and she refused to question why.

Tomorrow, the volunteer therapists would arrive. They would help her arrange the schedule and activities for the special needs horse camp scheduled to open in a few weeks. Those responsibilities would keep her busy enough to prevent her from analyzing why Travis being gone for a while felt like a relief.

It was good Travis was gone, she told herself. There would be no time for socializing. The Horse Adventure Camps were a lot of work. She enjoyed the labor, but when the day was through, she only wanted a hot bath and then to relax before the television.

She gave Jake a half hour before she marched herself over to the bunkhouse and went in.

She hadn't considered the fact that this was the time of year when the temporary summer help began to arrive to prepare for the opening day of the ranch's tours into the Badlands. This was the men's quarters, and her face flamed with color when she walked in, unannounced, and found five men covering up real fast as they had been preparing for bed.

She closed her eyes and gritted her teeth. Perhaps she needed a checkup, because lately, she had been more forgetful than a nineteen-year-old should be.

But she'd come this far and was not going to back down. Not one of those guys would ask why she was there, among

a group of half-dressed men. She was the boss's daughter, after all. Who were they to question her?

She squared her shoulders and continued down the length of the building toward Jake's private apartment, not once considering how this looked to the ones she passed, whose gazes were following her. She reached the door, raised her fist, and pounded on the closed wood. If she had looked behind her, she would have been mortified by the assuming looks being passed back and forth between the guys watching the drama unfold, the conjoined thought in each mind being the new foreman was going to get laid tonight, the lucky sap.

Donna pounded again, louder this time. Good grief, he couldn't be asleep already…

The door swung open angrily and a heated, "Fricken A, can't a person shower in peace around here?" came out of his mouth.

His icy blue eyes locked with her sapphire ones.

Donna's already heated face bloomed scarlet, right down to her hair roots. But she couldn't seem to remove herself from this embarrassing predicament. He was dripping wet; one noticed that right off, as rivulets of water were coming off him, no doubt making puddles on the hardwood floor. Thank God he had wrapped a towel around himself. That is, she assumed he had a towel covering his lower half because she was not going to look. Wanted to, but wouldn't.

And Lord above, he had gotten a haircut. It was cropped short, off his ears, and would be above the collar, if he were to have a shirt on. His dark brown hair appeared black because of the moisture plastering it back from his forehead,

though one rebellious wave was trying to work its way forward. It was truly amazing how a simple haircut could emphasize a person's looks.

Gad, but he was delicious looking. She hadn't seen him without his shirt before now, and her eyes strayed all by themselves, traveling to his chest. It was broader and more firmly muscled than she would have thought. Unlike her father, he had a mat of crisp dark hair covering the solid flesh. His biceps attested to the fact he was used to hard work. Those muscles she'd seen before when he wore a sleeveless shirt upon their first meeting, and that barbed-wire tattoo, circling his upper right arm, had her unknowingly licking her lips.

He had a rich, golden tan. At least the upper half of him did.

She told herself not to look further. She didn't want to know if his legs were pale, but her heart was beating rapidly and she desperately needed a drink of water; her throat was so dry. Darn her wondering eyes! They started the downward path, but his voice, sharp and low, stopped them: "Unless you're goin' to finish what you've started, Spitfire, keep those eyes of yours on my face."

Her gaze snapped back to his, unable, in her innocence, to discern the raw implication she saw there. Her scarlet coloring went two shades darker. Without thought, she spun around and practically ran from the building, the men's laughter following her every step.

Mortified that she had been so stupid as to seek him out in his domain, she kept running until she was safely in the comfort of her bedroom with the door closed. She leaned against

SPITFIRE

the wooden door, breathing heavily. What in the devil had possessed her?

Remembering why she had gone there in the first place brought her anger back to the surface, but she decided she would wait until morning before having that little chat with him. She still wanted to know what he told her father earlier that brought on his displeasure. If she ever got the courage to leave her room again, she would bring it up.

Good god, no one had ever affected her like that before! One glance at the photo of Travis resting on her dresser and it was hard to admit the truth, but she did: Travis never stirred her libido like this. She would have to focus; Travis deserved her attention, not some stranger she was positive was an ex-con.

Despite her resolve to forget about Harper, she was still weak-kneed with images of Jake standing there, dripping wet. As she prepared for bed, forgoing the covers because her body was hot enough already, she tried closing her eyes. But restlessness had her tossing and turning, her body tingling in areas that had never tingled before. She groaned. Although she had never been with a man intimately, she recognized sexual desire and regretted two things: her attraction for someone she suspected was a felon, and the fact she had not looked. Had he been wearing a towel or not?

As for Jake, he was having one hell of a time himself trying to sleep. He tossed and turned in the twin-size bed with an ache in his loins that would not go away. The memory of Donna standing at his door, her gaze lazily roaming over his chest, was not helping one bit. If he had not stopped her from

looking lower, they would have both been further embarrassed. Those wondering eyes of hers had given him a hard-on, and it took every ounce of willpower he'd had not to reach out, pull her into his room, throw her on his bed, rip her clothes off, and pounce on her.

He did not know why she knocked on his door, but the fact she did raised havoc. He was so sexually aroused it hurt. Had she not hightailed it out of there, he would have forgotten all about his resolve to stay away from women, and no doubt be looking for a new job on the morrow. He didn't want to do that. Not when he'd only gotten here and liked the boss, despite his crazy humor.

Jake couldn't figure out Colten for the life of him. When the man invited him for the evening meal, Jake had not felt like making small talk with jock-boy, knowing Travis would be at the table, which was what Jake told Colten, and it had the older man chuckling. "Know what you mean," Colten confessed, then asked, "You and my daughter get along all right this afternoon?"

Why he told Colten yes, until Travis arrived in the picture, Jake would never know. Perhaps it was because it still ticked him off that Donna had taken her upset out on him. But that was no excuse; he had bigger shoulders than that to let such a trivial incident upset him. Yet Colten listened intently, chuckling the whole time, then told him to take the evening off.

Jake tossed the single sheet away from him, got up, and walked to the television. Snapping the set on, he moved to the small fridge and grabbed a beer. As long as he didn't get drunk, they allowed the beverage. Oh, but he wanted to get

SPITFIRE

drunk. Drown out the image of Donna standing at his door so he could get some shuteye.

He slumped down in the chair, watching the tube. Every inch of skin on his body was on fire. She had done this to him, with those huge sapphire eyes of hers roaming over him in a I want to devour you way.

The television wasn't helping to distract him, either. All he could see was Donna standing there, the image keeping him rock-hard, and she was not available. No doubt already asleep in her bed. The image of her spread out on his bed had him groaning, and he did something he had not done in years. He reached for himself and took matters into his own hand. Picturing Donna doing this to him took him to the brink, then over the edge.

His head fell back with the release, and the only coherent thought he had was "Fricken A."

Chapter Nine

Something woke him up. The crick in his neck had him groaning; he'd fallen asleep in the damn chair, and that didn't help his mood.

What was that noise? He stretched, rolled his neck a few times to loosen up, moved from the chair, and glanced at the clock. Six o'clock in the morning. It was then he recognized the sound as a horse racing through the yard.

What the hell?

He moved to the window. There wasn't enough light to see much except the dark image of a horse and its rider leaving the ranch. Something about the way the person rode reminded him of someone, and when he realized who that someone was, he said, "Frickin' A."

The last person to be on his mind last night, and the first person to be imprinted there this morning. It was a conspiracy, that's what it was. A fricking conspiracy.

There was no way he would get back to sleep now, so he jumped in the shower, making it a cold one because his "southern buddy" had stood to attention the moment he recognized Donna as the person exiting the ranch.

He dressed and headed outside for a smoke, shivered at the cold air, and wished he had put on a jacket. Should have known better. This was, after all, only the middle of May. It could be sunny and warm one day and blizzard the next. He hoped the weather would continue on its warming trend because winter was a bitch in this part of the country.

SPITFIRE

No one else in the bunkhouse was up yet. Lucky them. He was wide awake.

What did the fool girl think she was doing, riding her horse at this ungodly hour?

He didn't care. No, he did not.

Then he smelled coffee, its aroma coming to him on the slight morning breeze. He looked toward the mess hall. The lights were on. Obviously, the cook was up early this morning too. Starting tomorrow, everyone would have to be up at o'dawn thirty, and breakfast needed to be ready for them. But that was tomorrow. Today he could have slept in.

"Fricken' A," he mumbled, crushed the cigarette under his boot, and tossed it away. He decided to grab his light jean jacket for the trek across the yard to the mess hall.

No one stirred as Jake made his way back through the quarters, grabbed his coat, and headed back out in search of coffee.

"Good morning!" The chipper greeting was called out the moment Jake opened the door to the mess hall.

Jake would reserve judgment of the morning until he'd woken up, thanks. "Morning," he managed, walking forward and taking a seat at the counter.

The guy behind the counter seemed to be in his thirties, but Jake didn't claim to be an expert in judging a person's years. "I'm Juan López. Head cook. Bacon, eggs, and toast will be right up, but the coffee's done if you want some." At Jake's nod, the man poured a mug and handed it to him. "You're up early."

"Some fool runnin' a horse through the yard interrupted my sleep," Jake griped, taking a sip of the hot brew.

Juan chuckled. "I wouldn't call Miss Donna a fool. She's smart as a whip. She simply likes to rise early every morning and take her horse out."

"Good God, why?"

Juan laughed but didn't answer the question right away. "I understand you're the new foreman. Welcome to the F&L."

Jake grunted a response, but he couldn't let his question go. "Why does she get up so damn early?"

Juan shrugged. "She always has. From the day she was old enough to ride a horse on her own and had the freedom to go by herself, she's done this routine for at least seven years. The only thing that slows her down is the snow and ice that comes in the winter and rain in the summer."

The coffee was beginning to do its job. Jake could feel the brain haze beginning to lift. Good god, was she insane?

Juan said, "But that's nothing. Wait until you meet her brother, Hunter. He's sixteen, wants to be a Navy Seal. He's been training himself since he was about," he paused a moment, considering the years, "Oh, probably about when he was six or seven. He knows all the requirements, one being endurance, so he runs every day, rain or shine."

Jake couldn't help looking at Juan as though he had grown two heads. "You're kidding."

Shaking his head, Juan continued, "Nope. That boy can run four miles in a little under thirty minutes."

Now Jake knew the older man was pulling his leg and felt as though he had walked onto the loony farm. Getting up early

for no good reason was far too weird. He should quit now while he had a marble or two left himself.

Jake took another sip of coffee and was feeling as though he could function now that the dark liquid was weaving its magic.

"So, how lon' have you been at this ranch?"

Juan puffed up his chest. "Almost twenty years."

Jake was impressed; he wouldn't mind being able to stay in one place for longer than six months. Since leaving Texas, luck for longevity had been eluding him.

"Do you want some breakfast?" Juan asked. "It's ready."

"Sure. Why not? I've got a fence to fix, anyway; might as well get to it before the sun comes up."

When Juan placed a platter full of food in front of him, Jake dug in with an appetite he hadn't been aware he had until the food was right there. He'd scarcely taken the last bite of his second helping of eggs, and Juan had poured him a third cup of the black brew when he heard, "Harper, I want to talk to you!" bellowed from behind him.

There was no mistaking who was speaking, and Juan's "Good morning, Miss Donna," confirmed it.

Calmly, Jake pushed the plate back, tried to forget the effect she had on him last night, and picked up the mug of coffee as he waited for her to close the distance.

She reached the counter within seconds, placed her hands, palms down, on the Formica, and leaned forward, practically in his face. He looked at the aggressive stance, kept a poker face, though he admitted to himself she was breathtaking in her fury.

He said, "Ah, you're fixin' to apologize for yesterday afternoon, and I accept. It took long enough, but it's nice to know some people can admit when they're wron'. Unless you're apologizin' for poundin' on my door at midnight and leavin' before you finished what you started."

Obviously, he liked courting the devil.

Her jaw dropped, momentarily speechless; at the same time, her face flushed red hot with the memory of Jake's naked flesh. "I'm not fixin'," she mimicked his slang, though it came out a hiss, "to apologize for anything!" How dare he!

When she heard Juan's cough, she was further shamed, and Donna clenched her jaw so tight she wondered if it would ever open again. The head cook was, no doubt, enjoying this side-show.

"Oh?" Jake stood, picked up his black Stetson, and simultaneously turned and headed for the door. "My mistake."

She was stunned motionless until she heard Juan's amusement, confirming he was finding this whole thing hilarious. That, knowing Juan was laughing at the confrontation, was the perfect cure for her paralysis. She went after Jake as though she were a predator and her meal was about to get away.

"Now hold on a damn minute," she snapped, grabbing his arm and hanging on for dear life because he simply kept on walking, the damn jerk. "I want to know what you said to my dad last night that had him all over my case."

That stopped him. Eyes narrowing, he looked at Donna, wondering what her game was. "The only time I talked to

SPITFIRE

your father was when he invited me for supper. I declined, seein' how jock-boy was still around."

"His name is Travis," Donna snapped.

Jake shrugged. "Obviously, you know whom I'm talkin' about." The look on his face clearly stated he thought Travis was all brawn and no brains.

Donna's eyebrows instantly slashed downward. "Leave my boyfriend out of this."

"I'd be more than glad to if it wasn't for the fact it was his snappin' at you yesterday that had you snappin' at me. We'd had a peaceful time together out there," his hand gestured toward the trails, "In fact, I thought we'd gotten along quite dandy. But then jock-boy shows up and you turn into a pole-cat. Sorry, but I don't like two-faced females."

Donna glanced at Juan with a question in her eye. She had no idea what Jake meant by polecat. Chuckling, Juan told her, "He more or less called you a witch, Miss Donna. Or a skunk. I'm not quite sure, but it's one or the other."

She gasped, but was not going to admit she had acted like a witch when she asked him if he thought he could fix that fence.

Jake would have walked away right then if it wasn't for the fact she was still gripping his arm as though her life depended upon it. He looked pointedly at the death grip, then back up to her. "Do you mind? I've got thin's I'm fixin' to do this mornin'."

Donna released her hold as though he had unexpectedly caught fire.

Jake tipped his hat. "Y'all have a nice mornin'," he said, taking a step toward the door.

Juan asked, only because he had known her all of her life and was considered one of the family, "Were you a witch, Miss. Donna?"

She stiffened. Closed her eyes. Damn it. If she said no, she would be a liar.

"All right!" she gritted.

Jake stopped. Looked over his shoulder. "Excuse me?"

Her sigh was heavy, loud, and, no doubt, heard all the way outside. Juan certainly heard it, and he was watching this exchange with keen interest, having never witnessed Donna in such a temper.

"All right, you're right!" She snapped, then more softly because it wasn't easy to swallow one's own pride, "I owe you an apology."

Jake reached a finger to his ear, inserted it, wiggled it, then said, "My hearin' isn't workin'. It almost sounded as though…"

"Shut up, Harper, and don't beat it into the ground."

His lopsided smile revealed that darn crooked tooth and dimple, sending her pulse beat into a soaring palpitation. God, what that smile did to her insides. Without intending to, she returned the smile, finding humor in the ridiculousness of the situation. Apparently, she had inherited some playfulness from her dad and couldn't hold something against Jake that had been her fault in the first place.

Her smile caused Jake's heart to throb. Donna Fisher was a feisty one, to be sure, and yet, she caught him by surprise

SPITFIRE

when she admitted she had been in the wrong. His own anger disappeared with the revelation that she could admit being at fault, not run to Daddy to carry untruths. At that moment, he wanted to reach out and pull her to him. That smile of hers was fetching enough to invite him to do so. But he clenched his hands to his sides, refusing to give in to the urge. She had a boyfriend, was not available, and he certainly wasn't looking for any form of a relationship with someone when he did not trust females in the first place. And the mere fact that she apologized did not make her trustworthy.

Someone cleared their throat. They had been staring at each other, unaware of anyone else around them. The person cleared their throat once more, finally succeeding in getting their attention. As one, they looked in the direction of the throat clearer.

Jake simply said, "Morning, Mr. Fisher."

Donna was not as charitable, "I want to talk to you, dad."

Colten chuckled. "Sure, if it will stop you from keeping Jake from his work, I'd be glad to chat."

Her eyes widened. "I wasn't…"

Colten waved a hand of dismissal but was still smiling. "Never mind. I was looking for you anyway, Donny. I got a call from Bismarck a minute ago."

Donna's face brightened, knowing precisely what he was talking about. She had been bugging the group home all winter long to allow one of their wards to spend the summer with her at the ranch. "And?" she asked, hopefully.

"You can get the guest room next to yours ready. Randy can stay the whole summer."

With a whoop, Donna hugged her father. She even gave Jake a smile, which caused his heart to catch, although he was now, admittedly, at least to himself, jealous of Randy, whoever he was. "Another boyfriend of yours?" he couldn't seem to help the sneer.

Donna looked at him as though he were crazy. And who was he to ask such a question? It was none of his business, and she answered with, "As a matter of fact…"

Jake slammed the Stetson on his head, made a sound of disgust, and walked out the door. Of course, she would have two boyfriends, probably more. Good-looking women like that often did, and Donna was welcome to them all. He did not care how many men she strung along. No, he did not. He certainly would not be one of them.

Colten and Juan glanced at each other. It might be fun this summer, watching this soap opera unfold.

Donna watched the door close, heard her father's soft chuckle, and remembered she wanted to talk to him. She got right down to business: "What had you all pissed at me last night at supper?"

"I was?" Colten's brows drew together, having no clue what she was talking about.

Donna's eyes widened. "You most certainly were."

"I don't recall being upset with you."

She threw her hands in the air. "How convenient of you to have forgotten."

Colten shook his head. "Honestly, Donny, I do not understand what you are talking about."

SPITFIRE

Making a disgusted sound, she scoffed. "I highly doubt that, dad. And, don't you think it's time you stop calling me Donny? Good grief, I'm nineteen years old!"

"I know how old you are," he grumbled, thinking she should still be five years old and not a young adult. Where had the years gone? One minute she had been his little girl bouncing on his lap, and the next thing he'd known, he and Jacqueline added four more kids to the mix, and now the last ones born, the twins, were the five years of age Donna should be.

"Then you should call me Donna, not some boy's name."

"Well…" he began, but she cut him off.

"Oh, never mind!" she snapped and stormed out the door.

Colten looked at Juan, confused.

"Don't expect me to have the answer," Juan chuckled. But he suspected Miss Donna was in love and didn't know it.

Chapter Ten

Jake finished mending the fence and returned to the bunkhouse well after the other residents had awakened and were preparing for the day. When he walked through the door, a few of the guys immediately started to rag on him about the scene last night when Donna knocked on his door.

"No one," he told the group at large, in a voice low and full of menace, "will talk about that to anyone, least of all me, unless you want to know what it's like to have your nose broken."

His words, spoken in precisely that way, had each guy there believing Jake meant to follow through on the threat, and they shut their mouths darn quick.

Jake walked into his efficiency apartment, his cowboy boots sounding harsh on the wooden floors. The hard work of digging a new fence hole and stretching wire had not eased his sour mood.

Two boyfriends! How could her father allow that? And one would be staying the whole summer, in the main house, in a room next to Donna's. Jake had not thought Colten would be the sort of man to allow something like that to go on in his house, right under his nose. But then, he hadn't thought Amanda Anderson would be such a lowlife either, until it was too late. And don't get him started on his mother, or his father, who turned a blind eye to what his wife did behind his back. Two boyfriends! It pissed him off. It shouldn't. It wasn't his business, but it did.

SPITFIRE

Jake grabbed the daily roster of chores Colten gave him last night. When he headed back into the main room, he noted the staff were all trying to avoid his notice and he didn't care if they now feared him.

He stopped in the middle of the room, read off the tasks, and assigned one or two to each of them, telling them to meet back here in two hours. All but two of the temporary employees were here for the second and third time. The seasoned hands had been on the trails before, so he would utilize their familiarity with the terrain by pairing them up with the new hands, tagging along with them himself whenever he could so he, too, would get a better grasp on the different routes. The once-through with Donna would not be enough, and he sure in the hell would not ask her to show him again.

As Jake walked across the yard on his way back to the café to speak with Juan, he noted two vehicles parked in front of the guest cabins. At a glance, he saw Donna and assumed she was assigning where each of the four women standing with her would stay. He figured the women were a few of the volunteer therapists who would help with the Horse Adventure camps Colten had told him about. He had always had a soft spot for persons with disabilities, though he had never been around any for any length of time. At least Donna had one quality he admired, if he was going to think of her, which of course he was not.

As he reached the mess hall, he noticed Mason Lafayette on his way to the guest cabins. He watched the teen greet the women and; what the hell? Jake stopped, fascinated, as the sixteen-year-old turned on the charm, and the women, who

were at least ten years older than him, seemed caught up in his allure.

Good god, the teenybopper was a regular Casanova. No wonder Colten tolerated his daughter having more than one boyfriend if he allowed a kid under the age of consent to seduce women like that.

Shaking his head with disgust, Jake opened the mess hall door and headed in. As it had been that morning, he and Juan were the only two in the place. In a few weeks, that would change; the eatery served not only the ranch employees but also tourists once the ranch opened for the season. The small restaurant would be busy almost twenty-four seven then.

Jake tossed the clipboard with the duties down on the counter and took a seat. Without having to ask, Juan poured him a mug of black coffee and slid it to him.

"Thanks," Jake took the mug, sipped, then sat the container back down. "So, Juan, what's Mason's story?"

Juan wiped his hands on his apron as he pondered how to answer. He knew all about Mason, but that was privileged information only a few trusted ones knew. If Jake had to ask, then obviously Mr. Fisher hadn't divulged the truth, but they could talk about some things. He answered Jake by asking a question of his own: "What did you want to know?"

Jake shrugged. "I saw him over at the guest cabins, introducin' himself to the therapists."

Chuckling was Juan's reaction. "Mason's a modern-day rake, that's for sure. He has the attitude that any willing woman will do."

Jake's eyes widened. "And the boss approves of this?"

SPITFIRE

"Nah. Mr. Fisher tries to encourage the kid not to be so loose, but the boss doesn't have a lot of control over him. His mamma is Jacqueline's best friend. Mason has been here for almost a year. His parents will be coming for him in about six weeks."

Jake raised the mug to his mouth, took a swallow of the brew, relishing its flavor. "You know, Juan, I believe you make the best coffee I've ever had."

Juan beamed.

"So," Jake said, setting the mug back down, "you said you've been here for twenty years. How did you wind up here?"

Laughing as he poured a mug of coffee for himself, Juan walked around the counter and sat down next to Jake.

"Now, that's a long story." Juan settled back. "I grew up on the streets of New York City. I was damn good at picking pockets, though I stopped that habit once I got here." Juan guffawed, remembering the day he stepped off the bus of that church youth group, only to discover he'd landed in Colten Fisher's lap. "The best thing my mother ever did was get me out of New York and bring me to North Dakota. I cleaned up my act, got married, have two kids, and do not regret the life I have here."

Juan took another sip of the hot brew. "How about you, Jake? What are you running from?"

Jake stared at the man. "I have no idea what you're talkin' about," Jake told him.

Juan nodded gently. "Yes, you do. I know that look you have because I grew up around it. I won't push, but if you need someone to talk to, I'm a listening ear."

"What if I told you I was filthy rich and ran away from home?"

Juan threw his head back and laughed. "I would probably tell you you're a damn fool."

Jake couldn't blame Juan for not believing him, regardless of it being true. But he pushed farther and asked, "And why would you think I were a fool?"

"I suppose I would have to know the whole story before passing judgment, but I came from nothing. I stole merely so my mom and I could eat. Sometimes we had a roof over our heads, sometimes we didn't." He shrugged. "At that time in my life, I would have done almost anything to have a stable life."

"However," Juan continued, shrugging again, "every situation is different. If you were running away because Daddy wouldn't buy you a new toy, that would be foolish. If they abused you, then that's a different story. But whatever your reason for being here, I hope you find peace."

Chapter Eleven

By the following weekend, Jake had gotten to know the habits of almost everyone on this ranch, and he was able to avoid Donna well enough. Luckily for him, she was spending all her time finishing the final touches for her adventure camp and rarely came into his line of vision.

On Saturday afternoon, a week after he arrived, Jake watched a black CJ-7 Jeep roll through the ranch entrance and drive straight up the path to the main house, leaving a cloud of dust in its wake. He heard Donna's voice call out in excitement, "Dad, they're back!" Jake turned to watch father and daughter exit the corral, both practically running toward the big house.

The jeep stopped in the driveway. The passenger door swung open and a young girl, was she eleven? Twelve?— jumped out and began sprinting down the hill toward Donna and Colten.

"There she is!" Colten exclaimed, catching the girl as she launched herself into his arms for a quick hug once they met up. "There's my Lissa!" He set her back down, giving her a quick tickle. "Daddy!" The girl, Melissa, wrapped her arms around her father's waist and squeezed him tight, obviously happy to be home.

Jake felt a squeeze of envy in his heart. At one time, his own father had shown him the same affection, but his mother, Clair, put a stop to that by telling Gregory Harper if anyone would make a sissy out of his son, it would be him if he didn't

start treating Jake like a man. The hugs stopped when he was six years old.

Donna paused to give Melissa a quick hug. Jake's eyes followed her as she continued on to the jeep where the driver, was this Hunter, the infamous son Juan told him about?—had already gotten out and was busy unbuckling a smaller child from a safety seat in the back.

Colten took Melissa's hand in his and began walking up the drive. "Did you have fun with your cousins?"

"Yes, sir. But I sure am happy to be home."

"I'm glad you're home too, Lissa." Colten looked around the yard, spotted Jake, and yelled for him to follow. Jake supposed it was time to meet more of the family. He placed the pitchfork he had been using against a rail and began moving in the direction of the Fisher family reunion.

Once Jake reached the driveway, he could see there had been two young children, twins, in the back of the jeep. One, a girl, Rebecca, was wrapped in Donna's arms, and the boy, Wyatt, was looking wide-eyed at Hunter.

"Hey, Jake. I want you to meet some more of the clan," Colten told him. Indicating the children, Colten introduced them: "This is Melissa. The one Donna is holding is Rebecca, and this little man," he pointed to the child still staring in wonder at Hunter, "is Wyatt."

"Daddy," Melissa said, "Hunter got a ticket for speeding."

Hunter sighed heavily. "Seriously, Melissa, you are way too much like Clinton with your blabbermouth," he said. "No one asked for that information."

"But it's true!"

SPITFIRE

Colten looked at his second youngest son. "How fast were you going?"

Before Hunter could answer, five-year-old Wyatt said, "Zoom! Zoom!"

"That fast, eh?" Colten asked, and Wyatt nodded, repeating, "Zoom, zoom!"

Hunter reached into the back of the jeep, grabbed the few suitcases, and said, "Gosh, I can't wait until Clinton's back, and you'll know every other wrong thing I do." Their oldest brother Clinton had a habit of being the family informant—not that he meant to be a snitch, but due to his autistic mind, rules were rules, and if you broke one, Mom and Dad should know about it.

Hunter placed the luggage on the ground, pulled out his wallet, flipped it open, and pulled out his driver's license. As he handed it toward Colten, Hunter said, "I'll pay the fine. How long before you give me my license back?" He had traveled down this road enough times to know the drill by heart.

Colten glanced at the license being held out to him, then he looked at his son. And Colten knew, at that moment, that out of all his children, he had always been the hardest on Hunter. And yet, he was the one he was the proudest of.

It wasn't that Colten loved his other children less. His actions stemmed from his own ridiculous insecurities after his first child was diagnosed with autism. He pushed Hunter in ways he never pushed his other children. And had Hunter deserved it? Deserved it when the boy bordered on genius? He had a photographic memory, excelled in everything he did, ranked among the top martial artists in the world, and would

leave soon to study in Korea before signing up for the Navy. As he had earlier with Donna, Colten wondered where the years had gone. No, Hunter had not deserved Colten expecting him to do more than anyone else in the family.

"You can keep it," Colten told him, and they locked eyes. Both of their eyes were such a dark brown the iris swallowed the pupil, and in his son's eyes, Colten saw the reflection of himself at that age. "And I'll pay the fine."

"Besides," Colten coughed to swallow the lump of emotion that had rapidly risen up, "you got your brother and sisters back home safe and sound, and that's all that matters."

Again, Jake felt that pain of jealousy in his heart. Did Colten's children have any idea how lucky they were? His dad would have beaten the tar out of him for having dared bring home a speeding ticket.

Hunter stared at his father, then shared a sideways glance with Donna. Genuinely concerned because this was not the norm, Hunter asked, "Are you okay, dad? Are you dying or something?"

Colten's laughter echoed off the buttes. "Oh boy, I needed that," Colten said, slowly bringing his amusement down to a controllable chuckle. "No, I'm not dying, and that was a one-time deal. Don't think you can use it to your advantage."

"Anyway," Colten wanted to change this emotional moment as quickly as he could, "meet Jake Harper. He's the new foreman."

The teenager studied Jake with a blank gaze that had Jake admitting to himself he had met no one who could look at him

like that and still unnerve him more than the inmates he'd been locked up with.

"Ah," Hunter said, picked up the suitcases. "Guess that's fine."

He dismissed Jake, turned to Donna and commented, "Heard you got a new boyfriend. Can't wait to meet him." His tone, however, suggested otherwise.

Regardless, Jake did not want to hear about Donna's boyfriend. "If that's all you needed from me, boss," Jake told Colten, "I've got some chores to finish up."

"Sure. Go ahead. Perhaps you'll join us for dinner tonight," Colten offered.

Jake glanced at Donna, then back to Colten, "Sorry, sir. I've already got plans for the night."

Chapter Twelve

Donna sure in the hell would like to know what she had done to piss Jake off. He had been avoiding her like some plague for almost two weeks, and she wanted to know what crawled up his butt. And people thought women were fickle! Harper certainly had a mood swing; one moment they were getting along, and then the next thing she knew, he became a cube of ice.

Ever since she allowed him to believe she kept more than one boyfriend, he gave her the cold shoulder. He couldn't possibly believe she was telling the truth! That would be ridiculous. But she would not ask him. She had more things to worry about than stressing over what that mouthwatering foreman's problem was.

Had she thought of him as mouthwatering a second ago? Oh no, she was not going to admit that was true.

There were only a few days left before opening day for the Horse Adventure Camp, and things were falling into place, as they did every year.

In her mind she made a list so she could keep track of the progress of what would happen soon.

First and foremost, her mother would arrive home tomorrow.

Uncle Cadman, who was head of the secret elite group Task Force Ghost, and his wife, Kasey, would stay the four weeks until the Fourth of July reunion wrapped up. Cadman was taking an extended vacation to grieve the devastating loss

SPITFIRE

of his entire team in a recent West Germany explosion while attempting to defuse a bomb.

The day after her mother arrived, Social Services would bring Randy to the ranch. Donna was ecstatic to see the seven-year-old boy with cerebral palsy who stole her heart when she was a volunteer last year.

Entering the corral, Donna approached the horse as she made soothing sounds to it. She had been working with this horse, Ester, over the winter months and believed the beast ready for the adventure camp. Although Ester was an older and gentler horse, they would not use her for the regular trail rides. No, Ester, along with five others, was chosen for her calm, people-friendly personalities and would be used exclusively for the camp. Donna trained each one of the adventure camp horses to react in a relaxed and controlled manner in all types of situations. She wanted the children to have good experiences, not frightening ones, knowing without doubt that horses could provide laughter and smiles to children who did not have hope for a brighter tomorrow.

"So, Ester," she spoke to the horse, "are you ready for your big day?" As though understanding, the horse nodded its head, bringing laughter bubbling forth from Donna. "That's my girl," she patted the horse's neck.

Donna was coiled with excitement. Children with Down's syndrome, cerebral palsy, autism, or other disabilities would have opportunities to ride a horse, assisted by either herself or the volunteer therapists staying in the guest cabins.

For the most part, there was no charge to the families, as meeting medical bills already strained their budgets.

Fundraisers helped defer the cost of Donna's program. Mason's parents and Uncle TJ would each donate enough to cover the cost of several family's bill if asked to pay for this service, which sometimes meant a dozen family's at least could take advantage of the camp. Her parents supported the program by supplying the horses, equipment, and cabins for the families to stay in.

But they couldn't pay everyone's expenses, and so Donna came up with different ways to generate funds.

Donna was placing the saddle she'd brought with her onto Ester's back when she heard Hunter's voice from behind her: "Looks like you've done a great job with ol' Ester."

Turning, Donna found her brother walking toward her, their sister Rebecca riding his shoulders. "Thanks, Hunter." Donna finished cinching the saddle, straightened, and reached for Rebecca. Placing her on the horse, she strapped the child in with the unique belts attached to the saddle. She buckled Rebecca in simply out of habit, though the straps were primarily used to secure children who couldn't balance themselves. Children's safety was always foremost in her mind. Once the employee she asked to bring the other saddle arrived, she would try that one out, too, ensuring it was ready for use.

Once Rebecca was secure, Donna began leading Ester around the corral. While she walked, Hunter hoisted himself onto one of the corral posts and sat down to watch.

Donna completed one circle and began another. "So," she said after a short silence, "Are you counting the days until you

SPITFIRE

leave for Korea? It's not everyone who gets to study with the masters."

No matter Hunter's explosive personality, she was proud of him. The first time Hunter faced a martial arts instructor, the teacher knew the boy was a diamond in the rough. Because the Fisher children were all homeschooled, Hunter was able to travel to different places, escorted by Uncle Cadman, to further his skills in the ring without the hassle of dealing with public school administration.

School was a breeze for Hunter. He was gifted with an eidetic memory, also known as a photographic memory. The fact that he had a high rate of recall was undisputed. Added to that, Hunter was multilingual, already speaking five languages fluently and working on a sixth. Donna had always been a little jealous, having struggled with science, though she spoke English and French and was picking up Spanish slowly.

"Yeah, I guess." Hunter's eyes scanned the area, thinking of what it would be like to no longer be a part of this life. He wouldn't miss it. Not that he hated the ranch, but he needed more adventure than what North Dakota offered.

When it didn't look as though Hunter would say more, Donna asked, "What's Mason doing?" Those two had been best friends since they were babies. She would have thought they would hang out together now that Hunter was back, but she had seen little of Mason lately.

Hunter laughed. "What else? Checking out the women therapists."

Donna cringed, knowing that probably meant he was chasing women. Lust should have been Mason's middle name, and his good looks certainly didn't help, as grown women swooned over him.

Stopping the horse in front of Hunter, she asked softly, "Do you think he's going to be okay?"

Last year, Mason found out the man he'd grown up believing was his biological father was not related to him by blood. In fact, it was only when Mason discovered the truth that Donna and Hunter had been told the story behind Mason's conception. Donna admired Mason's mom for having had the courage to give birth to Mason. To keep a child conceived through violence could not have been easy.

At least now, Donna knew how Rosalinda had gotten the multitude of scars that covered her body. Usually, Rosalinda wore long sleeves and long skirts to hide the disfigurements on her arms and legs. When visiting, she rarely used the swimming pool the Fishers installed a few years ago; which was surrounded by a privacy fence, but most of the time, Rosalinda stayed away from bathing suits entirely.

Hunter shrugged. "Don't know. Didn't ask."

Donna sighed, knowing he truly cared about his best and only friend, but he also kept a distant, wait-and-see attitude.

Time to move on to another subject: "So, are you ready for this year's season?"

"Oh yeah," he uttered with sarcasm. "I can hardly wait. Maybe we'll be lucky this year, too, and some bigger-than-an-elephant will want to ride our horses."

SPITFIRE

"Hunter!" Donna guffawed, remembering last year's incident.

Donna began walking Ol' Ester in the opposite direction. Three minutes of silence passed before Hunter broke it. "So, sis, why haven't you told me about the new boyfriend? You kind of clammed up earlier when I mentioned him."

Donna stopped dead in her tracks, stunned that her brother was taking an interest in her personal life. "Well," she frowned, now why couldn't she think of something? "Well," she repeated, "I like him."

Hunter snorted. "No kidding. Didn't think you'd go out with him if you didn't."

Sighing, knowing she should have expected that, she opened her mouth to list off the qualities in Travis she first admired in him when they'd met at that party in Bismarck.

"He has a great smile," she began, causing Hunter to break out in laughter. "So does Uncle Cadman's dog when he gets a bone he likes."

"Ha, ha," Donna said drolly, then caught sight of a sporty yellow Trans-Am rolling into the yard. Surprise registered on her face as recognition of the vehicle dawned. She had not expected to see Travis until next weekend. It should have thrilled her he was here, but for some reason, she was not as enthused as she probably should be.

She told Hunter, "Well good news, brother dear, here he is now."

Hunter glanced over his shoulder as the sports car came to a stop close to the corral, and the guy got out.

Jumping down from the fence, Hunter said, "Oh, goody." The tone implied he was not all that excited by the prospect of meeting the guy.

SPITFIRE

Chapter Thirteen

Donna cringed. Hunter, to date, had liked none of the guys she'd been interested in and was not shy about his opinion.

"Hunter, be nice."

He gave her a Cheshire cat grin.

"Hunter!" she hissed. "You better be nice to him!"

"Define, nice."

"Damn it, Hunter!"

"I promise to be nice until after I meet him." His face turned angelic, reminding Donna of how a demon could change shapes to suit its deception. She could only hope he would not be difficult, but his picture of innocence wasn't fooling her for one minute.

But there was no time to worry about this first meeting any longer. Travis had walked into the corral and was approaching her.

"Hey, baby," Travis greeted, planting a kiss on her lips. "Man, I've missed you."

Hunter snorted, earning him a glare from his sister. "Travis, what are you doing here already?" she asked, removing Rebecca from Ester's back, placing her on the ground where the child promptly hugged her leg, shy now that there was a stranger among them. "I thought you weren't coming until next weekend."

Travis put his arm around her waist and pulled her close. "I was missing you. And when we talk on the phone, it's not the same." He chuckled and nuzzled her neck. "Aren't you glad to see me?"

"Of course I am," she said, "but you know we open for business soon. I've got a lot of work to do."

Jake came out from the barn, carrying the saddle Donna requested one of the summer help bring her. He'd been heading in this direction, so he offered to deliver it. It had nothing to do with wanting to get a look at her. Nope. He'd been avoiding her with good reason. He was doing this strictly to be helpful to the employee.

"Hey, Donna, where did you want this?" Jake glanced up and stopped dead when he saw Travis with his arm possessively around Donna. The question died in his throat. Irritation, sharp and unfamiliar, flared.

The fact that jock-boy was holding the woman he had the right to hold shouldn't bother him. Yet Jake glared at the chump all the same.

Donna's head turned at the sound of Jake's question, and she couldn't fathom why she felt abruptly uncomfortable with Travis's arm around her. It was utterly absurd, this feeling of guilt. Jake was nothing but a hired hand; Travis was her boyfriend. He had every right to be here. But noticing Jake's glare had her hackles rising. It seemed they always flared up whenever Travis and Jake were present at the same time. Jake acting as though Travis was treading on his property exasperated her enough to snap, "I don't care where you put the damn thing."

"Good!" The saddle dropped with a thump in the dirt, causing a small cloud of dust to bloom. His own tone turned peeved too. "Hope you don't need anythin' else as I've got plenty of work to keep me busy."

SPITFIRE

At that point, Mason appeared next to Hunter. The two teenagers were taking this all in with amusement and knowing looks. They comprehended at the same time that summer would not be as dull around here as they'd thought, not with those two at each other's throats with a boyfriend thrown into the mix.

Donna's spine stiffened. How dare he speak to her like that? She didn't care if he was the guy her father was hoping would one day take on more responsibilities. He had no right to stand there and accuse her of whatever was going through his mind.

"Well, don't let me keep you from earning your keep," she told him, though she regretted the hasty words. Regardless that they were often at each other's throats, Donna would never say Jake was not a hard worker. He worked harder than most of the temporary employees. She had surely turned into a bitch ever since Jake Harper stepped foot onto Fisher property.

Travis snickered.

Jake gave her a withering look before spinning on his boot heels and exited the corral without a backward glance. He did not need this headache. No, sir. Having dealt with not one, but two, bitches in his life was more than enough to last a lifetime. He should pack his bags now, that's what he should do, and head on down the road.

Travis grinned. "What a jerk."

"Shut-up, Travis!" At his shocked expression, Donna groaned. What had gotten into her? "I'm sorry," she told him softly.

Travis tensed. Everything in him wanted to react to her shouting at him. But they were not alone, and it wouldn't help his goal if he reprimanded her, especially in front of others. Forcing himself to swallow his anger, he plastered a smile on his lips. "It's okay, baby."

Mason and Hunter exchanged glances. They had never seen Donna so short-tempered.

"So, why the unexpected visit?" she asked Travis, giving him her full attention, forcing herself to dismiss Jake.

"Other than missing you? Actually," Travis explained, "I'm on my way to Montana. My uncle Ralph is there, visiting relatives. Thought I'd swing by here and see my favorite girl before going the rest of the way."

He turned a smile on Hunter. "And who do we have here?" Now that he knew who Mason was he managed not to stare at him. He needed to play cool, which was not hard because he was the ultimate definition of the word. Better to chum up to the brother, if that's who the other kid was, though Hunter wasn't what he expected. There didn't appear to be anything "sissy-like" about him.

Donna sighed. She might as well introduce them. "You've met Mason," she nodded to the family friend from France. "And that's my brother, Hunter."

"Hi there, sport," was Travis's opening line, causing Donna to cringe and lock eyes with Mason, both wary of Hunter's reaction. No one in their right mind would ever call Hunter sport in such a demeaning way.

Outwardly, Hunter showed no reaction, but every muscle in his body went taut at having been talked down to like that.

SPITFIRE

Before he could tell the jerk precisely what he thought of that nickname, Travis continued, "Donna told me you want to be a Navy Seal. My Uncle Tom's a Seal. He's stationed in Hawaii."

"Yeah?" Hunter sounded as though he was interested, but he was not. Anyone could claim anything.

"I also heard you've got a junior black belt in Taekwondo," Travis continued the, I'm-your-buddy-buddy talk. "Good for you, Sport. I remember when I got my junior black belt. Now I'm an adult black belt."

Hunter's eyes lit up; Donna and Mason winced. Her brother had more than one black belt in several different styles of martial arts, not only Taekwondo.

"Do tell," Hunter said.

Travis nodded. "Yep. So, if you ever want some pointers, I'd be glad to help you out."

"Truly?" Hunter's tone would lead people to believe he'd recently found his hero, but that twinkle in his eyes betrayed him. Donna and Mason knew he was being sarcastic. And if they knew Hunter, and they did, he was no doubt thinking, this chump is actually going to let me pulverize him!

"I didn't bring any sparring equipment with me, of course," Travis had the gall to sound disappointed by the fact.

"I," the look in Hunter's eye was pure evil, "have lots of sparring equipment."

"You do, sport? Well, that's great! We'll have to practice sometime."

"How 'bout now?" Hunter pressed, the evil glint still in his eyes.

"Oh, heck, sport, it's way too hot, and as I said, I'm on my way to Montana," Travis replied, dismissing the suggestion.

Hunter raised a brow. Seventy-five degrees above zero was not hot in his book. "But you'll be back soon?"

The hopeful innocence oozing from him brought Donna to life. She knew Hunter was itching to smash Travis's face and didn't blame him in the least. She was confused, though; she'd never heard Travis mention any of this before. He confused her, but right now, she needed to get him out of there before there was bloodshed.

"Come on, Travis. Let's take Rebecca up to the house and see if Sara has some lemonade for us." She didn't wait for his answer, simply took Rebecca's hand, then grabbed his and exited the corral, pulling both of them along in her wake.

"I do not like him," Mason said, once the couple was gone.

Hunter stared. "Gee, why not?" he sneered.

His dad was right. There was something about Travis Carlson that did not ring true. If Hunter enjoyed anything, it was a good mystery. For now, however, as much as it went against his grain, he would be Travis's buddy until he figured out what the guy was up to.

Then he would pulverize him.

SPITFIRE

Chapter Fourteen

Although she had things to do, Donna spent time with Travis. She hoped that by doing so, she could rekindle what she felt for him no more than a month ago. Good grief, how on earth could she have forgotten how much she liked him? She decided it was probably because their relationship was long distance. If she lived in Bismarck, they would see each other all the time, but her home and her dreams were here. Feeling she owed it to him, she decided to give them time together before he left for Montana and his reunion with his uncle.

They strolled hand-in-hand along one of the many scenic walking paths, which circled from the house to the small store attached to the mess hall, where tourists could buy drinks or souvenirs.

Half an hour later, Travis tugged her to a bench. Sitting down, he placed his arm around her shoulder, pulling her close. "This is quite the spread your folks got here." His tone was admiring, and Donna smiled with pride.

"What time were you going to leave for Montana?"

"Anxious to get rid of me?" The tone was gruff.

"No!" She sat back and looked at him. "Travis, I didn't mean it like that, honest. The drive to Helena is long, and I don't want you traveling too late and getting drowsy."

He studied her intently, fighting his anger. Not long ago, he'd had her full attention. Now, when he was so close to having a golden opportunity handed to him, she was pulling away. If he were to succeed in his endeavor, he needed to

have access to this ranch. If she dumped him before July 4th, when Mason's mother was scheduled to arrive, his bank account would not grow beyond the norm. He had to stay calm. All of Donna's turmoil began when Harper showed up. Obviously, something was going on between the two of them. What else could it be?

Donna was watching him cautiously. He seemed so angry, as though he wanted to hit her, and that thought frightened her. But then Travis relaxed. He gave her a lazy, sensual smile, and it eased her fear. Perhaps she jumped to the wrong conclusion.

"I like hearing that," he whispered, leaning toward her. His hand came up to stroke her cheek a second before his lips found hers. He made the kiss whisper-soft, enticing. He wooed her mouth with his tongue. When she opened for him and wrapped her arms around his neck, he smiled against her mouth and whispered, "That's my girl."

Donna tried to lose herself in that kiss, working to recall the things she liked about him. For one short instant, she envisioned him the way he had been when they first met. Handsome, to be sure, with that engaging smile. Instantly, a dimple and a crooked tooth replaced the image of Travis's smile in her mind and she gasped, pulling back and staring at Travis as though he were a stranger.

"What's wrong, baby?" He frowned, not understanding her abrupt resistance.

Oh God, how could she answer that question? She was so confused she didn't know anymore what she wanted. Travis had always been kind, attentive, and understanding, and he'd

been all she could think of. Now, one ridiculous lopsided, crooked tooth smile had her emotions in such turmoil she couldn't think straight. What was happening to her...to them?

She stood up and wrapped her arms around herself, feeling moisture forming behind her eyes. Why on earth was she so mixed up?

"Hey, none of that, baby." Travis also stood, watching her. He gritted his teeth as he fought his anger, yet managed to keep his voice calm. Control didn't come easily, but he forced it. If he'd learned anything about Donna, it was that she responded well to sensitivity. "You know," his voice was soft and gentle, "I think you're worn out, baby. You've got a lot on your mind, and here I've taken you away from your work."

Her smile was tentative. She felt a weight being lifted. That had to be it; she was tired. There could be no other explanation for her jumbled thoughts of late. "Thanks," she whispered. Travis's understanding warmed her heart.

He strolled to her in that jock strut of his, pulled her into his embrace, and kissed her temple. "You're welcome. Now come on. Let's go back. As you said, I've got a long trip ahead of me, and you have an opening day to finish preparing for."

Twenty minutes later, she kissed Travis goodbye and waved as he drove from the yard, already looking forward to his return. The sensitive lug. Now she remembered what drew her to him in the first place. How could she have forgotten?

Chapter Fifteen

It was after two in the afternoon the following day when the engine of a small plane was heard approaching from the east.

Melissa ran out of the house, exclaiming, "Mom's back!" She rushed back inside and brought the twins out, hoping someone would soon pull the car out of the garage.

Hunter and Mason, having been out on a trail earlier, hadn't yet unsaddled their horses when they heard the plane approaching. "Race you," Hunter told his best friend and vaulted onto his mount. Hunter's horse was in motion before Mason had his foot in the stirrup.

Donna looked up as the plane circled the ranch and dipped its wing in hello. With a smile on her face, she began moving toward the house, caught sight of her dad placing the twins in the backseat of the family station wagon, and figured she would catch a ride with them.

They arrived at the airstrip after the plane landed, the engine cut, and its passengers were getting out. Hunter and Mason were already by the plane, receiving hugs and kisses from Jacqueline, and Cadman's wife Kasey.

As Donna and the group she arrived with approached the plane, the twins and Melissa rushed forward, practically attacking their mother in their enthusiasm. Jacqueline laughed as she knelt down to gather her youngest children close. "I have missed you so much!" she told them.

Donna moved in, hugged her mother. "Glad you're back, mom."

SPITFIRE

Then she stepped back, allowing her father, to move forward and take his wife into his arms for a heated kiss that had Cadman saying, "Come on, kids, help me unload and tie the plane down. It will be a while before they come up for air."

Kasey batted her husband's arm. "Be nice. They haven't seen each other for almost a month."

Cadman pulled his wife into his arms and gave her a hard kiss. "So you know," he told her, "I'd do the same if you ever left me for more than a day."

Laughing, Kasey pulled back and grinned. "Should I make it two days and get fringe benefits along with the kiss?"

"Oh, my god!" Hunter exclaimed, "The four of you need to get a room or something."

"Hunter, you have no zence of romance," Mason told him.

Hunter turned to his friend. "Let's get the baggage and drop the romance mush."

With a shake of his head, Mason began helping unload the luggage. As he walked it to the station wagon, he took a moment to feel sorry for the woman who might one day turn Hunter's head.

As the teenagers gathered the luggage, the younger Fisher children were attacking Cadman and Kasey, seeking their attention almost as much as they wanted their mother's.

Cadman picked Wyatt up, gave him a gentle toss in the air, and pulled him close once he caught him. "I sure missed you all when I was here to pick up your mother. No more growing for any of you." He gave them a firm stare.

Rebecca laughed, and so did Wyatt as they hugged his legs and tried to force him to walk with them holding on. With a

shake of his head, he told them, "See what happens when you grow. I could do that when you were three and four, but I'm afraid the days of you riding my feet have passed." The twins groaned their disappointment.

Melissa took Cadman's hand, and then Kasey's into her other. "I got Missile Command for my Atari." she told them.

"That will be fun," Kasey said. "But we also have to play Space Invaders. I'm still planning to beat your high score on that!"

"I have gifts for everyone," Jacqueline announced, placing her hand in Colten's as they walked to the waiting vehicle.

To make more room in the station wagon, Hunter placed Wyatt in front of him on his horse, as Mason did the same with Rebecca.

Donna drove the station wagon back toward the ranch with her parents riding in the passenger seat holding hands. Cadman and Kasey sat in the back with Melissa sitting between them chatting about video games.

When they reached the halfway mark to the house Colten told his wife, "I hired a foreman while you were gone. Actually, the day you left he drove into the yard looking for a job."

Donna did not want to hear about Jake. She'd spent most of yesterday, after Travis left, trying to rekindle in her heart what she knew she should feel for her boyfriend, not some ex-con, if that's what Jake was. Perhaps she could discreetly ask Uncle Cadman to do another background check. She knew her father would have been thorough, though; he'd been, after all, once a Secret Service agent, and Uncle Cadman headed that division long before she was born.

SPITFIRE

When everyone was back at the main house of the ranch, Jacqueline passed out gifts. As she handed Hunter his, she told him, "I believe these will be to your specifications. I found a tailor skilled enough to accomplish your design." With a whoop, Hunter took the package and headed into the house and up to his room, eager to try on the pants he knew were wrapped inside.

Jacqueline then turned to Mason, handing him two packages. "One is from your parents," she told him gently. "They miss you very much." When she saw the moisture gather behind his eyes, she leaned in for a hug, whispering in his ear, "We all love you, Mason."

Swallowing a lump in his throat, he took the gifts, then he too disappeared into the house. The year away from his parents was by his choice. He had not wanted to be anywhere near France after discovering the truth of his conception, and why his mother, Rosalinda, had hundreds of scars on her legs and arms. He had not wanted to be in Paris when his mother gave her press conference to announce that, yes, the rumors were true: Charles was not Mason's natural father. He still could not fathom how anyone could love him when his biological father was a monster. To find out that the man he admired, cherished, and loved was not his actual sire was still an open wound in his heart, one he did not know if it would ever heal.

Rebecca, oblivious to Mason's heartache, tugged on her mother's skirt. "Do I get a present too?"

"Of course, darling," Jacqueline told her, forcing herself to focus on her other children. She wished she knew how to help

Mason understand how deeply Charles, the man who raised him as his own, loved him.

Jake watched the family reunion from a distance, leaning against the small gardening shed. Not for the first time, he wished this family were his. If his mother had shown him half the affection this woman displayed for her own, his life might have been different. Yet, as he grew older, he wanted nothing to do with the attention she finally gave him. Similarly, if his father had been half the man Colten Fisher was, Jake might have respected him. Jake long ago gave up trying to understand why his parents bothered to have a child.

He pushed away from the structure, intending to go back to work, when a white van drove through the main gate. As it approached, he heard Donna exclaim, "Randy's here!" And she rushed down the drive to greet the van.

Great, Jake thought, recognizing the name belonging to her other boyfriend. Right when he thought his day could not get any worse. He was still pretty pissed about that morning when Travis showed up, and Donna implied he was nothing more than a hired hand.

It did not matter that in reality, that's what he was. He wasn't a blood relation and had no claim to this ranch, but the way she'd said it was demeaning still the same.

He should head back the way he came and finish his chore. He did not need to see what this guy looked like. Probably another jock, Jake sneered to himself. That seemed to be Donna Fisher's type.

SPITFIRE

But if curiosity killed the cat, Jake knew he was destined to die because the intrigue was too strong to resist. He had to see what this guy looked like in comparison to jock-boy.

So, he watched as Donna greeted the female driver of the white van, then raced around to the passenger side and opened the door.

"Randy!" She cried, reaching in as though giving that person a hug. "You have no idea how happy I am that you get to spend the summer with me."

Yeah, Jake thought. In the room next to hers in the main house. It still bugged the hell out of him that her parents would allow them to be that close to each other.

In fascination, Jake watched a pair of feet enter his vision below the door frame. The sun glinted sharply off the windshield, obscuring the passenger's features. With the passenger door also blocking his view, Jake strained to see. Was Donna helping the guy out? Not a tall fellow, that was for sure, as Jake could only see the top of his head.

And then the passenger door closed, and Jake almost could not fathom what he was seeing.

He'd expected some guy around Donna's age, if not his own, to be standing there. But what he saw was a little boy who might be seven years old, if he were a day, with braces on his legs, and forearm crutches to help him balance as he walked.

Jake was glad no one could see him because he felt as though he had egg on his face, and shame crept up his spine.

He had been jealous of a seven-year-old who could barely walk because he wanted to think the worst of Donna Fisher.

Chapter Sixteen

It was nearing suppertime when Colten's youngest brother, TJ, and his black Porsche pulled into the yard.

The expensive car's twenty-six-year-old passenger waited until the vehicle stopped before jumping out. There was no mistaking Clinton's excitement at being home. He had been with his uncle for a month-long quest to find an Appaloosa horse he deemed perfect.

"Dad! Dad!" Clinton exclaimed, wanting to tell his father all about his adventure.

Luckily, Colten was sitting on the porch with his wife, stretching his legs and enjoying the peaceful evening as they waited for Sara to announce supper was ready. Had he not been there, Clinton would have probably run to all the buildings on the place looking for him.

Colten stood up, telling his wife, "I guess we're about to hear all about a horse."

With a chuckle, Jacqueline stood as well. "And a road trip. He's been gone long enough to obsess on that for years to come."

Colten groaned inwardly. He loved his eccentric son with all his heart, but there were days the boy could talk your ear off over something no one else in the world cared about. But he dealt with it and opened his arms to his oldest son, knowing Clinton would want the bear hug. "Welcome home, son," Colten said. His oldest child might be a grown man, but he still had childlike needs sometimes.

Clinton raced up the steps and went into his father's arms, saying, "I found a horse! I found a horse! They're bringing him in two weeks!" His whole body vibrated with uncontained enthusiasm. Seeing his mother, he repeated the information to her and beamed a smile as wide as Texas before leaving his father to wrap her in his embrace. "I missed you, mom!"

"You missed your mother, but not me?" Colten teased.

"Yes! I did." Clinton grinned. "I will tell you about my horse. Someone will bring it in a few weeks. I wish it was here now."

Inwardly, Colten sighed. He knew they would hear about this horse continually until the beast arrived. But Colten accepted his son's quirks a long time ago, and so he sat down on a chair and settled in to hear Clinton's animated tale.

Hunter and Mason made their way to TJ's side and began helping him unload luggage.

"So," Mason said, "He haz found a horze."

TJ chuckled. "Yep. Finally. I was beginning to wonder if I would be touring the United States for the rest of my life, not that I minded. Helped keep my mind off my fucking ex-fiancé."

Mason opened his mouth, but TJ shot him a look that, for once, shut the sixteen-year-old up about romance. "I'm not going to talk about her," TJ said.

Hunter rolled his eyes. "We aren't the ones who brought Heather up."

TJ scowled. "I don't want to hear her name. Ever."

The teenage boys glanced at each other. Obviously, TJ was still angry over having discovered the love of his life in bed with his best friend the day before the wedding.

Time to redirect his uncle. "So, my brother found a horse," Hunter prompted.

Thank God TJ dropped whatever rant he would have gone down and changed back to the subject. "He did, and once he found the one he wanted, I couldn't get him home soon enough."

Laughing, Mason asked, "Iz that because he waz anxiouz to be home, or because you were tired of iz telling you about zee horze?"

TJ's eyes widened, and he placed a hand on his heart. "I could never tire of him telling me about his new horse." A complete lie, but he was accustomed to his nephew's chatter. He tried to be carefree. He should be glad to have found out about Heather's deceit before he married her and discovered himself in divorce court, where she would have squeezed a sizable alimony sum out of him. He made his first million ten years ago at age twenty-one in the stock market, and his portfolio continued to grow through real estate development and his successful construction company in New York City. He was now a multimillionaire.

He did not work unless he wanted to, and on this trip with Clinton, he came to a decision: he was going to sell the company and move. The rat race he once thought he wanted was over, though where he would wind up was still up in the air.

"Did your speedometer ever drop below a hundred?" Hunter asked TJ, a knowing smile on his lips.

SPITFIRE

"Not if I could help it," TJ told him. "But I'm sure Clinton will tell you all about that, too, once his mind settles down enough from his obsession with the horse he purchased."

"How many speeding tickets?" Hunter wanted to know.

"Not a one."

"How did you manage that? I can't get from Bismarck to here without at least one if not two."

TJ patted him on the back. "That, dear nephew, is because I know how to take the back roads and outmaneuver the highway patrol. Besides, it's only a driving expense."

"Tell that to my dad," Hunter griped.

They picked up the suitcases and began moving them to the house.

As the three took the luggage inside, Jake stepped onto the porch. He stopped a few feet away from Colten and the guy who was talking non-stop about a horse, waiting until Colten signaled for him to approach.

"I'm glad you're here, Jake. I wanted you to meet my wife earlier, but I couldn't seem to find you."

Jake nodded to Jacqueline. "Ma'am." He tipped his hat to her and could see where Donna had gotten her nose and chin from. The mother was as attractive as the daughter.

Jacqueline stood up and shook her head. "Oh, no, you don't," she told him. "You can call me Jackie, Jacqueline, or Mrs. Fisher, but there is no ma'aming me. It makes me feel old." She smiled at him, stood up, and surprised him by giving him a hug. "Welcome to the F&L. I hope things are going well for you here."

"Yes, Ma'am—" he cut himself off at her scowl. "Mrs. Fisher," he amended.

"Better," Jacqueline smiled. "Colten told me you're doing a fine job, and that's good to hear." Colten had also told her about Jake Harper's past, but they were keeping that knowledge to themselves for now.

"So," Colten asked, "Did you have a question for me?"

"I wanted to know how many horses you wanted brought up to the corral for openin' day tomorrow."

"Twelve should do," he answered.

"And I would like you to join us for supper tonight," Jacqueline told Jake, then introduced him to Clinton, who proudly announced, "I bought a horse!"

Having been told about Clinton's autistic traits, Jake was not surprised by the childlike shrill in his voice. "Good for you. What kind did you buy?"

"A black snowflake Appaloosa." Clinton beamed from ear to ear.

Jake was quiet for a moment, remembering his childhood, and the horse he'd had. It, too, had been a black snowflake Appaloosa. He cleared his throat to dislodge the emotion that unexpectedly arose. "That's a good choice. That breed is a bit high-strung, but I've been told you're an expert horseman, so you shouldn't have any problem with its temper."

And speaking of temper, Jake saw Donna round the corner of the deck and thought, if she were a horse, she'd be an Appaloosa. She was like them: smart, brave, independent, and as edgy as the horses his dad bred and raised.

SPITFIRE

Startled to see him there, Donna gasped. Her parents looked at her with surprise.

Jake touched the brim of his hat in salute to her. "Don't worry, Miss Fisher, I'm heading back to work. I'll continue to earn my keep."

Donna's face flamed hot, reminded of her poor attitude toward him yesterday in front of Travis visited. She still felt awful for so callously dismissing the hard work Jake did for the ranch.

He walked off the porch without a backward glance.

She felt her parents' eyes on her. "What was that about?" Jacqueline asked.

"Nothing." Donna refused to explain her behavior around Jake when she didn't understand it herself.

"I got a new horse coming!" Clinton exclaimed.

She had never been so grateful for her brother's disability than she was at that moment. "Tell me all about your horse," she encouraged, sitting down and settling in, keenly aware of her parents watching her with interest.

Fifteen minutes later, their housekeeper announced supper was on the table. Tonight's feast was set up in the formal dining room, the only place in the house that could fit enough long tables for the dozen guests this evening.

Donna's eyes scanned the table and the resulting chaos: The twins were playfully swatting at each other, and Randy was joining in as far as his disability allowed. Mason and Hunter were bickering over something, while Clinton seemed content simply watching the action. Her parents tried to focus on everyone at the same time, and she quickly tuned out Uncle

Cadman and Uncle TJ, who were already deep in a discussion about politics.

Kasey spoke with Melissa about the new Kurt Russell movie, Escape From New York. Kasey admitted she'd had a crush on Russell since 1969 when he starred in The Computer Wore Tennis Shoes.

When Kasey felt Cadman's eyes on her, she gave him her attention and patted his arm. "Not to worry, hon. I have no intention of running off with Kurt anytime soon." Those at the table laughed at Cadman's scowl.

Donna noticed a frown on her mother's face. "What's up, mom?"

Jacqueline looked at her daughter. "I told Mr. Harper to join us for supper. I wonder why he isn't here yet."

Donna closed her eyes and knew why Jake had not joined them for supper: it was because of her. It was not normal for her to treat people the way she treated Jake, and the guilt threatened to consume her. She knew she needed to swallow her pride because, once again, she owed him an apology.

Pushing away from the table, she excused herself. "I'll look for him," she said and headed out the door.

Jake was not in the mess hall with the rest of the ranch hands and volunteers. Juan told her he hadn't seen him since that afternoon when he came in for a late lunch. As much as she loathed doing it, remembering the last time she was there, she knocked on his apartment door. He wasn't there either, but his truck was parked in his assigned slot in front of the building, so she knew he was still somewhere on the ranch. She kept looking.

She found him in the barn, cleaning out a stall, his back to her. For a moment, she hesitated, mesmerized by the way he moved. She did not move closer but watched him as he worked. He wore his trademark t-shirt with ripped-off sleeves. His muscles rippled with each movement, and Donna openly admired his wide shoulders, narrow waist, lean hips, and long legs. Why did he have to look like that? Couldn't he have been ugly? And it was not only his looks that drew her, though she hadn't figured out what that something was. But watching him now, her body trembled in ways it never had before.

"Are you goin' to stare at me all night, or did you want somethin'?" The voice was harsh, lashing out, but he didn't stop his labor.

She jumped, startled that Jake knew she was behind him when she could have sworn she hadn't made a sound. Closing her eyes, she told herself not to react to the anger she heard in his voice. He had a right to it, but that didn't make what she had to do any more comfortable.

"Jake," she cleared her throat. "Jake, I'm sorry about yesterday. It was wrong of me, and—I apologize for implying you don't do your fair share of work around here."

His movements stilled, but he did not turn to face her. "Listen, Sara made steak, and Mom was asking about you, so why don't you wash-up and come to the house for supper."

Slowly, his head turned. Looking at her over his shoulder, he said, "What?"

She sighed. Great, Jake would not make this easy for her. And again, she cleared her throat. "I said, I'm sorry. I have

no idea what's gotten into me lately, but I've been a bitch to you. I know it. You certainly know it…"

He startled her by placing the pitchfork against the stall and strolling to her. And damn him; he was smiling that fool smile of his, complete with that crooked tooth showing. Her heart went into overdrive, then pulsed more because he kept on coming, and his hands reached for her shoulders. Before she could react, he was pulling her forward and closed the remaining distance to her mouth with a kiss that curled her toes.

Each nerve ending in her body felt an immediate, intense shock of electricity.

The kiss grew demanding and almost brutal in its passion before his lips left hers to trail across her cheek to the warm hollow of her slim neck; her breath quickened. She felt her limbs grow weak. She swayed against him, grasping fistfuls of his t-shirt as an anchor as the world spun dizzily around her.

The only awareness she had was of him, devouring her.

Chapter Seventeen

Her back hit something. A stall, a post, a wall? She had no idea how she had gotten there or where there was, but she felt his arousal pressing up against her hip.

The groan escaping her mouth had nothing to do with the discomfort from the unyielding object behind her, but everything to do with the solidness grinding against her. In the back of her mind, she knew she should push him away, escape while she still had the chance, and if she could form a coherent sentence, she would tell him to stop. But the heat shooting through her, surging moisture between her legs, kept her mind a haze. She didn't realize she had removed her hands from their death grip on his t-shirt and was now anchoring his head to keep him locked to her.

"Donna, are you in here?"

Jake stepped back so abruptly Donna would have fallen had he not reached out to steady her. She hadn't heard the voice. She was too dazed to comprehend what transpired between them, least of all the fact they were no longer alone in that barn.

Jake himself was having a hard time recovering his composure and calming his labored breathing. He could not believe what he'd almost done. Practically swallowed her whole. Did he like playing with fire? Obviously.

Earlier, when she entered the barn, he sensed her. That alone caused tension to work its way through him. But when she apologized, actually apologized for her earlier behavior, it touched him in ways he had never been stroked. And how

did he thank her? He had almost pushed her to the ground and made love to her right there on the dirt next to a pile of horse apples; that aroused he'd become.

"Donna?" the voice came again, and this time Jake recognized whose voice it was and almost laughed outright. It seemed too ironic that it would be the sixteen-year-old Casanova, to nearly catch him in the same act the kid himself participated in frequently.

"She'll be there in a minute," Jake called over his shoulder, watching as Donna recovered from his attack.

The moment her eyes focused, they widened and flew to his in total disbelief at what almost happened between them. Then her eyes narrowed with accusation. "What the hell—?"

Mason turned the corner of the stall Jake guided her to in his kiss hazed frenzy; took one look at the two occupants and grinned. Looking at Donna, he chuckled, "Perhapz I zhould inform your mère you are...buzy?"

Donna's face went crimson, Jake tensed.

The moment of truth was at hand. Would she begin telling tales? Sure, he was the one to initiate that kiss, but she'd participated nonetheless.

"Don't be absurd, Mason," she snapped. "Your having a one-tracked mind is not a sufficient reason to assume everyone else shares your carefree ways."

She brushed past Jake without a backward glance as she told Mason, "Jake was simply showing me a cut ol' Ester got and wanted to know what I wanted to do for it. That's all."

Mason watched her walk out the barn door, glanced at the horse in question, who happened to be on the opposite side of

SPITFIRE

the barn, then looked at Jake. His grin got wider. "I have found that a bed ees much zofter—"

The growl came from deep within Jake's throat; sexual frustration was not comfortable, nor was it going away anytime soon. "Shut up, Mason."

Jake exited the structure without a backward glance. Unknowingly tugged at his crotch, shifting his arousal regardless of the fact it would not ease the discomfort, and heard Mason's laughter following all the way to the bunkhouse.

Fricken A. What had gotten into him?

Donna Fisher, that's what had gotten under his skin, and against his better judgment.

He stomped into his apartment, intent on taking a long cold shower when from the doorway, he heard, "You zhould azk her for a date."

Jake's fingers stilled, his shirt half raised, and he let it fall back into place as he looked up and found Mason leaning against the side of the door. "Go away, Mason."

Straightening, but not leaving, Mason repeated, "You zhould azk her for a date."

Nothing could have prevented Jake's laughter right then, and despite the over-heated state of his body, the laugh rolled out.

The sixteen-year-old rake was giving him advice about the opposite sex. It was too absurd.

Wiping tears of mirth from his eyes, he chuckled, "Kid, you are too much."

"But you like Donna."

"She's got a boyfriend, kid." There should have been enough warning in his tone to alert Mason the subject was closed. It was for Jake, and he marched off to the fridge to grab a beer, damning the can't get drunk rule.

He would be more than willing to lose himself in drunken oblivion.

Undaunted by the quality of Jake's tone, Mason continued. "But, you like her, oui? Zhe ees extremely beautiful…"

Jake grabbed the beer, slammed the refrigerator door closed, and glared at Mason. Considering the state he had been in, was still in, this conversation was not helping in the least.

Turning to look the kid right in those green eyes of his, Jake hissed, "Did you not understand? I thought your English was pretty good up until now, but what part of 'boyfriend,'" he set the beer down with force on the table and used his fingers to emphasize the word, "didn't you comprehend?"

Mason made a face. "He eez nothzing," he scoffed. "You azk her…"

Exasperated, Jake grabbed up the beer, opened it, and drained half the liquid in one pull. "Mason," he warned once he swallowed, "It's not that simple!"

The grin on Mason's face told him he had not succeeded in warning the kid off the subject. "Zee kizz you gave her in zee barn tells me it ees simple." Mason witnessed it, having come upon them lost in the moment, and had backed away, giving them a few moments before calling out.

Jake looked away and sighed. "That was a mistake."

SPITFIRE

"Non!" Mason exclaimed with passion. "It ees not a miz-take…"

"Oh, for crying out loud." Counsel from a sixteen-year-old. It was too priceless.

"Look, Mason. I know you mean well, but I've sworn off women," Mason's face twisted into horror at the mere thought, "for the time being. I need some time—"

"Ah, you have been hurt by a woman. You will get over deez, I think. Donna, zhe help you forget."

Jake threw his hands in the air. "Boyfriend," he repeated.

Mason shrugged the statement away. "He ees no good. Hunter and I do not like him."

That revelation had Jake raising a brow. "So you think I should woo Donna so you two can get rid of him?"

That brought on another fit of laughter. "Non, non. Hunter doez not need help to zend Traviz packing. He lookz forward to zee day. Forget about Traviz. You take Donna to bed, show her how you feel."

"For the love of…" Jake couldn't believe he was party to this discussion, never mind the fact he wanted desperately to get Donna in his bed. "Listen, Mason, you mean well and all, but as I said, it's not that simple. I haven't been with a woman in over a year…"

"Non!" Mason's eyes rounded the size of small saucers, and his hand flew to his chest. In no way could he imagine abstaining from sex for any reason, unless, "You are sick?"

"No."

Mason frowned. That kiss he'd seen had been heated, but perhaps he'd misunderstood. Could it be? He had to know. "Gay?"

"No!" It came out a half-laugh.

"Then, why not?"

There was nothing for it. Jake was so irritated he told Mason the reason he had a hard time trusting women. Amanda, the lies, and the six months in prison; all of it came tumbling out, and Mason was staring at him as though he were the most fascinating creature to have ever lived.

"Zo, deez Amanda, zhe vindictive woman," Mason shrugged. "I think it eez time to move forward, Jake."

With that, Mason finally left, with Jake's eyes boring holes into his back.

Chapter Eighteen

As in years past, opening day proved to be a resounding success. Throughout the day, more than one hundred and fifty guests arrived, looking forward to their horseback excursions. Jake and his team of temporary guides were kept busy, alternating between essential ranch duties and leading tourists into the heart of the terrain. The rides offered spectacular vantage points, allowing visitors to experience the raw beauty of the Badlands up close. From the vibrant layers of sediment painting the canyon walls to the silent, windswept beauty of the valley floors.

Donna hadn't had a moment to herself since her morning ride. She said goodbye to her Uncle TJ that afternoon as he was headed back to New York. The first busload of children arrived around nine in the morning, keeping her mind filled with the organization of the group, and she was more than grateful for the distraction.

It kept her from reliving Jake's assault the previous night. Well, she didn't think of it as a violent attack. Not once had it crossed her mind that he may have considered raping her. But it was an onslaught the likes of which she'd never experienced. The memory of it kept her up most of the night: hating him for having the power to extract desire from her, loathing herself for hoping he would be bold enough to do it again, and depressed because she shouldn't be thinking of him at all.

But now that she experienced that mind-blowing kiss, what was she supposed to do? Gad, life was not easy to figure out when men were thrown into the mix. It felt as though she

placed Travis and Jake on a scale, and they were balanced there, waiting for it to tip one way or the other.

Ol' Ester missed a step, forcing Donna to concentrate on the moment at hand. Right now, she was riding behind Randy, with him sitting in front of her to keep him on the horse she bragged about in letters during the winter. She enjoyed being with him and was glad he was there, though she hadn't the opportunity throughout the day to spend time with him.

Now that supper was over, the ranch closed for the evening, and the volunteer therapists were settling the visiting group of children down for the night with story time and games, she took advantage of the free time.

The type of palsy Randy had caused involuntary facial movements that often gave the impression he was slow-minded, but Donna knew otherwise. He was incredibly intelligent. The disability also required him to wear braces and use crutches, but the physical therapist highly recommended riding a horse bareback. It was a tremendous help, strengthening weaker muscles and relaxing tighter ones.

"So, Randy," Donna leaned forward, speaking softly into his ear, "are you enjoying being here so far?"

Randy's response was "Eees." Donna knew he said yes and smiled. The boy worked with a speech pathologist three times a week and had made marked progress; last summer, he'd been unable to get more than sound past his lips.

Her gaze lifted to the path, catching sight of a rider and their horse slowly coming her way that instantly stole her focus. The memory of the pressure of his lips on hers flooded her mind, making her heart stutter and her face burn. The

SPITFIRE

certainty she loved Travis was nowhere to be found. Instead, the sight of Jake Harper alone was enough to make the mild evening air feel thick with undeniable tension.

Never in her life would she have dreamed she could be a whimsical female. She hadn't looked at another guy since Travis came into her life, and now here she was, having second thoughts, all because of this man and that knee-bending kiss he'd given her. Curse him.

Jake touched the brim of his cowboy hat in greeting and stopped his horse beside hers. "Howdy, Miss Donna," he said. He was neither friendly nor hostile, and strangely enough, he hadn't used his nickname for her, which left her feeling disappointed. A simple greeting, as though nothing transpired between them. Evidently, that kiss hadn't affected him one wit, and that annoyed her, though it shouldn't. She should be thankful he was not rubbing it in her face. She certainly wasn't going to mention it ever again.

He removed his black Stetson to wipe his brow, set it back on his head, and out of her mouth popped, "You know, I never told you, but I like your haircut."

Why on earth was she flattering him? It was beyond comprehension, no matter that it was the truth. She had yet to see his hair neat and tidy, because whenever she saw him, he had the hat on—except for when he'd first gotten it cut, but that did not count because it had been dripping wet then. Wet from that shower. Her face flamed at that memory. Gad, she was a glutton for punishment, allowing the image to flick through her mind like that.

He stared at her so long it made her uncomfortable. "I did it for the tourists," his shrug was barely discernible. "You know. Cowboy image and all."

Despite her resolve not to, she had to know, "So why'd you grow it out in the first place?"

The answer did not come quickly. He wanted to tell her he'd let it grow out while he was in prison but wasn't ready to admit his past history with the law. Finally, he said, "It seemed the right thing to do at the time."

Well, good thing she hadn't truly wanted to know.

Fuming inwardly for having asked, she vowed right then and there she would not be asking about that odd scar of his under his chin no matter what.

Jake's eyes released hers at last, his attention falling on Randy. His expression softened, not in pity, but with genuine interest. "We haven't been introduced," he reached out to shake the boy's hand, waiting patiently as Randy reached out in his uncontrolled manner to grasp it.

Donna's heart grew warm at the sight. Jake had looked at Randy, not through him, as many people did with handicapped individuals. She would have never guessed he had a soft spot for children, let alone those with disabilities.

"Randy, this is Jake Harper," she explained, introducing the two and explaining what Jake's job entailed.

There was a twinkle in Jake's eye as he glanced at her briefly. "Oh, yes, your other boyfriend."

Donna allowed a tentative smile and a small shrug. What else was there to say? It was a great joke at the time.

Randy said, "Ake," bringing both adults' attention back to him.

"Yes, Jah-ache," Donna sounded the name out slowly.

"AAke."

Donna chuckled; he tried his best. "Yes, Jake." She glanced at the bearer of that name, saw he had that lopsided, crooked tooth-revealing smile spread across his face, and turned to mush, regardless of the fact it hadn't been directed at her.

Clearing her throat and mentally shaking herself, she sounded the name out once again, emphasizing the 'J' sound. "Ake! Ake! Ake!" Randy repeated, seeming to enjoy the new word.

The child's enthusiasm amazed Donna. Sure, he had never been shy, but he seemed to have warmed up to Jake as though he had known him for years. Unbeknownst to Donna, a conspiracy was at work right there in the main house where Randy was living: two sixteen-year-olds were strategically working on a "let's get rid of Travis Carlson" plan.

"I think he likes you," Donna observed, looking at Jake, trying not to become hypnotized.

Jake's grin vanished, and he was staring once again. "Maybe I'm a likable guy, Spitfire."

Now, why on earth had he said that? Jake wondered. He'd been kicking himself over that kiss, knowing he should not have done it, but nothing could have stopped him. When she had apologized, she sounded so remorseful that all he wanted to do was let her know he forgave her. Again. Jock-boy seemed to bring out the worst in her. However, Jake admitted he might have added to her upset with his own behavior. But

he was jealous; he could admit that to himself. However, as long as Travis was still in the picture, he had to keep his hands off, no matter how attracted to her he was.

"Itire," Randy latched on to Jake's nickname for Donna and laughed.

Donna gave Jake a dirty look. "I'll get you for that," she told him dryly.

Jake couldn't have prevented the grin had he tried. "I look forward to it."

The scowl Donna gave him did not last. She found the humor in the situation instead and burst out laughing. "I bet you do."

Their eyes met, locked. Her laughter died. A breeze stirred, and with it an awareness that made them both uncomfortable.

Jake was the first to break the spell. "About last night—"

"Oh heavens," she waved a hand, cutting him off. "I've forgotten all about it." What a whopper of a lie that was, but she could not deal with that subject right now.

He gave her a curt nod. Evidently, Mason was wrong in this situation, but at least she wasn't going to hold him accountable for his actions or find a way to get him locked up. With a will of iron, he forced himself to dismiss her, concentrating on Randy instead.

"So, youn' man; since I'm free for the evenin' how 'bout you and I goin' for a ride? Only us guys."

Randy's garbled, but enthusiastic, yes told them he wanted to be with Jake instead of her. Donna's mouth dropped open; she was honestly a little hurt by the fact.

"Well, that's settled, Spitfire. Us men have trails to blaze," Jake chuckled.

"But," she almost sputtered, "he needs to ride bareback."

Jake shrugged. "So, we'll switch horses."

"You have to be sure to hang on to him."

"I'll hang on to him."

"You can't ride too fast."

"I won't," Jake's eyes danced with amusement over her mother hen attitude.

"Well…" Donna stammered, "All right, then."

The switch was made, and the next thing Donna knew, she was sitting on Jake's horse, watching the two of them riding away from her. To her utter horror, she heard Randy say, "Bb..i, Iiitire," which translated, bye, Spitfire. Donna's cheeks turned red with embarrassment, but Jake's laughter caused the scarlet color to consume her entire face.

Chapter Nineteen

The early morning sun was barely climbing over the buttes when Colten caught the first fish of the day. Reeling it in, he held it up for Cadman to view. "This is a good start to the fish fry Sara is planning for tonight," he told his former boss.

"I swear you have some kind of deal with the fish around here. Whenever we do this, you make the first catch."

Colten chuckled as he put the fish on a stringer, then tossed it back into the lake to keep it alive and fresh. They had left the ranch while it was still dark to drive the thirty-six miles to Camel's Hump Lake located west of Medora, united by their shared passion for fishing.

Cadman watched Colten put bait on the line and toss it back in. "How's Harper working out? My secretary let me know you had him run a deep check on the guy."

Colten sat back in his chair. "He's doing good. In fact, he's excellent. The kid got a bum deal from that last place he worked."

"Can't believe that woman was able to frame him like that. Vindictive bitch," Cadman said. "I've never heard of a woman who would be that spiteful simply because the guy she was interested in wouldn't…"

"But she did," Colten interrupted, a red blush forming along his cheekbones. He did not want to talk about why Jake was put in prison.

Cadman shook his head, marveling at Colten's avoidance of talk involving sex.

SPITFIRE

"Thankfully," Colten continued, "the newly appointed sheriff is an honest man, who Amanda Anderson wasn't able to corrupt. And that he looked into Jake's case and got the boy free from the hell she put him through for no good reason."

"Agreed," Cadman said, glancing at his fishing line.

"I've only told my wife about Jake being the sole heir of the Harper Appaloosa horse ranch in Texas," Colten explained. "But I'm not mentioning it to the kids or anyone else. That's his story to tell, not mine. It appears he wants nothing to do with the place."

"TJ find out anything while he was down there with Clinton buying that horse?"

"Only that Jake's dad has hired a detective to try to locate him and is heartbroken by his son's disappearance. It will only be a matter of time before they track him here, but since Clinton purchased his horse from there, and they will be delivering it soon, it will help the process along."

"And you think that's a good thing?"

Colten shrugged. "I don't mind giving a push to whatever's between them so they can clear the air."

"So, wise one, what if Jake goes back to Texas?"

"That will be up to him, but personally, I'm hoping he'll want to stay here. He's been an asset to the ranch, and if my daughter would come to her senses and get rid of that boyfriend of hers, I think she would discover her perfect match was right under her nose."

Cadman threw his head back and laughed. "Are you playing matchmaker?"

"No comment," Colten said, but the red splotches that crept up along his cheekbones revealed Cadman assumed correctly.

"So, you still don't like the guy she's dating?"

Colten shook his head. "You haven't had the pleasure of meeting him yet. Jacqueline will have my hide, but I want you to run a check on him."

The two men sat silent for a time, watching their lines.

"Mason's still pretty torn up about Charles not being his biological father," Colten spoke softly. "He keeps it to himself, but you can see it in his eyes when you mention his folks."

Cadman nodded. "I've tried talking to him, but he clams up." He shook his head. "He doesn't understand how Charles can love him. It's a heartbreak for Charles, too. He loves that boy with every fiber of his being."

Colten shook his head. "Rosalinda fought a long battle to recover from what happened. The turmoil she went through when she found out she was pregnant, and the courage she had to give birth and then keep him. Having him distancing himself from them breaks their heart each day. I hope when they arrive, Mason will allow the wound to heal."

The two men remained silent for a time, each remembering the dark past.

"And thank God Mason shows no signs of being like Pierre," Colten added.

"Amen to that," Cadman agreed. "He may almost be a clone in his looks to Pierre, but his heart is good, and that's probably why he has taken it so hard, discovering the truth about his conception."

146

SPITFIRE

Cadman's body gave an involuntary shiver. He had been the first on the scene when Rosalinda was found after Pierre Bellefeuille kidnapped and tortured her. He doubted the image of seeing her—hanging by her arms, legs shackled to the floor, face battered, and her body covered with blood from the countless cuts inflicted on her by Pierre, would ever leave him.

"Cadman?"

He blinked to bring himself back to the here and now. "What?"

"It's been sixteen years. If we're lucky, Pierre's dead."

"We could hope that's true, but I get bits of information now and again of him still being active. I was in Libya last October because I got news he was there, but as always, by the time I arrived, he'd disappeared into the wind. But I will keep looking. Keep hounding. I don't want him to think he'll have the chance to hurt any of the Lafayette's again. As long as I'm on his trail, he's not going to have space to breathe."

"At least you have people keeping close to the family, even if the Lafayette's don't know it."

"It's difficult when they are always in the spotlight. They have their own bodyguards with them at all times, but the more eyes on them, watching for danger, the better, though I think I probably fear for them more than they do themselves. Which is saying a lot. But they can't be expected to change who they are. I only hope Pierre doesn't make a move to take Mason. By now, unless Pierre never has the chance to listen to the news, he's got to know he's the boy's father. Rosalinda

did not name him when she held that press conference, but anyone who knows Pierre would see him in Mason."

He looked at Colten, venom in his voice. "I want that son-of-a-bitch to pay for what he did to Rosalinda; what he tried to do to you and Jacqueline. It's because of him your wife can't freely visit her family, having to wear disguises. You two could never travel with Hunter to his tournaments outside of the country. And as happy as I have been to be the one to do it for you, it pisses me off, knowing everything he's taken from the two of you."

"We have a good life here," Colten told him. "And a good friend in you, and Kasey, for doing for our kids what we aren't able to do for them."

"Well," Cadman coughed to cover the emotion that rose up in his throat, "since we don't have kids of our own, we appreciate having some to spoil."

Chuckling, Colten motioned to Cadman's line. "Were you going to let that fish toy with the bait all day, or are you going to catch the damn thing?" This conversation had gotten too emotional for his liking.

Grabbing his pole, Cadman rose from the beach chair to snare the fish, glad to have something else to occupy his mind instead of memories from the past.

Chapter Twenty

"Hello," Travis's smile was warm as he walked up to Donna a week after he'd gone to Montana. Gently patting her on the rump, he gave her a quick kiss on the cheek. "Mmm, you smell good, baby."

Donna stepped away from the corral, where the therapists were working with the children. "How was your visit with your uncle?" she returned the smile. Despite her recent confusion, Travis still had the power to pull at her heartstrings. He may be a jock, preferring a backward baseball cap to a cowboy hat, but he had good qualities.

"What? No hug?" he asked, chuckling with a twinkle in his eye.

She hugged him, knowing she needed to have The Talk with him soon; he had no idea she was considering putting their relationship on hold.

When she released him, he answered her question. "My visit with my uncle was great; informative too."

"Informative?"

Travis nodded, motioning to the 35mm camera hanging around his neck. "He gave me some great pointers on picture taking. I might even make a few bucks."

Donna's mind did a double-take. This was the first she'd heard of him having an interest in photography. Her mind tried to put up a red flag, warning her something was not right.

"Money?" she said stupidly.

His laugh was soft. "Yeah, money. Never mind that, it's not important." His focus seemed to glide past her for the

slightest of moments. Then he grinned and raised the camera. "Mind if I take your picture?" The shutter clicked before she could reply. "That will look great hanging on my wall." he claimed.

Donna told herself not to be suspicious. People took pictures all the time. "Well, remember not to photograph the children who come here for Horse Adventures, unless you have permission first. Privacy reasons, of course."

She momentarily considered telling him not to take photos of Mason either, but she couldn't fathom why she should. Mason posed for countless photos with tourists whose only interest was capturing memories of those who guided them, not because they had any clue his mother was a famous movie star. It wasn't something her family discussed. If her relationship with Travis were to go farther, he would meet them and know the truth, but she hadn't broached the topic yet.

Travis shot one more photo in Donna's direction before allowing the camera to rest from the strap. "So, what have you been up too?" he asked, putting his arm around her as they began walking toward the house.

"Busy, busy," she answered, allowing his arm to guide her, trying to resurrect what she had felt for him.

But Jake chose that moment to walk by, heading toward a group of waiting tourists. She felt guilty all the same. Those feelings she once had for Travis weren't as strong as they had been before Jake Harper came into her life.

Jake did not glance her way, and it hurt. It should not have, but it did.

SPITFIRE

Unknowingly to Donna, Travis did not miss her eyeing the foreman. He was not a fool; he knew something was going on between them. He wanted to confront her but was afraid of losing the free pass his dating her gave him. As long as they were a couple, he would be here for the Fourth of July. Fortunately, the situation would take care of itself soon enough once his uncle arranged it. With Harper gone, Donna would not be distracted. He would have her all to himself, and that would guarantee his status with Donna Fisher.

They were at the front of the house when Travis said, "How'd you like to go to a movie tonight?"

"I can't. You know I'm only free on Friday nights, sometimes Saturday."

His sigh was loud, drawn-out, and disappointed. "I know. It's only… We don't get to spend any time together, and I miss you, baby."

Why did she feel so utterly awful? "I'm sorry, but you knew it would be like this. I explained it to you when we first started dating. Summer is my busy season."

He stopped walking and stepped around her so he could look at her directly. "It doesn't mean I have to like it." It was not said in anger, but the implication was clear: he was tiring of the long-distance relationship.

With a sigh, he relinquished, "Yes, you told me. You're busy during the summer; I'm busy in the fall when college starts back up. I've been helping Dad with his roofing business, but maybe I need to take on another job as well, merely to keep me occupied so I won't miss you so much."

"You could always work here," she suggested, surprising them both if that look of disbelief on his face was any indication.

"Here?" It was spoken with such disdain it caused Donna to step back.

Eyes narrowing, she pinned him with her gaze. "And exactly what is wrong with here?"

Travis's face flooded scarlet, with embarrassment or anger, only he knew. But it was self-directed anger, because how stupid could one get? Working here would have given him plenty of opportunities to complete his mission. But he'd put his foot in his mouth and couldn't figure out how to redeem himself without looking suspicious.

"Sorry, that was not meant the way it sounded." At least he could be somewhat truthful with her, because honestly, he didn't know squat about farm work and animals; he would never survive. "I've never been on a horse, Donna."

"You could learn."

"If I wanted to," he said. "Look, baby, let's drop this subject."

She shook her head. "Absolutely not, Travis."

He stared at her for a long moment, seeming to struggle for an explanation. "Okay, fine. The truth is…" he managed a sheepish look, "Horses scare the shit out of me!"

She stared. She would have never imagined.

The laughter tore from her throat before she could stop it, doubling her over with tears escaping her eyes and running down her cheeks. By the time she noticed he was no longer beside her, but sitting on the porch, she'd calmed down

enough to say, "Sorry," but the giggle didn't help the apology sound sincere.

"Well, go ahead, laugh it up. You asked."

Donna brought her laughter under control. "I am sorry, Travis. It's only that, you're a jock!"

"Athlete," he clarified.

"But still…" her humor returned. "You're afraid of horses?" Although Uncle Cadman, who used to travel the world tracking down terrorists, hated horses, he wasn't afraid of them.

Travis looked away, disgusted.

"Travis…"

"Oh, never mind. Let's drop it, all right?" He stood up. "We were talking about us not having time together often enough, remember?"

How could she forget? He'd taken her mind off her dilemma momentarily with his unexpected revelation. But now that he brought the subject back up, she needed to give him some type of answer. The problem was, she did not know what her response should be. Travis or Jake? Making choices of the heart was painful. She opened her mouth to say something, but what that might have been would remain a mystery to her as Hunter walked out the front door right then, saving her from making a snap decision.

"Hey, Champ," he greeted Travis as though it thrilled him to death to see him, and Donna's eyes widened with amazement. She would have thought her brother would have welcomed him a lot differently after their first encounter, but here

he was acting as though he truly was glad to see him. Would wonders never cease?

"Hi there, Sport," Travis grinned. "Good to see you, too."

Hunter hung his head as though he were embarrassed to have this guy giving him attention, and Donna was no longer in wonder; she was as suspicious as hell.

"Well," Hunter fairly gushed, "I was wondering… Is your offer to help me with my martial arts still open?"

Travis reached out and messed Hunter's hair. "Of course, it is! What do you need help with?"

"Would you mind helping me with my Pal Gae number eight? I'm having problems remembering that one."

Donna's jaw dropped. Hunter's photographic memory never failed him.

She sputtered, "You're having problems…"

"Yep, sure am," her brother cut her off. "Travis offered to help if I ever needed pointers with Taekwondo." He gave Travis such an innocent look it could have fooled anyone, if Donna didn't know her brother so well. "Isn't that right, Champ?"

Travis chuckled. The saying, ignorance is bliss, had never been truer than it was right then. "Yes, I did, sport. Come down here," he pointed to the bottom of the steps, "and show me what you know of the move."

"Okay, Champ!"

Donna raised a brow. Did she call Hunter on the carpet, or see how this thing played out?

SPITFIRE

Almost bouncing down the steps, Hunter took on the basic Taekwondo stance and began the Pal Gae. It was the sloppiest performance of the move Donna had ever seen her brother do.

"Hunter Sundance Fisher," Donna's tone was a warning. Whatever he was up to, it was not good.

The front door opened, and this time Mason stepped out. He glanced in Hunter and Travis's direction, but his face did not reveal a thing. "Donna, Randy ees not feeling well, and ees looking for you," he said, nodding toward the house.

She sighed. "All right." Obviously, Mason was in on this charade of Hunter's, and if they had gotten Randy involved in the scheme, she'd kill them both.

The last thing she heard before the door closed behind her was Travis saying, "Boy, sport. I'm surprised you ever got your junior black belt with such poor form."

Chapter Twenty-one

"Elle est amoureuse."

Hunter turned around in his saddle to stare at his best friend. "Yah think, Lafayette?" he said with a trace of sarcasm. "Of course, Donna's in love with the guy. The dumb girl hasn't figured it out yet."

Mason nudged his horse beside Hunter's mount as the trail widened. "Oui," he agreed. "However, there ees ztill one problem."

Hunter grunted, "Yeah, Travis." His face contorted as though he'd bitten into something foul tasting.

For a moment, they were silent, watching the group of ten tourists as their horses picked their way slowly along the designated path into the Badlands. This venture was a two-day campout. Oh, joy. Colten and Clinton were leading the group and were far enough away not to overhear this conversation, even though Colten would agree wholeheartedly with the teenagers, since he didn't like the jock either.

Deep in thought, Mason's romantic nature caused him to change the subject back. "I believe Harper lovez her, alzo. I zee the way he lookz at her; admiration, compazzion, gentleness..."

"You're gonna make me barf, Lafayette," Hunter declared.

Mason laughed, the sound disturbing a nearby rabbit, which took off in the opposite direction. "Hunter, you do not have a romantic bone in your body."

Hunter snorted.

SPITFIRE

Mason's brows drew together as a thought occurred to him. "I wonder what would happen if your plan failz and Donna windz up wiz Traviz." He grinned as his best friend's face twisted hideously at the mere idea. "Perhapz, it would be fun to have Traviz as a brother-in-law." He knew he was treading on shaky ground, but he could say things to Hunter no one else could.

Hunter gave a sharp pull on the reins, making his horse rear up. The sight caused the tourists to become uneasy, wondering if there was a nearby snake about to spook the animals they were on.

Bringing the quarter horse under control, seeing his father in the distance looking at him for an explanation, he forced himself to calm down. Not that it was easy; Hunter had a short fuse.

Signaling to his dad all was well, and lowering his voice, he hissed, "There is no way I'll let that happen. She's not going to stay hooked up with him much longer. I promise you that. Travis was acting pretty suspicious last night." Travis had spent the night in one of the empty guest cabins, claiming he was too tired to travel the remaining distance to Bismarck after coming from Montana.

"Ees there somezing you have not told me, Hunter?" Mason asked. They had been in this plot from the beginning, but Hunter seemed to be holding back.

"Yes, there ees," Hunter mimicked Mason's chopped English. "Having Travis spending the night allowed me to watch him more closely."

Mason chuckled and dared, "You liked being wiz your buddy, eh zport."

Hunter's facial expression turned livid. "Don't you ever," he warned, highly agitated, "use that word around me again." A shiver coursed through his entire body.

Mason knew he had gone too far. Still, it was entertaining watching Hunter pretend to tolerate the guy when all he really wanted was to smash in his face. Hunter was merely biding his time, waiting for the precise moment. Mason prayed he wouldn't miss the complete and utter grinding of Travis Carlson into the dirt when the time came. He disliked the man no less than Hunter did.

"Anyway," Hunter continued, regaining his composure, "I spent the night watching him watching you."

Mason's face showed he did not understand. "When waz deez?"

"Thisss," Hunter corrected, then went on with his story. "Carlson was sneaking around the guest cabins while you were there." When Mason shrugged, Hunter added, "With that camera of his."

Again, Mason shrugged. "My family eez always photographed…"

"In America?" Hunter questioned, then stressed, "In North Dakota? Nobody who would want photos of you, because of who you are, knows you're here." He watched Mason grasp the implication. "Now you've got it."

"Mon Dieu!"

"Exactly. Carlson is up to something, and I'm gonna find out what."

A comfortable silence fell between them, but Mason managed to rid himself of thoughts of the dreadful consequences if Travis was indeed using photography in the way they suspected.

Hunter's pants caught the sun's reflection, casting off beams of light and changing Mason's focus momentarily. "How many zipperz do those pantz have?" Mason asked. They were too unique-looking not to draw attention.

Hunter glanced down at the specially designed baggy pants made of lightweight cotton camouflage print. The pants, which he'd designed, were the gift his mother had made for him while she was in France. "Twenty-five."

Mason arched a brow.

"It's an experiment," Hunter explained. "Each compartment contains items sealed in watertight pouches: Flashlight, matches, lighter, fishing line and hook, pocketknife—my numb chucks are here," he pointed to his right pants leg to the bulge on the side between thigh and knee, "my Swiss army knife is here, duct tape here," he pointed to each pocket as he listed off the numerous items.

Mason's face showed his confusion. "Ees that not what backpackz are for?"

"Yeah, but I want to carry things on my person at all times. It's a round-the-clock survival kit. I don't carry a backpack all the time, but I certainly wear pants." Hunter took the Boy Scout motto 'Always Be Prepared' to heart. "And," he added, pinching the material between his fingers and moving it back and forth, "they are loose enough to allow me to do my martial arts with ease of movement."

Hunter watched the riders for a time, wishing he was gone from here and a Navy SEAL already.

"So, Lafayette," he glanced back to Mason. "You ready to see your folks again?"

Mason kept his eyes forward, not wanting his friend to see the pain the question caused him. "I have mizzed my little zizter," he answered.

"Sssssisssster," Hunter corrected, stretching out the S sound, again. "Seriously, Mason. You need to work on your S's."

Mason hissed at him, sounding like a snake.

Laughing, Hunter said, "There. That's better! Keep that in mind the next time you say, sister."

"Anyway, let's get back to the subject. By now, you must be homesick and missing your parents."

"Oui, but..." Mason searched for the words to describe his turmoil. "All of my life, I believed Charlez was my père. Discovering he ees not...that the one who fathered me ees a wanted criminal..." his voice trailed off. "The same man who caused your father to lose his eye..."

He glanced up at the clear blue sky for a few moments to compose himself before continuing. "Knowing what that man did to my mother iz hard enough. To know hiz blood flowz through me..." he shook his head, at a loss, dampness gathering behind his eyes.

Hunter was silent for a moment, knowing he wanted to say something to ease his friend's heartache. Though he did not allow emotion to rule him, Hunter understood.

He cleared his throat. "Perhaps you need to focus on the fact Charles loved you enough to give you his last name. I think it's more important that you find a way to concentrate on that and fuck whoever your biological father was. Although, I'm sorry he obviously passed his ugly face onto you."

Mason stared at him.

Hunter stared back. Laughed. "You should see the look on your face. It's priceless."

"I am not ugly. Women find me irresistible."

"I'll be damned. You managed to pronounce irresistible without a hitch, but you're still ugly."

"Va te faire enculer," Mason told him, though there was a smile on his face when he told Hunter to do something that was not physically possible. He knew Hunter was only trying to lighten the moment.

"Well, Lafayette," Hunter said matter-of-factly, "Your mom's still your mom, and Charles is your pop in every sense of the word. You should…" The sentence was cut short when he noted one of the horses ahead of them turning from the trail, heading in some direction other than the designated path.

"Hey," he called to the rider, "where are you going?!"

"I don't know!" came the frustrated answer. "Ask the horse!"

Hunter rolled his eyes, cursed, and under his breath, for Mason's ears only, said, "Tourists."

He hated these stinking trail rides.

Chapter Twenty-two

As the days passed, it seemed to Donna that whenever Jake was not guiding a tour, she would find him hanging around the corral used for the Horse Adventure program. He would often walk alongside the smaller mounts, his presence a comforting anchor as he served as a side walker, his hands near the child's hip or saddle horn, ready to stabilize them and keep them upright if needed.

He would kneel beside a child patiently showing them how to manage the metal latch of a gate, his own calloused fingers guiding the child's clumsy grip. Then there were other times when he could demonstrate the careful technique needed to tighten a cinch on a small saddle, making sure the slightly handicapped child understood the feel of the leather and the importance of the correct tension.

One day she witnessed him take a handkerchief from his pocket and wipe the nose of one little girl who was beaming despite her difficulty with motor control. Moments later, he stood ready to clean the saliva from the corner of a mouth that drooped, his attention entirely on the comfort and dignity of the children he served. He treated each act, whether it was handling tack or addressing a physical need, with the same quiet, uncompromising respect he showed the tourists or other guests of the ranch.

There was no end to his tolerance. Even when three-year-old Hanna threw up on him because of her nervousness about getting on a horse, he took it in stride. He continued to soothe the child until he had her up there in that saddle, and only

then, once assured she was all right, had he turned her over to a trained professional and strolled to the bunkhouse to shower and change, as though he didn't reek or cause a few green faces in his wake.

Randy, especially, seemed to favor him more so with each passing day. Sometimes Jake would take him along when he led an hour-long tour, going bareback because it was beneficial to the child. Each act of kindness Jake did regarding Donna's special charges melted away her previous belief that her dad made a mistake in hiring him.

The scales were tipping in his favor. Yet, he'd wholly distanced himself from her, other than the time he spent with the children. Even then, he ignored her, acting as though that kiss never happened. He avoided being alone with her as though she had a contagious disease.

And she was glad for it. Honest, she was. She kept telling herself that anyway and willed for it to be true.

She had not seen or heard from Travis since he left a week and a half ago. Though she did not exactly miss him, she found his absence odd.

It was the last Friday of June when she found herself sitting on the front porch of her home, feeling restless, wanting something different to do for a change. All the children were gone, a new group to arrive on Monday.

The last tour for the day left almost an hour ago, and the ranch would close to any more tours in a matter of minutes. Once this last group returned and left, there would be peace and quiet for the night.

Her parents, along with Cadman and Kasey, had driven into Medora tonight to attend the musical. Meanwhile, Hunter and Mason were off doing who knew what, and Melissa was currently trying to master her new video game. In the living area, Sara and her girlfriend, Beth, were entertaining the twins with a board game. They had talked Clinton into joining them, hoping the game would distract him from obsessing about the horse whose delivery had been postponed.

Donna sighed. She'd never been bored in her life, but she was sitting here doing absolutely nothing but waiting for Randy's return, as Jake had taken the boy with him on this last tour. Her sitting here waiting had nothing to do with wanting a glimpse of that cowboy and his crooked tooth smile. Not a thing.

When she, at last, spotted the group coming into view, she stood up and headed toward them. She would collect Randy and be on her way. Nothing more than that crossed her mind, and simply because she might have to speak with Jake in the process, well, she couldn't help that. Maybe he would smile at her.

What a dumb thought.

She met them at the dismounting area, automatically reaching for Randy to help him down, and the boy was instantly trying to tell her something. But in his excited state, she could not make head or tails out of the garbled sentence.

She looked to Jake for the explanation, enjoying the way he could smoothly slide off a horse. Today he wore a gray t-shirt with torn-off sleeves to complement his blue jeans, and she wondered if the guy owned any shirts that were not torn.

He seemed to wear them constantly, despite owning a beautiful, expensive black jean jacket she'd seen a few times. Perhaps that was why; after the extravagance of the jacket, he probably couldn't afford new clothing.

This t-shirt was torn at the sides. The only thing holding it together were the seams across his shoulders and around his waist. It left a gaping hole on both sides that gave her teasing glimpses of his washboard abs.

She could have used an ice pack right about now, and it had nothing to do with the ninety-five-degree heat they'd been blessed with today.

Randy was still trying to make known what he was excited about, and that was a welcome distraction. It also gave Donna an excuse to talk to Jake. Not that she wanted one, but who was she to question an opportunity?

"What's he so excited about?"

Jake reached out and messed Randy's hair with his hand. "I told him I was fixin' to take him to the movie tonight." Jake smiled, and her heart fluttered.

He moved away from her, gave the tourists the final farewell and thank you speech, reminding them there were souvenirs at the general store if they wished to find a memento. Then he spoke with the employee who had brought up the rear of the tour as they began the work of un-cinching saddles, taking care of the horses, and putting the gear away for the night.

Donna was still standing there with Randy when Jake finished the chore, surprising him. He'd expected her to have escorted Randy to the house, not linger, and her lingering was

not good. Her proximity did things to him he wished to ignore. Helping with those children took effort, but forcing himself to ignore her presence during those times took extreme determination. He continued to be drawn to her, but he'd made up his mind to keep his hands to himself. Don't look. Don't touch. Definitely, don't kiss. But she was standing there watching him, and he wanted to do all three. That and more. So much more.

There was no avoiding her. To do so would be rude, and so he gathered his will about him like a cloak and walked forward. "Did you need somethin'?"

"Well," she drew the word out, "what movie are you going to?"

His stare was long. He had a hard time not becoming lost in those huge sapphire eyes of hers. He realized then her question wasn't personal; the Fishers were responsible for Randy. He should have asked for permission first before promising the kid. He relaxed. "Guess I should have asked…"

"Oh, that's not a problem. Randy seems to adore you, and we trust you." When had she begun to no longer think of him as an ex-con, but as trustworthy? "I was wondering, that's all."

"Raiders of the Lost Ark," he answered.

"That one with Harrison Ford?"

He nodded.

"That, ah," she cleared her throat, "That is, ah," oh, come out with it, dimwit. "That would be fun."

Jake stared at her anew. Was she hinting?

"Did you want to join us?" he asked, heart thumping, and couldn't believe he was asking.

"Oh, wow! That would be great!"

He chuckled. How could he not? Though he wondered, if she tagged along, how he would make it through the evening without touching her? But Randy would be there, so they would not be alone. Frickin A., he wished they would be, and yet it would be better this way.

Then another thought occurred to him. "What about Travis?" He hated bringing jock-boy into the conversation, but he could never forget she had a boyfriend.

She merely shrugged. "I don't see him around, and besides, if I can't go to a movie with friends..." she trailed off and shrugged again.

Inwardly Jake winced at being classified as a friend; he wanted more but would settle for any morsel she threw his way. Was he pathetic? Absolutely, but he didn't rightly care at the moment, too thrilled at the prospect of spending an evening with her, even if it was with a seven-year-old chaperone.

They agreed to meet in forty-five minutes, and Donna and Randy were waiting for Jake on the porch when he eased his pickup to a stop in front of the Fisher's home.

Donna left her cowboy hat behind, Jake was pleased to note, and her shoulder-length hair fell free, framing her face. It surprised him to notice she'd used a small amount of make-up to enhance her looks, and at that moment, she honest to God took his breath away.

She wore an off-the-shoulder, above-the-knee, button-down dress with a ruffled hem and elastic waist. A wide silver Concho brown belt circled her slender waist, and light-brown ankle western boots graced her feet.

He fleetingly wondered how he was supposed to survive this evening with her looking like that. His longing for her had never been stronger.

Knowing he needed to help Randy into the truck, he exited the jacked-up Ford and took the steps two at a time to reach them, trying not to be obvious in his attraction to Donna. He gave her a quick glance, knowing that if his eyes lingered on her, he would find himself uncomfortably trying to keep an erection hidden.

Concentrating on Randy, he said, "Howdy, buddy, ready for that movie?" At Randy's affirmation, Jake continued, "Well then, let's get a move on." Once more, he looked at Donna and surprised himself by saying, "You look gorgeous, Spitfire."

Donna looked away, unable to believe the warmth he'd generated in her heart with that simple compliment. She murmured a thank you and refused to analyze why she wanted to dress up a little for tonight's outing.

But she couldn't help but notice how nice he looked. Gone was the torn t-shirt and ripped jeans. Now he was wearing a black cotton, spread collar, western shirt with contrast stitching on the pockets. The shirt was tucked into jeans that looked as though he had been sewn into them. The entire outfit looked as though it had been custom-made. The outfit, and that jean jacket he owned, probably cost a fortune.

SPITFIRE

The unwelcome, fleeting idea that he might have stolen the money to purchase them tried to surfaced, but she shoved it down instantly and told herself to stop being ridiculous. Of course he hadn't robbed a bank! In all the time she had known him, he had given her no reason whatsoever to doubt his integrity. She absolutely refused to think the worst of him.

Donna wasn't sure anymore where her emotions were regarding Jake Harper, but she told him, "You look nice, too," and looked away when she felt her face flush.

"We," Jake cleared his throat. "We best be headin' on down the road if we expect to make the movie on time."

Jake helped Randy down the handicap ramp that ran the side of the porch steps. As he did so, he told Donna to get into the pickup's cab. Only after she was already committed did she realize that once Randy was in the cab, she would be in the middle, right next to Jake. Her heart did several flip-flops.

Within moments Randy was buckled in, and Jake had climbed into the driver's side. He pushed in the clutch, shifted gears, and his hand brushed her thigh. She felt a shiver run through her at the slight touch. Their eyes met for the slightest of moments, but in that casual glance, Donna's heart squeezed.

Jake cleared his throat. They needed a distraction. He motioned to the cassette case near Donna's feet and told her to pick one out and put it in the player.

Glad to have something else to consider, Donna reviewed Jake's collection: Hank Williams Jr., Mickey Gilley, Conway Twitty, Ronnie Milsap, Tanya Tucker, Alabama—all great artists, many of them her favorites. She chose one by The Oak

Ridge Boys and placed it into the cassette deck. Within moments, she and Jake were comically singing along to "Elvira," with Randy exclaiming, "Ira!" each time they sang the name.

It was nice to have country/western music, her preference. Travis leaned toward hard Rock n' Roll. No, she would not think about Travis tonight, but if he were here, and could read her thoughts, he would have a legitimate reason to be jealous. The attraction she had for Jake was so tangible it frightened her. She had so much more in common with Jake than she did with a college boy from Bismarck. Her doubts about her relationship with Travis increased.

The drive from the ranch into Dickinson took forty-five minutes. With moments to spare before the movie began, Jake dropped his passengers off close to the building then parked the truck. He met them at the ticket window and paid the fee for all of them.

"Would you like popcorn?" Jake asked her, motioning to the concession stand.

With a laugh, Donna told him, "It's the only way to watch a movie! Of course, we want popcorn!" She looked at Randy, "Don't we?"

Randy grinned. "Orn. I ike pa orn."

"Me too," Jake told the boy.

While Jake stood in line, Donna helped Randy maneuver down the aisle of the theater where they found seats. Donna decided it would be wise for Randy to be seated between her and Jake. She could still feel the touch of Jake's hand as it brushed her thigh each time he'd shifted gears. It would have been better if Jake's truck was an automatic.

SPITFIRE

Once Jake joined them, it was not long before the movie began, and everyone was holding their breaths watching Harrison Ford's character outrun a gigantic boulder. Randy squealed with delight.

At one point during the movie, Jake stretched, placing an arm around Randy's shoulder. But when his arm came down to rest on Randy, it startled him to encounter Donna's arm already there. Over the child's head, their eyes met, but he did not move his arm, and neither did she.

Then she smiled, a small, hesitant smile that brought warmth into Jake's heart and longing to his soul. The signals she was giving off had him rock hard, and now he wished Randy were not there because he was ready to haul her out of that chair, out of the building, and into the nearest Motel.

Was she doing it on purpose? Was she telling him she wanted to explore this electric current going on between them? Or was she stringing him along? True, he hadn't seen jock-boy around for a while, but as far as he knew, they were still a couple. Was she playing games with him?

He needed and wanted answers. But Randy was along, and his questions had to wait. But he was determined to find out tonight once and for all where he stood with her.

He treated them to ice cream after the movie. A cold shower would have been better, and as much as he wanted to get back to the ranch and corner Donna alone, it would not be fair to Randy.

But he made sure Randy was sitting next to him instead of Donna for this trip back. He would not put himself through any more discomfort, and when she was near, he was

uncomfortable to the extreme. They ate in the truck with Donna spoon-feeding Randy his chocolate Sundae and watching the cars drive by the Dairy Queen.

Donna was the first one to notice the black jacked-up Ford pickup drive by. For one fleeting moment, she would have sworn Travis was in the passenger seat. But the vehicle passed too quickly for her to be sure, and she could not imagine why he would be in Dickinson.

"Hey, that looks exactly like your truck, Jake," she said, pointing in the direction the pickup had gone.

Glancing up, Jake caught sight of the back end of the vehicle as it turned a corner. "Mine's better," he claimed, with no small amount of male vanity, and dismissed the matter from his mind.

By the time the threesome arrived back at the F&L, Randy was half asleep. Jake carried him up the stairs of the porch, setting his frail body down so he could stand. "Did you have a good time?" he asked the child.

Randy nodded wearily.

"Me too," Jake assured him, then shot Donna a look that told her he wanted to talk and would not take no for an answer.

"I'll take Randy inside," her voice was soft, nervous. She didn't doubt she knew what was on his mind. She'd been giving him the come-on all evening, yet she was not sure what she would say to him. She wondered if she told him she was a mixed-up mess, he would accept that for an answer.

"I, ah," her eyes met his, "I think I'll walk over to the corral, and check on the horses after he's tucked in for the night."

SPITFIRE

His look was intense. "That would be a good idea," he told her.

His attention turned to Randy. "Well, scamp," he smiled. The child was almost asleep on his feet. "You have peaceful dreams. I'll see you in the mornin'." He tipped his hat to Donna and stepped off the porch and headed for the bunkhouse, figuring he had time for a smoke before Donna would come back out.

It was not long before he spotted her exiting the house, going to the corral. He didn't move right away. He watched as she leaned on a fence post and watched the horses. He crushed the cigarette out with the heel of his boot, tossed it away, and headed toward the corral.

Donna heard rocks crunching under the weight of his boots, and slowly she turned. She was not sure if this was a bright idea, but they needed to talk. "Thanks again for the movie..."

"Let's cut to the chase." He pinned her with his eyes. He was not in the mood for small talk.

She turned away, trying to hide from the anger in his tone and the fire in his eyes.

"Did I misread your signals durin' that movie?"

She closed her eyes and groaned. "Jake, I don't know what to think anymore. I feel as though I'm being tugged in two directions."

He spun her around, feeling justifiably angry.

"Here's the deal," he snapped, "I care about you. I believe in the work you're doin'. You have a wonderful gift with horses and an open heart for children. But I cannot deal with your mixed signals. It's utter hell bein' here, knowin' you're

not available." He released her with enough force she stumbled.

Tears pooled behind her eyes. "Please don't make it more difficult—"

He laughed. The sound harsh. "Difficult?! You don't know the half of it."

He turned around and began walking away. "Don't play games with me. I've had enough women in my life who have done that, and if that's all you're going to do, to hell with you."

Donna watched him disappear into the bunkhouse and felt her heart break.

Chapter Twenty-three

Donna did not have any problem getting out of bed the next morning for her before-dawn ride. She had not slept at all. Jake was right. She needed to come to a concrete decision.

In record time, she had her horse saddled and was racing out of the yard to the special place she discovered at the tender age of ten. It was far removed from any of the trails used for guided tours, hidden in a little valley, then up a small hill and across the Little Missouri. Only here could she clear her mind, finalize her daily intentions, or simply watch the glorious sunrise play across the immense North Dakota plains.

But not this time. She knew she needed to break up with Travis, and it weighed heavily on her mind. She'd thought of nothing else during the night. And she finally admitted to herself her feelings for Travis no longer existed, and what she felt for Jake was so much more.

Dismounting, knowing her horse was trained not to wander, she allowed the reins to slide from her hands as she grabbed the blanket she always brought along. She walked a short distance, spread the thick blanket out, and sat down in its center to watch the sun continue to climb.

As the sky slowly subsided into a kaleidoscope of colors, and the shadows receded, the sound of a horse approaching drew her attention. Her eyes widened with surprise when she looked over her shoulder and saw who'd dared invade her sanctuary. Seeing Jake and his horse leisurely moving toward her had her slowly standing to her feet to watch his approach.

Their eyes met as he neared; he stopped the horse for a heartbeat before setting it into a slow walk down the short incline, not once breaking eye contact with her.

Jake dismounted next to her horse, doing as she had, and allowed the reins to drop from his hand. He closed the distance between them and stopped before her.

"Well, at least now I know where you go every morning when you've woken me up from a sound sleep." There seemed to be a hint of a smile on his face, but it was not a happy one. He looked sad, and her heart ached, knowing she caused his pain.

"You followed me?" Eyes wide, scarcely believing he was there.

He gave a slight nod. "I know I shouldn't have..." He looked as though he was raging a battle within himself. "Fricken A., I know you have a boyfriend, and I shouldn't be feelin' the way I do about you, but that doesn't stop the pull you have on me, and as much as I love it here, after last night, I decided it's time to move on. I'll be givin' your dad my two weeks' notice this mornin' when I get back to the ranch."

"Why!?" Dumb question. She knew the answer to that, but she hadn't told him the decision she'd come to last night either.

He reached out and grabbed her shoulders. "Because you do have a boyfriend, and I'm not the kind of man to steal another man's girl."

"Well, that's noble of you, if you're referring to me. But before you give my dad your resignation, I think you might

like to know that I'll be breaking up with Travis the next time I see him."

He stared. "What?"

She shook her head; almost laughed at the expression on his face. "Did you go deaf, Harper?"

He was not going to assume. "Why are you goin' to break up with jock-boy?"

"You will not make this easy for me, will you?" She smiled at him. "Because you're the one I want to be with, Jake."

They were in each other's arms without consciously knowing they had moved. Their lips met; their tongues danced.

"Oh, God," someone moaned, but which one had was up for grabs.

He tore his lips from hers. "You mean that?"

She nodded, unable to manage an audible voice. His presence was overpowering. The sensations fluttering in her belly, and the warmth spreading through her, refused to be denied any longer. She leaned into him, and his mouth fused with hers once more.

His tongue forced its way between her lips, and she opened her mouth to accommodate him, moaning softly. She could feel the evidence of his desire pressing against her hip and knew there was no turning back. Today she would know what it was like to be with a man, and today she would make love to the man of her heart.

He pulled her down to the blanket, managing to have her lying on top of him with her legs between his. But the full weight of her pressing on him was torture; exquisite torture,

but he rolled over anyway, placing her beneath him; frantic urgency to his every movement.

Donna felt him opening her belt and tugging at her shirt. His hand moved up under her shirt and under her bra. The contact of his hand on her breast brought forth little sounds of pleasure, driving him wild. He was too inflamed to be gentle, but so was she.

She damn near tore that sleeveless t-shirt from him, trying to reach his bare flesh. His skin was hot, burning her, and the muscles on his back were hard and tense. She dug her fingers into those muscles, clasping him savagely, running her fingers through his hair. She ran her hands over his shoulders, his thickly corded neck, then back to his hair, grasping it in her fists to anchor him to her mouth.

His lips devoured hers, bruising her, demanding more, and she gave back with the same intensity he was giving her. He tugged at her pants, and she helped him push them down to her feet; removing her boots, he extracted the jeans completely.

His desire to have her skin molded to his gave him lightning speed. He took off the rest of her clothing and his as well. Laying her back on the blanket, he covered her with his hard body, ravishing her mouth once again, as he continued his assault. She brought her knees up, giving him access to that part of her that was moist and warm, making it easy for him to enter her. But for one delicious moment, Jake restrained, wanting to savor that first thrust.

Belatedly, he realized he was not wearing a condom. This seduction had not been on his mind when he followed her

here, but there was no turning back. It was too late for that. But then she said, "God, Jake. I've never done this before, but I knew when I met the right man, it would be like this."

Jake froze in mid-thrust. "Oh, my God," he gasped. Beads of sweat lined his brow from the effort he made not to continue forward; tremors shook his body; his eyes locked with hers.

It never entered his mind that she would be a virgin. Why he assumed she would have done this before he did not know, but he should have known not to assume anything about her.

"Donna…" he did not know if he should continue forward or retreat. Knowing this was her first time shook him to the bone.

"Jake," she whispered. "Don't stop now."

He would have laughed if he were not trying to do exactly that. "Are you sure…"

To prove she was sincere and knew this was her choice, she thrust her hips upward, taking him in. She gasped and sighed his name. She never dreamed anything could feel this good and she delighted in the full length of him.

For a moment, Jake did not move. He savored the feel of her warmth surrounding him as he let her do the same. And when he began moving within her, his movements, at first, were slower than she would have liked. But she found the exquisite torture had its rewards, intensifying her need, prolonging the craving. And when she hurtled over the crest, the explosion that followed shook her to the core, draining her. Nothing on earth could compare.

She was positive she made the right choice, and afterward, as she lay with her head on his chest, their bodies entwined, she could not help the silly thought that crossed her mind. She never imagined lovemaking was this wonderful. No wonder Mason was so fond of it.

She got the giggles because of that thought.

Jake had been laying there, digesting the fact he'd been her first, pleased with the knowledge; jock-boy never had her. But when he felt her body beginning to shake and heard the soft giggles, he felt a moment of defensiveness. "You know," he said, "it unnerves a man to have the woman he made love to moments ago laugh afterward."

She glanced up at him, a twinkle in her eye. "I assure you. I wasn't laughing at you."

"Well, that's a comfort."

She looked up at him again. It felt so right, lying here with him. She was not ashamed of lying out in the open with nothing on but sunlight and was thankful it was already warm, despite it being barely seven o'clock in the morning.

Now that she made her choice, she was not afraid to ask him anything. And because she always wondered, from the first time she saw it, she asked, "How did you get that scar, Jake?" She reached up to touch it as she asked, but he jerked his head away.

"It doesn't matter." The tone was angry, defensive, and caused Donna to recoil from the intensity of it. One simple question and the mood was shot to shit.

"Well, excuse me," she huffed, sitting up, reaching for her clothes, trying desperately not to allow the moisture forming

SPITFIRE

in her eyes to trail down her cheeks. What a fool she was to expect he would open up to her only because she had given herself to him.

With a curse, Jake reached for her. "Look, I'm sorry. I simply don't want to talk about it."

She pinned him with her eyes. The daggers coming out of them should have caused more scarring, if not death. "Hey, no problem," she snapped. "Silly of me to have asked such a personal question after what I allowed you to do." She had her jeans back on in record time.

"Now, Donna…" he reached for his own clothing. "It's not like that."

"Whatever." She pulled her boots on, stood up, grabbed his pants and boots, and threw them as far away as she could before stalking to her horse with such intensity it had the beast skidding away. She did not care one bit that he would have to walk barefooted over thistles to get to his boots; she simply wanted out of there.

A sling of curses were being strewn behind her as Jake struggled to fetch the clothing she'd carelessly thrown. She was on her horse in the blink of an eye and speeding over the Badlands as though a band of wild coyotes were nipping at her heels.

How could she have been so stupid? Giving herself to him when he was not willing to share his past with her was by far the most foolish thing she had ever done. If she ever saw him again, it would be too soon.

He caught up with her before she reached the halfway mark to home. "Damn it, Donna," he shouted as his horse came

alongside hers. He tried reaching for the reins of her horse, but she took her foot out of the stirrup and kicked out.

That made Jake madder than hell. Confounded woman, she had reached the wrong conclusion and wasn't about to give him a chance to explain. Well, he was going to explain if he had to drag her off that horse.

Which was precisely what he did.

He maneuvered his horse a hair's breadth from the side of hers, wrapped an arm around her waist, and pulled. Doing that at breakneck speed in the movies was always so romantic looking, but in real life, it was a damn near catastrophe.

Her horse was long gone by the time he managed to stop his mount while still retaining his hold on her, screaming and twisting as she was and cursing him for almost getting her trampled to death because of his lack of good sense.

"What in the hell do you think you were doing!?" her voice was a high-pitched shrill, her eyes incredibly large with the fright he'd given her. Once her feet could touch the ground, now that his horse had stopped, she found standing difficult because her legs wobbled from the terror she'd experienced. She doubted her heartbeat would ever be its normal rate again.

Jake dismounted; reached for her, wanting to comfort and assure himself she was all right, but she was not having any of that. She took on a martial arts stance and said, "Stop right there."

He did and raised his hands in surrender. "I should have known you'd know karate."

SPITFIRE

"Yeah, well, a person can't grow up with the brother I have and not learn something from him. He's even teaching Melissa and the twins some defensive moves in case the need should ever arise."

They were at a standoff, and they knew it.

"Will you calm down enough to listen to me?" he managed to bring his emotions under control. The fact he could have killed her with that dumb stunt with the horse had frightened him to death.

Her answer was a curt nod.

He took a deep breath. "I'm sorry I got mad at you back there. Especially after what we shared. It wasn't right of me to refuse to answer your question when you have the right to know my past." He jerked his thumb toward the faint defect under his chin, braced for whatever her reaction would be, and told her, "I got it my first month in prison."

For a moment, she could only stare. Her mind tried to grasp that. He had been in prison. Oh, she'd known he was an ex-con! She'd known it! Hadn't she suspected him of being trouble that first day she'd seen him with that shoulder-length hair of his and a blue bandana wrapped around his forehead? Yet she'd been drawn to him like a deer to headlights, mesmerized, unable to see the danger approaching despite warning bells, and now here he was, confirming her earlier assumptions.

And to top it off, the coup de grâce: she had allowed a felon, a convicted felon to be exact, to be the first man to make love to her. No doubt he killed someone, and here she was, alone with him, with no witnesses about. Thank God she

knew some martial arts and hoped it would be enough to save her when he made his move.

"For cryin' out loud," he snapped, "Stop lookin' at me as though I murdered someone."

She blinked, then snapped back, "Well, didn't you?"

He shook his head. "Fricken A, thanks for thinkin' the worst."

She shrugged. What else was there to do? "My dad knows you were in prison?" Her own question gave her pause. Of course, her father knew. He'd done that background check. He would never have allowed Jake to get within five hundred feet of the children who frequented the ranch, let alone employ him. She should have thought of that sooner, but at least now she felt somewhat better. Obviously, he was not a killer. "All right," she sighed, "I'm waiting. What did you do?"

Now how was he supposed to answer that question? He'd done nothing, except refuse a woman's advances. He wouldn't believe such a ridiculous tale if someone told it to him, so when he told her the truth, it didn't surprise him one bit when her laughter erupted.

"And the scar?" she asked in-between breaths. "No, no, let me guess." She had to hold her sides. They hurt from the amusement his confession caused her. "One of the prison mice held his little knife to your throat and demanded you give him some cheese."

His smile was tight. "Somethin' like that." He turned toward the horse, picking up the reins, through with this conversation. She was not ready to believe him, and he wasn't going to try to convince her he'd spoken the truth.

SPITFIRE

He mounted up and reached out his hand. "Come on, we'll find your horse and head back to the ranch in time for breakfast."

She stared up at him, the determined look on his face making her hesitant. Not about her safety, but with her quick judgment on thinking his reason for being in prison had been a sorry excuse of an explanation. Yet, who in their right mind would conjure up such an unbelievable story if it were a lie?

"You're seriously telling me they locked you up in prison because you wouldn't.... wouldn't...," she simply couldn't say it.

"Come on," he continued to hold out his hand. "We'll talk more after we eat."

She looked at the hand for several moments before accepting his help in mounting up behind him. Call her a glutton for punishment; she had to hear how he had gotten that scar.

Chapter Twenty-four

The horse Jake and Donna rode crested the last hill looking down upon the F&L. They hadn't searched for Donna's horse, as she assured Jake it would find its way back home. She hoped they would arrive before anyone sent a search party out to look for her when they saw her horse come home without its rider.

Looking down the hill, they could easily see a horse trailer attached to a big pickup parked in the yard near the corral.

"Thank God," Donna sighed. "I think Clinton's Appaloosa finally arrived."

She felt Jake tense behind her. Turning her head to look at him, she could see his jaw was set, and he appeared upset.

"Jake? What's wrong?"

He looked at her. "I'm getting off here. You take the horse down."

"What?" Why on earth would he want to walk the rest of the way when they were so close to home?

Dismounting, he handed her the reins, looked back down at the horse trailer. "I need a few moments."

"But…" she could not fathom the hardness of his face.

He looked grim.

"Jake…"

"Go!" he shouted, the command snapping like a whip, and the sudden, raw fury in his voice made her body jerk involuntarily. He immediately closed his eyes. "I'm sorry," he said, shaking his head. "I'll explain later, okay? I simply need to be alone for a bit, that's all."

SPITFIRE

She stared at him long enough that it had him looking away.

"All right," she said after a moment and set the horse in motion down the hill.

Jake watched her slowly descend, then moved his attention back to the trailer. He'd known Clinton purchased an Appaloosa from out of state. Why hadn't he bothered to ask from where he'd bought it?

Could he hope his father was not down there? But that would be a foolish dream. Gregory Harper took pride in delivering his prized horses himself to those who had the money to spend on them, hoping that by doing so, it would impress the buyer into wanting to buy another one from him in the future.

From where Jake stood on the hilltop, he watched Donna approach the barn, dismount, and hand the horse over to someone else to take care of before she walked the distance to the horse trailer. The beautiful horse was being unloaded, and Clinton was there for the unveiling. Jake could feel the man-boy's excitement all the way up here.

Taking off his hat, Jake threw it on the ground in anger and knew he was having a tantrum but did not care. He was twenty-five years old and finally found a place where he felt he belonged. He did not want his dad in this life, and, oh god, would Clair come here so she would have the pleasure of looking down on the Fishers? Because he could bet she would not consider them high society enough. As far as Jake was concerned, the Fishers were as important here in the Dakotas as the Harpers were in Texas.

Feeling as though a weight had been placed on his shoulders and knowing he could not run from this, as much as he wanted to, it was time to face the hangman's noose. He picked up the cowboy hat, dusted off the dirt, placed the Stetson back on his head, squared his shoulders, and began his descent down the hill.

While Jake descended, Donna joined the rest of the family to welcome the new horse and to congratulate Clinton on his choice. Clinton, of course, was beaming and bouncing in place. He was eager to ride the horse, but he knew horses like the back of his hand, and he would give the beast time to adjust to him and its new surroundings before racing it across the prairie.

Jacqueline hugged Clinton. "He's beautiful," she told him. "And a wonderful addition to the ranch."

She looked over his shoulder and met Colten's eye. She smiled at her husband, knowing to have anything other than Quarter Horses on the ranch bugged the hell out of him. The horses she preferred were raised by her family in France, and because she'd grown up around them, Arabians held a special place in her heart. She'd kept one for her own personal use on the ranch since Colten and she had wed. Much to his dismay.

Now there was a different breed in the mix, and she knew Colten would grumble about it for a few weeks, then accept it.

"What 'cha gonna name him?" Hunter asked, eyeing the horse, and admitted it was spectacular.

SPITFIRE

Clinton puffed out his chest. "I will name him Sundance. Your middle name. It will remind me of you when you are gone. He is strong and fast, just like you!"

Hunter stared, and the family gasped. Clinton's confession touched everyone, as they had not been sure he understood his brother would be leaving, and there was no way of knowing when, if ever, he would come back home. Not someone who was known to become emotional, Hunter felt a lump form in his throat, and moisture threatened to flow from his eyes.

"Maybe he'll buck you off, so you'll remember what it's like when I get mad at you," Hunter said, voice gruff, and yet there was a smile on his lips when he said it. And he allowed Clinton to put him in a headlock and run his knuckles over his scalp as his brother laughed and said, "I won't miss that!"

Jacqueline wrapped her arms around Colten, leaned her face into his chest as her own tears flowed at the thoughtfulness of Clinton, and because she would miss her son each and every day. Colten felt his own heart squeeze, and he wiped at his eye to remove the moisture gathering there. Cadman was right. Where had the time gone? Only yesterday, he carried both Clinton and Hunter on his shoulders, and now they were grown, and one was leaving.

"Hey, Clinton. I'll help you take Sundance to the holding pen," Hunter offered, and the two brothers moved forward to begin the task.

The man who'd delivered the horse approached Cadman, stuck out his hand in greeting. "Gregory Harper," he said. "I wanted to personally congratulate you on your son's

purchase. If you are ever in need of another fine Appaloosa, don't hesitate to give me a call."

Cadman backed up, held up his hands palms out, and said, "Whoa. Wrong guy."

"Definitely the wrong guy," Cadman's wife chuckled. "He isn't a horse lover." Kasey pointed toward Colten. "He's the one you want to talk to. It's his son who made the purchase."

Gregory turned around and froze. He stared at the man standing behind the one with the patch over his eye.

"I see you're still usin' your salesman pitch, old man."

Donna looked at Jake as though he lost his mind. This person was a guest on the ranch. He should not be-- Still, using your salesman pitch? Did they know each other? But when she looked between the two men, it startled her to see the resemblance between them.

"Jake?" Gregory whispered. "Oh my god, son! Is that truely you?!"

And the older man rushed forward as though he were about to give Jake a bear hug. Jake stepped back. He did not want this man's affection. Not anymore. The time for that need had long passed.

Gregory Harper could not think of any of the numerous things he vowed to say to his son when, and if, the time came when he saw him again. He was too shocked to have unexpectedly found his son here. The first thing to come out of his mouth was, "I hired a private investigator to locate you!"

"Obviously, you can save your money. You found me. Now you can leave." Jake's voice was cold as ice.

SPITFIRE

"Jake, please!" Gregory, realizing there was an audience, lowered his voice and said "Is there somewhere we can talk?"

Colten stepped forward. "The two of you are welcome to use my study." He motioned toward the house.

"Thanks, but no thanks, Mr. Fisher," Jake told him. "I appreciate the offer, but he won't be stayin'."

"Jake! Son!"

Donna gasped. "This is your father, Jake?"

"That's what my birth certificate claims, but he's never been a father to me." Jake looked at Colten. "Your children are lucky to have you, sir."

With that statement, Jake turned on the heel of his boots and began walking away, going in the direction of the mess hall.

Gregory followed his son, reached out, and touched his arm. "Jake, please don't make this difficult. I made mistakes. I know it!"

Jake pulled his arm from the touch and kept walking.

"Damn it, son!" Gregory stopped, watched his son disappear into another building.

Colten came up beside Jake's father. "Give the boy some space. I'll talk to him. Get you that one on one you want. The rest is up to him after that."

Chapter Twenty-five

He should not have stayed away for so long. Travis knew that, but there'd been no help for it either. Not with his dad hounding him to finish those roofing jobs. He'd been dog tired in the evenings, ready to drop. Standing on a roof all day in degrees above ninety did that to a guy.

He would have come here last night, but he and Jerry, the guy his uncle hired, had been busy in Dickinson. Besides, this morning was early enough. But when he'd driven through the front entrance of the F&L, he'd seen the riders up on the hill and recognized Donna and that goddamn foreman, Jake Harper, riding together on one horse.

He had noticed Donna had been acting distant lately. He assumed it was because they weren't able to spend as much time together, something he didn't enjoy any more than she did. However, ever since Jake Harper began working for the Fishers, she had become reserved toward him.

He sighed, raked his hand through his hair, and watched the pair. Watched as Jake slid off the horse, then as Donna rode down the hill by herself. When Jake threw his hat on the ground, Travis hoped it was because Donna told him to get lost, but deep in his heart, he knew he was grasping at straws.

The feeling of possessiveness was intense, almost causing him to step out of his car, march to where Donna had ridden the horse and turned it over to someone else. He wanted to confront her. And he would have done it, even had one foot out of the car door, when the envelope in his lap slipped to the ground, spilling its contents in the dirt.

SPITFIRE

"Damn it," he hissed, quickly leaning down to retrieve the photos lying in the soil. He glanced immediately in all directions to see if anyone was watching him and moved back into the secrecy of the vehicle. Thankfully, everyone seemed to be gathered in the center of the yard, watching a horse being unloaded. No one appeared to have noticed his car parked to the side of the main path leading to the ranch.

Looking down, Travis began reorganizing the photos. He admitted they were not the best of shots, but he'd been forced to conceal the fact he was taking these photos and wasn't able to obtain a clear picture every time. But his uncle gave him some pointers. Travis hoped by the time the person he wanted to photograph arrived, he would get that million-dollar shot.

He hadn't begun his relationship with Donna with the idea of using her. Now that he was, he felt some remorse, but he could use that money. He did not intend to pound any more nails into shingles if he could help it.

Finding Mason Lafayette on this ranch had been a boon. The opportunity of a lifetime. When he called his uncle in California to let him know who was staying at this ranch, and who would be coming in July to pick the kid up, his uncle had been shocked and ecstatic at the same time.

It was why they met up in Montana. So Travis could prove he was not making this up, as he'd taken some amateur photos of Mason to show his uncle, and his uncle in turn gave him a crash course on photography. Because of a restraining order, his uncle could not be within three hundred miles of the couple without risking being thrown in jail. His uncle was a paparazzi, having taken intrusive shots of celebrities for years.

The going price for a picture of the Lafayette's at some function was fifty to a hundred dollars. Unless the photo caught one in a scandalous situation, and that could bring in the big bucks. Although to date, no photographer claimed to see either Charles or Rosalinda with anyone other than their spouse.

But Travis had enough compromising shots of Mason in his collection right now to pay for college over the next year once he sold them.

And the opportunity for the big shot arrived at the ranch next week. God!—if he could be fortunate enough to capture a shot of Rosalinda without makeup, or in a bathing suit, he'd be a millionaire. It was rumored her kidnapper had sliced her body with a razor, leaving hundreds of scars. Everyone in the world wanted to see those scars if they existed.

For one fleeting moment, Travis felt a twinge of guilt, but college was not cheap. Who was he to pass up the opportunity that had been handed to him on a silver platter? He knew the Lafayette's would arrive next Saturday, July the fourth. He needed to still have a reason to be here, and if Donna called off their relationship, he would be banned from coming here. And all because of that stupid cowboy who was moving in on his territory.

Flipping through the glossies, he came to one of Hunter and sighed. It hadn't been hard to win the teenager's friendship. Coming up with that bit about his uncle being a Seal, coupled with the fact he did have a black belt in martial arts, had been a great icebreaker. Sadly, the kid kept harping on wanting to spar, and Travis could not bring himself to fight the kid.

Hunter's martial art skills sucked. Obviously, whoever his instructor was only giving the kid higher ranking belts to pass him along, even though Hunter did not deserve them. Travis did not want to deflate the kid's confidence, but he knew it was only a matter of time before he would have to humor the kid and spar with him.

His eyes drifted back to what was happening in the yard. Harper had made his way down off that hill and was talking to some guy Travis had never seen before. In minutes, Jake turned away and walked into the mess hall. After a few moments, Travis watched Donna follow him.

He'd known something was going on between them.

Well, Harper would be out of the picture soon, and Travis would be right there to regain Donna's attention.

Chapter Twenty-six

Donna sat across from Jake at one of the tables in the mess hall. At the same time, he devoured a plate of scrambled eggs, sausage, and pancakes as though he had not had a confrontation with his father a short while ago. The English muffin she'd taken sat forgotten on the plate before her. She truthfully did not have an appetite. She only wanted to stay with him until she'd gotten some answers. Not that she expected him to give her any here, surrounded by the majority of the ranch's employees, but she would wait.

She wanted to know how he honestly got that scar. But most importantly, she wanted to know why she had not known he was the son of one of the wealthiest ranchers in Texas, and why he didn't want to talk to his father. It might not be any of her business, but after what they had done that morning, she felt she deserved answers.

He stopped eating and pinned her with his eyes. "When are you going to tell Travis to get lost?"

Her jaw dropped. Of all the nerve. Her chin came up a notch. "Now, why would I want to do that?" She was too angry right now to care what he thought. He didn't want to talk about his past. Why should she talk about her future? Fair was fair, wasn't it? Jerk.

Jake dropped his fork onto the plate with a clatter, stood up, grabbed his hat, and headed for the door.

She absolutely hated it when he did that! Whenever he did not want to deal with something, he simply walked away.

SPITFIRE

Case in point, his father, being here. He'd walked away from him, too.

The thought Jake might follow through with his intent on giving that two-week notice to her dad got her in motion. Obviously, he was wealthy enough not to need this job. At least now she knew how he'd been able to afford that new truck of his and the few items of custom-made clothing he owned. But regardless of that, at the moment she was mad at him for not telling her who he was, nor wanting to talk about his past, but she absolutely did not want him leaving here.

She had a hard time catching up to him, his strides were so long. "What do you expect from me?" she all but hissed under her breath, keeping her voice low and grabbed his arm when she was able to catch up with him at the half-way point to the corral. "One moment, I've experienced sex for the first time, and the next thing I know, I'm told to mind my own business by the person I'd given my heart to."

He stopped abruptly, turning to her. "Did you?"

"What's that supposed to mean?"

"It means, when you give your heart to someone, you trust them."

They stood there in the middle of the yard, glaring at each other. A slight breeze caused a few strands of Donna's hair to fall across her face. Automatically Jake reached out and smoothed them back into place; the small gesture deflating her anger, and she sighed. She honestly did not want to continue on like this, crawling down each other's throats.

"You're right," she conceded softly.

His crooked tooth smile spread across his face and accomplished its usual effect on her heart. "You know, Spitfire, you're beautiful." He glanced behind her. "And we'll have that talk, but right now, it looks as though one of the guys needs to talk to me." But he leaned down to her and stole a kiss before she realized that was his intent.

She could not control the sigh that escaped when his lips left hers. Damn it, regardless of the fact she learned only moments ago he'd been in prison and was the son of Gregory Harper, he could turn her to mush. He'd better have told her the truth about that time he'd been locked up, or she would... She had no idea what she would do; she only hoped he wasn't lying to her.

Jake noticed his father was sitting on the porch of the Fisher's home and turned his back on him, sending the message loud and clear he did not want him here.

An employee walked up to them. "Mornin'," the staff member greeted, smiling. It was apparent he had seen that kiss; how could he not when they were standing right there in the middle of the yard? "Looks like it's going to be another warm day." He looked at Donna. "Your mom asked me to find you and send you to the house."

"Thanks, Kevin," she did not dare glance at Jake, knowing her face was already flushed and didn't want to see his amusement at her expense.

She headed in the direction of the house without another word.

Her father was speaking to Gregory Harper, and as she approached, she watched the two of them go into the house.

It shocked her to see Travis sitting on the porch steps, and it brought her up short. She'd been too involved with Jake to have noticed that bright yellow Trans-Am of his parked on the side of the house, the area used by family and friends when visiting. Unbelievable. Now, what was she supposed to do? Fortunately, she did not feel guilty for having chosen Jake over him, but it did not make this any easier. She did not know what he would do or say.

"Morning, baby. Did you have a good ride this morning?" He kept the sneer out of his voice. He had meant that question two different ways. Having witnessed Harper and her together stoked the fires of his rage. And obviously, they thought he was a complete fool to carry on like that in front of him. But he was so close to his goal right now. Shouting at her would get him kicked off this ranch for good. So, for now, he would keep his mouth shut, and once Harper was gone, he'd confront Donna for her blatant disregard of him.

The way he asked the question caused a blush to creep up Donna's face. And to top it off, he must have seen that kiss she and Jake shared. It was time she got this over with.

"I...," she began.

He did not give her the chance to say anything more. Reaching for her, he wrapped his arms around her and kissed her with more passion than he'd ever used before. "I love you, baby," he whispered in her ear, and then stepped back, looking at her intently.

"Travis..."

He chuckled. "I know, I know, I need to come out here more. But Dad's been working me to death. I was going to

surprise you." His laugh seemed hollow. "Surprise! Here I am. I know you've missed me."

Gosh, he was not conceited in the least. How come she'd never noticed that about him before? "Travis," she tried once more but failed as he interrupted once again.

He headed toward his car at a quick pace. "I know I should have called. I didn't realize you would have so much activity going on around here." He opened the car door and climbed in. "I'll head back to Bismarck. Stay out of your hair, but I'll be back for the fourth. I've been looking forward to it for weeks!"

That reminded Donna of the fact she needed him to understand he could not be here on the fourth. "About that…"

He revved the engine, cutting her off again, put the vehicle in gear and began driving away. "Sorry for the rush," he shouted at her through the rolled-down window, "See you on the fourth, for sure! Bye!" And he drove away before she could bat an eye.

Stunned, Donna watched the Trans-Am disappear down the dirt road, feeling as though she'd been broadsided. She had never seen him act like that.

When she recovered, it was to catch sight of Jake standing by the barn, a saddle in hand, looking her way, and the look on his face told her he had seen that kiss.

He was pissed.

The only thing she could think to do was shrug. It wasn't as though she'd kissed Travis back. And she had tried to explain to Travis their relationship was over, but he'd cut her off at each and every turn. What else could she have done? Besides,

SPITFIRE

hadn't Jake moments ago, told her that when you have given your heart to someone you trust them?

Jake was still giving her the stink eye. Fine, guess he didn't fall into the same category of trust he had preached to her about. It annoyed her enough she threw her hands in the air and turned around, intent on continuing into the house but was stopped once again, this time by Mason. That knowing look on his face irritated her so much she snapped, "What do you want?"

"You zhould not be zo grumpy," he scolded, yet the smile on his face told her the outburst hadn't offended him, "Ezpecially when you had a pleazant morning."

Her blush had begun to fade, but now it came back with a vengeance, turning beet red, and it confirmed his suspicion. His smile broadened.

She was not going to stand there and discuss that subject with him when the last thing she needed was advice from a sixteen-year-old who'd been having sex way before her.

She walked past him and into the house to find her mother, Kasey and Sara in the kitchen, going over last-minute details for the upcoming holiday.

Sensing her daughter's presence, Jacqueline glanced up from the table. One look at her eldest daughter, and she asked Sara and Kasey to give them some privacy for a few moments. Once the women were gone, Jacqueline wasted no time in asking, "Was it what you expected?"

There was no accusing tone, merely curiosity, but Donna, at this point, could not grasp what her mother was asking. The lowering of her brows and the frown on her mouth showed

her confusion and brought gentle laughter from Jacqueline. "Your first time, dear; was it what you've expected?"

How in the world? "Mom!"

Jacqueline stood up, took her daughter's hand, and used her own to smooth down her daughter's hair, removing a few blades of grass. "Dear, I saw you ride in with Jake, and you may not realize it, but you glow in a way you never have before."

Damn blush. She would kill Mason for having caused it. "Oh, mom, don't be silly…" Her mother's brow rose. Donna cringed, wondering if everyone on the whole ranch assumed she'd had sex with Jake only because she'd been seen riding double with him?

The thought caused the blush to go two shades darker. Shit, and her mother, her own mother, was chuckling.

"Oh, all right!" Might as well admit it, she needed some advice anyway, and her mother had an open attitude on any subject.

So, she set about explaining to her mother everything to have transpired between Jake and her since the first day he arrived at the ranch. She finished with what happened moments ago when she'd tried to break up with Travis. "He didn't give me a chance to say a thing. And that means he still thinks he can be here on the fourth."

Jacqueline shrugged. "It doesn't matter. We will deal with that whenever we must. But you never answered my first question. Was your first time what you expected?"

Donna sat back, folded her arms over her breasts, and said honestly, "It was wonderful until I thought I had the right to

ask him questions concerning his past. Then he got mad."
Sure, he'd apologized later, but it still upset her he'd reacted
like that.

Jacqueline frowned. "What did you ask about?"

"His scar."

Jacqueline's frown deepened. "The one under his chin?"

Donna stared. "Do you know…?"

"No."

"But you are aware he's been in prison."

"Certainly."

"Well, you could have told me!" Donna exclaimed, feeling
as though she was probably the last one on the entire ranch to
know Jake had an unscrupulous past.

"It is not important."

"Not important! Mom, the man is an ex-convict!"

Jacqueline sighed. "Did Jake explain why he had been put
in prison?"

"Oh yeah, he came up with a cock-and-bull story about a
woman scorned. Please. This is the twentieth century. We've
got laws. The courts don't throw you in jail simply because
you refuse to sleep with someone!"

"Donna, your father checked his background. He spoke to
Jake's former employer. It was that man's wife who accomplished the unthinkable. Twentieth-century or not, money still
talks if one can find the right people, and this woman knew
how to manipulate almost everyone, accomplishing getting
Jake locked up. He was supposed to serve a year and a half
since the jury found him guilty of stealing his employer's
prized Appaloosa stud. It took six months before the new

sheriff could prove they had framed him and had the conviction overturned. The only thing Jake is guilty of is having had the misfortune of ever meeting the woman."

Donna looked away. How quickly she'd been to discredit Jake's explanation only because it sounded too bizarre to be believable. Jake was right. If she surely had given her heart to him, she owed him her trust, not suspicion.

"I suppose you and dad knew whose son he was, too."

Jacqueline nodded. "We knew. But as your dad said, that is his story to tell. It didn't matter to us. But your dad made sure T.J. took Clinton down to the Harper ranch with the hope Clinton would want to buy his horse from there."

"Well, I don't think Jake's in the mood yet to talk to his dad. He's going to lead as many tours as he can today so he can avoid the man."

With a shrug, Jacqueline told her, "Your dad will not let Jake off the hook that easily."

SPITFIRE

Chapter Twenty-seven

Jake guided the family of four, his third tour group of the day, into the stable yard, leading them toward the dismounting area. He helped the little boy off the horse, patiently answering the child's breathless questions about the animal. Then, he turned to the mother to share some of the local history she'd been curious about, particularly regarding the town of Medora, their next stop.

As he waved goodbye, he felt Colten appear beside him and immediately said, "No."

Colten chuckled. "So, now you're a mind reader."

Jake stroked the horse's neck. "It doesn't take a genius to know what you're probably going to say." He gestured toward the far end of the yard where the Harper horse trailer and pickup sat. "He's still here."

He turned to face Colten, meeting his boss's eye. "I don't want anythin' to do with him."

"Yes, you've made that extremely clear."

"Then obviously I was wrong, and that wasn't what you were goin' to mention."

"Oh, it was; still is. I think you should talk to the man. At least clear the air between the two of you."

"No."

"Stubborn jackass."

"If that's all," Jake said, nodding toward a group waiting by the ticket shed, "I have a job to do."

Colten signaled one of the summer hands. "Take 'em out, Joe. Jake will sit this one out."

Jake's jaw tightened. He spun toward his boss and glared. "I told you, I am not going to talk to him."

"Yep. You did. I heard you. But if you think you can brush me off by acting like a mule, you would be wrong. Have you met my son, Hunter? He's the definition of obstinate. You?" Colten shook his head. "You're just being silly. What do you think will happen if you talk with him?"

Jake had no answer to give.

"Right. You have no idea. You're a grown man. Act like one. He can't force you back to Texas unless you want to go. And I'm hoping you'll want to stick around here."

Jake paused. Was Colten insulting him? Was refusing to speak to his father considered childish? Then one phrase registered fully. "You want me to stay?"

"Sure beats looking for another foreman," Colten said. "And besides, I like you a hell of a lot better than Travis. My wife tells me our daughter apparently likes you better than the jerk, too, since she let you…"

Jake's eyes went wide. "She told her we had sex?!" He couldn't believe Donna would have told her mother that detail.

Colten's cheekbones reddened. "I didn't need to know that." He shook his head, genuinely wishing he hadn't confirmed his little girl was no longer an innocent. "I was referring to Donna letting you help with the Horse Adventure camp and taking Randy on rides when she isn't around. She's protective of that little boy."

"Oh," Jake said, his own face now flushed with embarrassment.

"Go talk to the man," Colten told him. "I don't think you'll have anything to lose by doing so."

"Fine," Jake gritted out. If it meant getting rid of his old man, he supposed he could endure being in the same room long enough to tell him to go to hell.

Feeling as though he were walking toward a firing squad, Jake strode toward the main house. Colten had said Gregory was waiting in his office, so that was the direction he took the moment he entered the Fisher home.

His father was standing at the window, hands clasped behind his back, looking out at only he knew what. To Jake's eye, the man appeared to have put on a few extra pounds since he last saw him two years ago, and perhaps he wasn't quite as tall as he once was.

Or maybe that's because once upon a time, I looked up to him, Jake thought. That changed a long time ago.

"I'll give you ten minutes," Jake announced, wanting this done and over with. "Then you can be on your way and stay the hell out of my life."

Gregory turned. There was a sadness in his eyes Jake had never seen before, but he wouldn't let it break his resolve.

"I deserve that." Gregory gestured to a nearby chair. "Would you like to sit?"

"That would imply this is a social call. You and I both know this isn't a friendly gathering."

With a sigh, Gregory said, "All right. I guess since you're not going to give an inch, I will have to make this the short version."

He walked around the desk and sat on its edge. "Clair left me."

Jake shrugged, his voice cold. "Are you expecting me to cry over that? You should have kicked her out a long time ago. But I suppose it would have been bad form to kick your son's mother out to the curb."

"Clair is not your mother."

Jake blinked. "Excuse me?" The news was so shocking he struggled to process the simple statement.

Gregory glanced around Colten's office, wondering if the man kept any whiskey nearby, because God knew he needed a drink.

"What do you mean she isn't my mother?!" The news, while stunning, caused a strange, immense weight to lift off his shoulders. At least now he knew the person he'd thought was his mother wasn't a sick pervert who tried to convince him incest was fine. But he needed absolute clarity. "Are you telling me that witch didn't give birth to me?" The woman had nearly scarred him for life.

Gregory, unable to speak, nodded.

Jake stood where he was, trying to digest the information. Then another, darker thought surfaced. "I suppose now you're going to tell me you're not my father."

Gregory managed a slight, sad smile as he shook his head. "No, you're mine, all right."

Jake studied his father's face, waiting for he didn't know what.

Gregory's sigh was heavy. "I failed you, and I am sorry for it. And you're right, I should have kicked Clair out a long

SPITFIRE

time ago." He shrugged helplessly. He couldn't change the past.

Jake closed the distance between them, his posture rigid with fury. "She made my life a living hell, and you didn't have the balls to tell me the truth, or stand up to her?!"

"I was a fool."

"You're a goddamn son-of-a-bitch!"

"That too."

Without caring that it was someone else's property, Jake kicked the leather sofa and spat a curse.

"Why would you keep that information from me?!" The volume of his voice carried far past the office walls. "Why would you do that to me?!" He paced the room like a caged animal, too many emotions churning for him to sort them out.

He spun toward his father, his eyes blazing. "If I had known, I wouldn't have felt so damn dirty the night I came home from college and Clair climbed into my bed!"

Gregory's hand flew to his chest, his face turning ashen. "What?" he exclaimed in a disbelieving whisper.

Jake stalked toward him. "That's right! The woman I grew up believing was my mother wanted me to fuck her!"

God! Jake closed his eyes, reliving the day when the nightmare began. He'd been 17 years old when Clair started her subtle flirtation with him. She would stroke his arm in a way that caused his skin to crawl as she told him he was turning into a fine-looking young man. And she would brush up against him, press her breasts into his back, and whisper in his ear that she could teach him a thing or two about how to please a woman.

The moment Jake was accepted to Utah State University to study Ranch and Land Management, he couldn't pack his bags fast enough.

His father was staring at him, stunned. "You slept with Clair?"

Jake's face twisted into an expression of profound revulsion. "I thought she was my mother! Do you understand what that did to me? Of course, I didn't sleep with her!" Nor would he have, even if he had known she wasn't his mother.

He kicked the sofa again, needing to strike at something, to destroy something because of the sickness Clair had caused him to feel. He was consumed by rage. The urge to beat his father was so strong it nearly crippled him.

"How could you do that to a child?! Why would the two of you keep that from me? I had the absolute right to know she isn't my mother!"

The leather sofa absorbed more kicks as Jake vented his blinding anger.

"Son, I cannot begin to tell you how sorry I am…"

"Fuck. You."

Gregory winced, physically recoiling from the harshness of the words.

Jake began pacing again, desperate to be anywhere but this room.

He spun back toward his father so quickly it made the older man jerk. "And my real mother?" Jake asked, though he wasn't sure he wanted the answer.

"She was my first love," Gregory said, his voice quiet, as if speaking louder would cause the memory to vanish. "I

would have done anything for her. But as it turned out, the moment she had you, she ran off with someone else and gave up all rights to you."

What a laugh, Jake thought bitterly. His actual mother hadn't wanted him either.

"I met Clair a short time later. Fell in love with her. I was so afraid she would run out on me too, I turned a blind eye to her treatment of you. I made her promise never to tell you the truth. I threatened I would divorce her if she did. I didn't want people thinking you were illegitimate." Gregory shook his head, amazed that this was the one vow Clair had kept.

God, Gregory thought. He had made so many mistakes in his life; it was surprising he was successful at running his ranch when he couldn't manage his own life.

Jake turned on his heel to walk out the door, finished with the conversation.

"Wait!" his father called out. "I was hoping you would come back to Texas. Run the ranch. It's your birthright, and I'm getting old."

Jake stopped and looked over his shoulder. "I don't want the damn thing!"

"But son…"

"Once, when I was a little boy, I dreamed of being in charge. But now that place is too full of bad memories, and the thought of going back there turns my stomach. I'm making a good life for myself here."

Gregory's face scrunched up in confusion and frustration. "But you're nothing but a hired hand here! My god, Jake! By all rights, you should be the boss!"

Marching back to his father with purpose in his stride, Jake leaned in. "This family here, the Fishers, means more to me than you ever did. And I would rather be the guy to shovel horse shit than help you out, when you allowed a little boy to suffer at the hands of a psychopath who got her thrills by mentally tormenting me!"

Gregory closed his eyes. His lips trembled, close to tears. "I never meant…. If I had known…."

"Save it. Stipulate whatever you want in your will if you get around to making one, but don't leave it to me. I'll burn it to the ground." At that moment, Jake meant every word.

"You'd be giving up a fortune!" Gregory exclaimed.

"No," Jake told him, poking his finger into his father's chest. "I have given up nothing. Money's great, but I don't want a damn thing from you anymore."

He turned around, heading toward the door once again. "Go home, Greg," he spoke as he walked. "As I said, do what you want with the land. I don't care. But I want you gone from here before tonight."

Jake opened the office door, slammed it shut behind him, and felt as though he at last closed up his past.

Without breaking his stride, he walked out of the house and headed for his truck. He needed some distance right now. From everything and everyone.

He spotted Donna at the corral used for the adventure camp, talking to one of the therapists, and immediately changed direction.

When he reached her, he pulled her tightly into his arms and held her. He gripped her as if by doing so, she would

SPITFIRE

anchor him, preventing the conflicting, raging emotions from causing him to crumble. If she hadn't given herself to him that morning and confessed she wanted him, he wasn't sure what he would have done when he learned the truth about Clair.

Donna wrapped her arms around him, feeling him tremble. Whatever happened had shaken him to his core.

"Jake?" she murmured.

He shook his head, not ready to share what he'd learned. "I'm taking off…"

When she cried out in sudden despair, he quickly reassured her. "Only for a few hours. I'm coming back, Spitfire."

Their eyes met. She saw his turmoil, but she also saw that he meant what he said. He was not leaving her.

"Okay," she whispered.

Not caring who was watching, he leaned down and gave her a hard, grounding kiss before turning and resuming his mission to reach his truck.

Donna watched as he backed the vehicle up and drove past the main gate, wondering why her heart was breaking for him.

Chapter Twenty-eight

Cadman met up with Colten in the machine shed, though why it was called a shed when it was a huge structure capable of housing the large tractor and other heavy equipment, he would never know.

Colten was in the middle of repairing something. Cadman paused, trying to remember what it was called, then grinned when it came to him. A Hay Baler. Ha. It had only taken him twenty years, but he finally remembered the name for that contraption.

He walked up to where Colten worked and said, "Well, I got information back on Travis."

Colten stood up, wiping hands full of grease onto a rag that looked filthy from many previous uses.

"And?"

"And," Cadman replied, "I can't find a thing that sticks out. College jock, captain of the football team at the University of Mary. He works part-time for his dad in the family construction business. Nothing points to him being anything other than an upstanding citizen."

Colten shook his head. "There's still something about him that puts me on alert."

"I've asked for a deeper check, but since I trust your instincts, I'm hiring extra security for Charles and Rosalinda's arrival. I want to be safe and hope it's not a necessary precaution." He shrugged.

"Not a bad idea," Colten agreed. "We've been lucky all these years not to have the paparazzi swarm the place. They

always let it slip they're vacationing in Italy, or somewhere else far from here, to throw the bloodsuckers off the trail. This has always been a sanctuary for them, but maybe it's time to change things."

Cadman raised a brow. "Well, I don't envision you selling this place."

Colten laughed and shook his head. "You'd be right on that. We worked too hard to carve out this little piece of paradise. However, after nineteen years, Jacqueline and I have been talking about purchasing a lake home up at Sakakawea. Something we could rotate out with my siblings and their families. And we'd book it for every other Fourth of July for the annual reunion with the Lafayettes."

Cadman's eyes brightened. "You mean I would be able to look forward to not being around horses at least every other year?"

Colten laughed again, slapping him on the back. "You'll miss them, and you know it."

The hell he would. Cadman hadn't willingly mounted a horse since the day he proposed to his wife five years earlier.

They left the machine shed together and watched as Gregory Harper's truck and horse trailer exited the ranch.

Colten blew out a relieved breath. He'd seen Jake leave in that jacked-up Ford of his but had no idea what the outcome of the father-son meeting had been. But there certainly had been a lot of shouting coming from inside his office. He'd wanted to eavesdrop but refrained, instead getting everyone else out of the house so no one else would be tempted to listen at the door.

Cadman watched until the horse trailer was out of sight before saying, "Wish I could have been a fly on the wall. Damn it, Colt. You took all the fun out of the day when you shooed me out the door."

Colten chuckled, but at the same time, he genuinely hoped Jake was able to put some demons behind him. He sincerely wanted the young man to choose this ranch as his home.

*　*　*　*

Much later in the afternoon, Donna felt her heart leap when she saw Jake's truck return through the main gate. She had seen the turmoil in his eyes when he left and wished she knew what he said to his father to cause the man to depart so abruptly.

She watched Jake climb out of the cab and head toward the bunkhouse, and she followed him.

She intended to apologize for laughing at what she had, at the time, cynically dismissed as a sorry excuse for his time in prison. Jake hadn't deserved her judgment. If they were going to continue their relationship, wherever it was headed, they needed to build trust. And she was not going to ask him what transpired with his father; if he wanted to tell her, he would.

This time when she reached the bunkhouse, she assured herself no one else was around before she walked in, wanting to avoid a repeat of the last time she'd sought him out. When she knocked on his apartment door, at least there was no one nearby to make assumptions. However, when Jake opened the

door, she admitted a small flicker of disappointment that she hadn't caught him taking a shower this time.

"I..." she began, but he pulled her swiftly inside. He didn't give her a chance to say anything. His mouth lowered to hers; hot and demanding. His tongue pushed her lips apart as he backed her up firmly against the wall.

All she could do was wrap her arms around his neck and hold on for dear life as her knees threatened to give out. God, this man knew how to kiss, and it thrilled her to feel how much he wanted her.

When he finally stepped back, her eyes were glazed over.

"Sorry," he said, slightly winded. "I wanted to do that the first time you knocked on my door all those weeks ago when I was in the shower."

Slowly, her eyes focused. They slid to the twin-size bed shoved against the wall. "Does it squeak?"

Jake groaned, his desire evident. "Worse than gates that need oiling. As much as I want you, I don't want anyone in the outer room knowing what's going on in here. I respect you too much for that."

She grinned up at him, warmth flooding her chest. "Then I guess we'll have to occupy ourselves with something else." She reached into her back pocket. "I've got tickets to the outdoor musical in Medora tonight," she told him.

His smile exposed that crooked tooth, and it took her breath away. "Yeah? I bet it won't be as much fun as that bed would have been if it didn't screech."

She laughed. "But you'll go to the musical with me, anyway?"

Jake's grin widened. "Why, Miss Donna, are you asking me for a date?" he drawled, the words low and husky, sending goosebumps down her arms. He bent forward and delivered another short, sweet kiss. "I reckon we could do that."

He followed the statement with another kiss.

"Hey! Donna, are ya gonna suck face all day?" Hunter's voice sliced through the moment from behind her.

Crimson color flooded her face. Jake hadn't fully closed the door before he'd pulled her into his space.

"I hate your brother," Jake chuckled against her mouth, and at that moment, Donna was in complete agreement.

With a swat to her backside, Jake said, "You go on and see what the ornery kid needs. I'll see you later."

"Pick me up at six-thirty?" At his nod, she turned around and pinned Hunter with a look that could have withered green grass.

Of course, Hunter merely shrugged, undaunted.

Donna gave one last look in Jake's direction. The promise in his eyes was so potent she felt weak-kneed, and the smile remained plastered on her face for the remaining hours until she was dressed for the musical and Jake stepped onto the front porch.

The sight of him immediately sent her heart into overdrive. He was dressed in a plain black button-down shirt, free of any embroidery, tucked into a pair of well-worn, faded jeans. The ever-present black Stetson and dark sunglasses hid his eyes from her.

Yummy was her first thought. Her second thought was that he was a brave soul for walking onto the porch. Her family

had conveniently chosen to wait with her, spread out on chairs under the guise of enjoying the beautiful evening. She wasn't fooled; she knew they were there to give him the family seal of approval.

"Ready to go?" Jake asked, removing the sunglasses and hooking them onto his shirt collar as he openly admired her. At her affirmative nod, he offered his elbow for her to take and escorted her down the steps toward his pickup.

"Have a good time!" Colten called out, his grin nearly splitting his face in half.

"Drive safe," Jacqueline added warmly.

"Do not do any zing you zhould not!" Mason shouted, drawing all eyes to him, since he was certainly the pot calling the kettle black.

Hunter laughed heartily, "And if you do, name it after me!"

Donna's blush reached her ears, and Jake's deep chuckling made the heat spread to the roots of her hair. Her family had never given her such a hard time about a date before, clearly indicating that they approved of her choice this time.

They arrived at the Burning Hills Amphitheater in Medora with plenty of time to buy refreshments and find their seats. This Broadway-quality show, North Dakota's number one attraction, had been performed nightly during the summer months under the stars since 1965, offering a two-hour musical extravaganza set against the outdoor splendor of the Badlands.

The musical had a traditional Western theme dedicated to the 26th U.S. President, Theodore Roosevelt. Roosevelt had spent time in the Badlands during the 1880s and famously

attributed his development of the traits and "bully spirit" that enabled him to become President to his time in the West.

During the performance—a fast-moving mix of singing, dancing, variety acts, and dramatic scenes featuring stuntmen shooting, fighting, and falling from large rocks—Jake kept glancing at Donna, wondering where this relationship was headed, and knowing precisely where he wanted to take it.

As the production continued, the sun sank in the west and cast the mysterious Badlands into purple silhouettes, softening their scarred, naked landscape into mellow beauty.

Donna shivered and unfolded the blanket she'd brought along. She had attended at least one performance of the musical every year since she was five and knew how quickly the warmth vanished once the sun disappeared.

"Are you cold?" she asked Jake.

"A little," he admitted, accepting her offer to share the blanket. He pulled her against him, enfolding her within his arms, the action possessive and comforting. Whispering in her ear, he asked, "Do you have any idea what you do to me, Spitfire?"

The look she gave him was so filled with pure innocence it made him chuckle. He sincerely doubted she understood the effect she had on his senses.

When the show ended, they joined the thousand or so people making their way back up the steep incline to the parking lot. They followed a long line of cars down a narrow, winding road away from the open theater.

Once on the main road, Jake swung left and headed up into the South Unit of the Theodore Roosevelt National Park. He

SPITFIRE

had been working for the Fishers for almost three months but hadn't once visited the historic town of Medora, though he'd studied its history enough to answer tourist questions.

With Donna sitting next to him in the cab, Jake felt as though he at last found where he belonged. He wasn't sorry he told his dad to leave. His whole life had been one big farce, but here, with Donna, he felt his life was finally changing for the better.

Jake hadn't lied to his father. The fortune that would have been his birthright meant nothing. Some people might call him a fool for throwing it away, but wealth didn't bring joy. He had never been truly happy until this morning, when Donna chose him to be her lover.

He hoped she would be much more than that one day.

When they reached one of the numerous prairie dog towns contained within the park, Jake eased his truck off the road and stopped. He left the engine running, keeping the heater set low. Tonight required it.

She leaned her head against his shoulder, whispering softly, "I'm sorry, Jake."

"What?" he asked, surprised.

She sat back, trying to see his expression in the fading light. "For doubting you this morning when you told me why you'd been in prison. I should have believed you, and I'm sorry."

He let out a long breath he hadn't known he'd been holding. "No problem." And truly, it wasn't. She humbled herself to apologize, and he couldn't bring himself to dwell on the fact that he wished she believed him right away. She did now, and that counted for everything.

Reaching his arm around her, he pulled her close, content to sit quietly as they watched the final descent of the sun.

Looking out the windshield into the gathering darkness, Donna could faintly make out the small historic town of Medora. Gazing a short distance south, she could see the silhouette of the Chateau de Mores.

"Have you ever been to the Chateau?" she asked Jake.

"No." The road leading to the musical went right past it, so he had obviously seen it. The only history he knew about it came from a pamphlet in the ranch's souvenir shop; he certainly hadn't taken the tourist tour.

"It was built in 1883 by the Marquis de Mores, a French aristocrat with an entrepreneurial spirit. He dreamed of slaughtering range cattle here in Medora and shipping the meat east in refrigerated rail cars. He named the town after his wife." She sighed, caught up in the romantic legacy left behind when the man's dreams eventually crumbled.

For now, she omitted the truth of her connection: her mother was a descendant of the same great-great-great grandparents as the Medora the town was named after.

Jake chuckled despite himself. She sounded like a walking history book. "You know its history pretty well, Spitfire."

"Well, don't forget, I grew up in the area. And I love the Badlands, and that 26-room Chateau."

She molded herself against him, feeling secure in his embrace, liking the way his hand lazily stroked her arm, then her cheek. His hand then moved to her breast, kneading lightly through the material of her t-shirt, inching slowly down until it reached her bra. His hand dipped inside, and the fires he

had been building instantly leaped to life; her breathing became shallow, and a low groan of desire sounded deep in her throat.

"I want to make love to you, Donna," he whispered, nibbling her ear. "But not in this truck. This morning happened too fast, and I want to love you all night."

His words thrilled her, and she spoke huskily, "What's wrong with this truck? It's got lots of room."

He'd been kissing her neck and now smiled against it. "Well, I'm not sure I like the idea of a park ranger stoppin' by and shining their flashlight in here when I've got my pants down."

The thought of a park ranger getting mooned gave her a fit of laughter. "That might be kind of fun," she claimed, breathless between chuckles.

"Does insanity run in your family?"

She chuckled all the harder.

He reached for her, silencing her with a long kiss, trailing his hand down her back, then bringing it back up under the soft cotton of her t-shirt. He was building a fire, and she welcomed the fuel.

"I want to make love to you, Spitfire. But not here," he repeated.

"There is a place," she breathed heavily. Whatever Jake was doing to the back of her ear was driving her insane.

"How far?" he all but growled.

She lifted her head, looking around, trying to get her bearings. Jake had a way of making her forget everything around her except him.

"A half a mile." She pointed out the direction. "It belongs to some friends of ours. It might be available."

Jake could not shift the truck's gears fast enough.

She looked at him as he drove like a madman. "What if it's rented out?" she asked.

"Then we'll see if that Park Ranger gets an eyeful."

SPITFIRE

Chapter Twenty-nine

It was early morning, not yet seven o'clock, when Jake and Donna arrived back at the ranch.

They spent hours after making love in the private cabin Donna directed them to. They were more than grateful no one had been occupying it when they arrived, and that the owners agreed to rent it for the night. Thank God they said yes.

When they weren't making love, they talked.

Jake confided in Donna about his difficult childhood, what Clair attempted when he thought she was his mother, and how he had gotten the scar under his chin. It had been a stupid fight that broke out between inmates one day. He, being the naive newcomer, thought he should break it up. The thanks he'd gotten for trying to soothe the savage beasts was for both inmates to turn on him. One tried to slit his throat. They would have succeeded that day if the guards hadn't arrived at the exact moment the makeshift knife descended. A guard grabbed the would-be killer's arm, causing the weapon to miss the jugular, but it managed to slice a deep gash under his chin.

Jake dropped Donna off at the main house, then parked the truck in his designated spot next to the bunkhouse. They would have gone together on Donna's customary pre-dawn ride, but all that was on their mind now was sleep, though they wished it wouldn't be in separate beds.

Jake was about to walk into the bunkhouse when a sheriff's cruiser drove into the yard. It pulled up to the main house, where a few lights were already on. Hunter was stepping

outside and coming down the porch steps, ready for his routine morning run, when the lawman exited from the vehicle.

The officer greeted Hunter, obviously asking a question, as Hunter pointed toward the bunkhouse.

The hairs on the back of Jake's neck stood up; a heavy sense of foreboding settled over him. It had to be his imagination. The law had no reason to seek him out. But the man headed straight for him, and Hunter went back into the house.

Something was definitely up if Hunter was going to forgo his everyday habit.

Jake watched the lawman approach, trying to appear calm when he was anything but.

"Morning," the officer said. "You Jake Harper?" At Jake's curt nod, the man stated, "You're under arrest."

"The hell I am!" Jake backed up. This couldn't be real. The idea of going back to jail was terrifying, causing him to break into a sweat.

The officer pulled handcuffs off his belt. "Don't make this difficult. If you resist arrest, I'm going to have to use force, and you don't want me to do that."

The ominous tone left no doubt in Jake's mind about that, but willingly going to jail; again, for something he hadn't done, didn't sit well with him either.

He was given a short reprieve as most of the Fisher family came running out from the main house toward where he and the Sheriff stood. They stopped a few feet away.

"What's going on, Calvin?" Colten asked, looking between Jake and the officer.

"Jake Harper is wanted for robbery."

SPITFIRE

"What?!" Jake was beyond livid. "I didn't rob anyone!" He caught sight of Donna, pleading with his eyes for her not to think the worst. "I didn't do it," he told her.

"Sure," the sheriff drawled. "You can tell that to the judge. He's probably never heard that one." He grabbed Jake's arm and snapped a cuff in place before Jake could fully react.

"Now Calvin," Colten began, his voice firm, "just who is Jake supposed to have robbed?"

Calvin sighed. "Not whom, but what. The M&H in Dickinson was robbed a few days ago, and the employee described this guy right down to that pickup he used to get away in." His chin snapped toward Jake's vehicle.

"I. Didn't. Do. It!" Jake gritted out, so angry he could scarcely talk.

"The employee is lying," Colten stated. "I can tell you right now, Calvin, Jake isn't guilty of the crime."

The sheriff shrugged. "My job was to bring him in, Colten. It's up to the court to decide his innocence or guilt." He looked at Jake. "Turn around."

Every fiber of Jake's anatomy protested. Looking once more at Donna tore him apart. She was staring at him, wide-eyed with shock.

Hunter stepped forward, his brows furrowed in thought. "Calvin, when did this supposed robbery take place?"

Calvin couldn't help but grin at the teenager. That kid was a born bloodhound, always interested in police business. "Well now, Hunter. You're a great little junior detective…" The withering look he received from the teenager at that remark had him amending the comment immediately. "Sorry,

Hunter, that was uncalled for. You come down to police head-quarters, and perhaps Captain Robinson will fill you in. You know how much he likes to pick your brains when it comes to crime-solving." He then pulled on Jake, leading him toward the squad car.

As Jake passed her, Donna finally broke free from her shock. She stepped forward, wrapping her arms around him, holding him tight despite the handcuffs. "I trust you, Jake. I know you didn't rob anyone."

Why would he? She thought fiercely. Although he'd rejected his father's ranch, Jake had a substantial bank account from the trust fund his grandparents left him; a fact they discussed last night. She couldn't blame him at all for wanting nothing to do with his father and was profoundly thankful for the parents she had.

She leaned in as he bent down to meet her mouth. They kissed, trying to convey, without words, the love and faith they had for each other.

The sheriff pulled on Jake's arm. "That's all I'm going to allow, and I shouldn't have allowed even that."

When the cruiser door was opened, it took every ounce of Jake's willpower to force himself inside the enclosure. This could not be happening again. The car door was slammed shut the moment Jake settled in.

Donna turned to her father, determination replacing the fear on her face. "There's another truck, Dad. We saw it the night we took Randy to the movie. I would have sworn it was Jake's truck if I hadn't been sitting in his at the time."

Colten looked at Cadman, a small, knowing smile playing on his lips. "Well, look at that. And here you thought you were on vacation. I'm sure you'll want to look into this."

"Was there ever any doubt?" Cadman asked, already shifting into investigative mode. He glanced at Hunter. "What do you say, Hunter? Want to drive into Dickinson with me? You too, Mason."

Both boys' eyes lit up instantly. The chance to leave the ranch and do some sleuthing would be far more fun than pointing things out for the tourists.

Chapter Thirty

Once again, he was locked up for a crime he hadn't committed.

Jake lay on the hard jail cot, staring at the ceiling, wishing he possessed the superhuman strength to rip the bars apart and escape. But he wasn't superhuman. He was, however, so explosively angry one might think the whole building should have blown up from the sheer intensity of his rage.

He cursed under his breath.

He'd been transferred from the Billings County Jail in Medora to Dickinson in Stark County because they simply didn't have room for him. Then he'd had to wait until Tuesday, yesterday, before standing before the magistrate because no one was available on the weekend and Monday was too busy of a day for anyone to bother with him. Bail had been set at a staggering $100,000.

Seriously? What had the judge been thinking?

With plenty of time on his hands Jake did a lot of thinking and he wondered if Donna still believed in his innocence. There had been no word from her nor any of the Fishers and it caused him to wonder if the entire family had washed their hands of him.

Sitting up, he leaned against the cold wall. He closed his eyes, resigning himself to the fact that he would probably be here for a while.

Damn and shit.

Jake wanted to know how he supposedly robbed that convenience store. Yes, he had been in Dickinson Monday night

doing some shopping, and he stopped at that exact service center close to the time the alleged robbery took place. His truck needed gas, and he bought a Coke. But that was it. He certainly hadn't robbed anyone.

If he didn't know better, he would be inclined to think Amanda had somehow masterminded this whole thing. But the last he heard, she was locked away. At least the thought of her behind bars brought him a minimal amount of pleasure in this deeply unpleasant moment.

His thoughts turned to Randy, wondering how the boy was doing. Tomorrow was the Fourth of July. He had planned on taking the kid on a picnic, with some fishing thrown in. He genuinely liked the child, though it went far beyond that. He just hadn't recognized the truth sooner. Being locked up gave him time to think, and Randy weighed heavily on his mind over these hours of confinement. The fact that the child suffered from an irreversible condition didn't matter to Jake. The boy had too much personality for anyone open-minded enough to dwell on his handicap.

Would the Fishers tell Randy about the arrest? Had he seen it? Or had he still been asleep in bed?

Jake heard a door open somewhere within the jailhouse. Footsteps clicked down the hall, then stopped. Keys jingled. "You've been bailed, Harper."

Jake opened one eye to look at the officer but didn't move otherwise. He was positive he hadn't heard correctly, having figured on being here indefinitely.

"Move it, Harper," the officer barked. "I said, you've been sprung."

Jake came off the hard bed as though in a dream. "Who?" Dazed, he walked out of the cell and fell into step behind the officer. When they reached the end of the hallway, the man opened the outer door, and Jake's eyes widened in disbelief. There stood Colten Fisher, leaning against the counter.

"Sir?" Jake could hardly wrap his mind around the fact that his boss had actually paid the bail. A tangible warmth flooded his chest, and a stubborn lump rose in his throat, making it hard to swallow. He hadn't expected anyone to come to his aid, least of all a man he'd known for a mere two months, but obviously the man believed he was innocent. Why else would he have come?

Colten looked him straight in the eye. "I told these guys I'd make sure you're in court when, and if, the time comes." He pulled himself up to his full six-foot-four height. "I assume you're not going to run out on me?"

Was that a half-smile on the man's face?

Jake couldn't help it; he laughed. Colten hadn't sounded worried about the potential of him taking off, but he still asked, "Why are you bailing me out?"

With a shrug, Colten said, "Good guides are hard to come by. Besides, we all know you're innocent. You might as well be at the F&L while the matter is being cleared up."

Jake grinned. How could he not, when no one had ever believed in him as much as this man did? The depth of that faith touched him, making his heart swell. "I swear I won't run," he promised.

Colten looked to the officer behind the desk. "I'll vouch for him, Mark."

SPITFIRE

The officer named Mark sat back in his chair and folded his hands behind his head. "All right, Colten. I suppose you know what you're doing." His voice sounded as though he thought Colten was nuts for springing an accused thief.

With a half-laugh, Colten replied, "I suppose I do."

He motioned for Jake to follow him, and as they walked toward the exit, he said, "There's a horse sale in town I want to check out before we head back to the ranch."

When they arrived at the horse sale, they found a seat near the front of the ring. There were many fine horses on the block; a few looked ready for the glue factory, but overall, the selection was superb.

"Are you looking for more horses, Mr. Fisher?" Jake ventured, though with the number of beasts the ranch already owned, he wouldn't think there was any need for more.

Colten shrugged. "Not necessarily, but if I see one I like, I might consider purchasing it."

After a long, drawn-out silence, Colten said, "I just want you to know, Donna wanted to be here earlier, and come with me today."

Jake didn't know how to respond to that, so he said nothing at all.

"I'm the one who kept her at the ranch."

That had Jake's undivided attention.

Colten shrugged. "Two reasons. First, I honestly didn't care much to have an emotional female tagging along…"

Jake's mind clicked into gear. Emotional? In what respect?

"…since she's head over heels in love with you."

That had Jake's lips splitting into a wide grin.

"And because Randy's been taking this pretty bad. A person's hero getting arrested doesn't happen every day, you know."

That wiped the grin clean off his face. "He's all right?" Jake was instantly consumed with concern.

Colten shrugged again. "Don't know for sure. It's another reason I didn't let Donna come with me. He's quite attached to her, too, and I just didn't think it was wise to remove her from the ranch right now. And I didn't think it would be a good idea to let the kid see you in jail."

"That's why you sprung me?" So much for hoping it was purely because the Fishers believed in his innocence.

Colten shook his head. "Already told you, good guides are hard to come by."

Jake fought a laugh, shaking his head at his boss's dry humor.

"So," Colten asked, turning back to the ring. "See anything that piques your interest?"

Jake watched the horses, his gaze settling on one specific animal. "That Appaloosa," he said, nodding in its direction.

Colten watched the horse for a time. "If given the choice, wouldn't you rather have one from your old man's stock?"

Jake looked at him. "No. And if you're wanting to know what we said to each other…"

"That's your business. The fact that you stayed, and he took off, tells me you weren't looking to move back home anytime soon."

"I don't want to give up what I have here."

SPITFIRE

Colten met his gaze, his expression serious. "Are you talking about my daughter?"

"Yes." He figured he owed the man the truth.

With a nod, Colten returned his attention to the horses. After watching the Appaloosa for a moment, he sighed and shook his head. "Do you suppose it will get along with Clinton's?"

"Sir?" Jake gave him a questioning look.

Under his breath, Colten mumbled, "I can't believe I'm doing this. Might as well add another one to the mix."

Jake stared at him. "What?"

"Well," Colten said, looking back at Jake, "I'm thinking it's time you had a horse to call your own if you're staying on."

His throat tightened so sharply he could barely draw breath and he swallowed a few times, trying to dislodge the sensation.

"I..." Jake coughed. Good god, he was going to cry. Never had he felt such acceptance and love as he did in that moment.

Colten gave him a quick, hard pat on the back. "Just so you know, you hurt my daughter, I'll cut off your balls."

Jake's quick laugh helped dislodge the lump. "I'll do my best to keep you from following through with that threat."

"Oh, it wasn't a threat. It was a promise." Colten stood up. "Come on. I've got a damn horse to pay for. I'll arrange to have it stabled here for a few days until we can bring the horse trailer. And maybe when we get back to the ranch, there will be some news from Cadman. He's investigating that

J.R. Zimmer

ridiculous charge of robbery, and you couldn't have a better man in your corner."

By four-thirty that afternoon, the two men were in Colten's pickup and headed down the road toward the F&L. Jake watched the darkening sky, absentmindedly reaching for a smoke, but remembered he didn't have any cigarettes on him. Sighing, he told himself it was probably time to quit anyway; he had smoked less and less since starting work for the Fishers and had no nicotine since being locked up.

"That storm looks like it's going to be a bad one," Colten observed the skyline, making the turn for the last twenty miles to the ranch.

Jake agreed. The sky was darker than he'd seen it so far this year, and the two fell silent for the remainder of the trip. But when they reached the ranch and turned onto the property, neither of them could prevent their shock at seeing four sheriff cars parked in the yard. The entire ranch seemed to be in an uproar.

Colten eased the vehicle to a stop just as his wife came running toward the truck. "What's going on?" he asked as he stepped from the cab, concerned by the anguish and strain lining her face. She was as white as a sheet.

"Randy's missing!" she exclaimed.

Jake's heart almost stopped beating. "What do you mean, missing?" She couldn't possibly mean what she'd implied.

Jacqueline looked nervously toward Jake. "He's been so depressed since you've been gone. This afternoon he wanted to sit on the porch, and I helped him outside. Donna had a headache and needed to lie down for a bit. I kept checking on

him, asking if he wanted anything, and he would just say your name." She glanced at her husband. "I checked on him again after you left, but with Rosalinda and Charles arriving tomorrow, we've been busy with last-minute details...." Her voice trailed off, ashamed that Randy had been forgotten.

"Have you checked the machine shed?" Colten asked, his voice tight with his own concern.

"Yes, yes! Everywhere! We called the sheriff an hour ago."

Colten looked at his watch. The boy had been gone for almost four hours. "Where's Hunter?"

"He's still with Cadman. The last I heard from them, the three of them were heading for Bismarck. I guess they wanted to check out something they found out in Dickinson regarding that truck that looks like Jake's. I'm not sure when they will be back."

"Damn it," Colten hissed.

"Where's Donna now?" Jake asked, his heart squeezing in anguish, knowing Donna was probably suffering more. She loved that little boy as though she had given birth to him.

"She's with the search party," Jacqueline said, motioning to indicate that a group was already roaming the Badlands in search of the lost boy. As hard as it was to believe a child with leg braces could make it far in this rugged terrain, they couldn't rule it out. Since he hadn't been found within the immediate area of the ranch, where else could he be?

Jake's mind raced. Randy's braces were sturdy, but they weren't meant for the vertical scrambles of the buttes. If he'd tried to climb, he could be pinned in a wash or, worse,

exhausted and shivering in a ravine that was about to become a river.

Thunder cracked.

Running toward the barn, Jake grabbed a saddle, and Colten did the same. It was urgent Randy be found swiftly. The Badlands were tough going under the best conditions, not to mention the wild buffalo still roaming the area. The rain added another layer of danger; if there was a downpour, a flash flood could occur in some of the low-lying places.

The wind began to gust; a sure sign the gates of heaven were about to open wide.

Throwing the saddles on the horses one of the part-time employees brought for them, they secured them and mounted up.

Jacqueline handed rain slickers and canteens up to them.

"If we haven't found him by the time Hunter gets back…," Colten began.

A flash of lightning, followed by a crack of thunder, drowned out the rest of the sentence, but Jacqueline knew what her husband would have said. If anyone could find a lost boy in the Badlands, it was Hunter. He had the instincts and tracking skills of a wolf.

The rain began in earnest, cold and stinging. Colten looked at Jake. "You don't have to do this," he said, the wind whipping his words away.

Jake finished snapping his oilskin shut and met the older man's gaze. The rage he'd felt in the jail was gone, replaced by a cold, sharpened focus. "Yes, I do. Two people I care

about are out there. I'm not coming back until I have them both."

He didn't wait for a reply. He kicked his horse into a gallop, disappearing into the gray curtain of the storm.

Chapter Thirty-one

They met up with the search party less than fifteen minutes later. The unit was returning to the ranch to regroup and wait until the weather cleared.

Jake breathed a sigh of relief when he spotted Donna with the bunch. He reined in his horse, and even through the rain, he could see by her face that they'd had no luck finding Randy.

Countless emotions; relief, anguish, and desperation, played across her face when she looked at him. "Jake," she choked, wanting to wrap her arms around him, grateful he was here, thankful her father had bailed him out. She needed him more than ever right now; she needed him to tell her they would find Randy unharmed.

She groaned in her distress, trembling more from anxiety than the horrible weather pelting them. God, where could Randy be?

Jake moved his horse abreast of hers. "Whatever it takes," he told her, shouting over the wind to be heard, "We'll find him!"

Colten moved his horse alongside theirs. "I just spoke with the sheriff. They're going back until this rain lets up. It's too difficult, not to mention dangerous, to be out here right now."

"I'm going to keep looking," Jake declared. Yes, it was dangerous, but Randy's life might be in the balance. He refused to wait for the weather to clear. In North Dakota, that could mean waiting ten minutes or until tomorrow; it was

entirely unpredictable, no matter what the meteorologists believed.

The two men looked at each other for a long moment. Colten wanted to insist Jake return to the ranch, but he didn't have that right. Then he glanced at his daughter, knowing in his heart she wouldn't listen to him either. Colten abruptly wished she were two years younger so he would still have parental leverage. As it was, the law considered her an adult, and he knew she wouldn't be returning with the main party if he gave Jake the go-ahead.

"All right," he sighed, resigned, and turned his horse around to join the search party on their trek back to the shelter of the ranch.

Donna didn't move her horse an inch. "I'm coming with you," she told Jake, the stubborn set of her chin confirming her resolve, but he tried anyway.

"No."

"I'm coming with!" she cried out in anger and frustration.

"Listen, Spitfire…"

"He's my responsibility!" she shrieked, her anxiety making her voice shrill. "I told Social Services I'd keep him safe, and now he's gone!"

Jake leaned forward, touching her knee, searching her eyes. He knew when to yield; if he insisted she go back with her father, he would have one hellcat on his hands, and precious time would be wasted calming her down. Hell, he wasn't calm himself, but losing control wouldn't find Randy any faster. "Then, we'll find him."

He kicked his horse forward, pulled his slicker closer, and wished to heaven this storm would let up. Thankfully, the lightning stopped even if the rain hadn't. It was a welcome relief not to fear an electrical strike, a scenario that had been highly likely as wet and exposed as they were.

For an hour, they traveled slowly, searching inch by inch. Occasionally they yelled out Randy's name, but with no response; if there had been one, it wasn't heard above the wind and the rain.

Nothing. There was no trace of Randy, and now even Jake was beginning to despair.

"We need to rest the horses," Jake broke their mutual silence, glancing at his watch. It was past eight in the evening. His stomach growled, hungry for nourishment. He could only imagine Donna was in the same state of discomfort but knew she wouldn't admit it if it meant turning back.

As much as Donna didn't want to give up the search, she knew he was right. "The cabin my great-grandpa built isn't far from here."

Jake nodded, remembering the one she was talking about; he'd seen it enough during the two-hour tours to recall it. "We'll rest there a little while, then begin again." Hopefully, Randy had been found and was at the ranch by now, and no one bothered to brave the rain to let them know.

As one accord, they turned toward the cabin, their horses slowly picking their way over the muddy ground. Moments later, they reached their destination, dismounted, and walked the horses into the small barn. Unsaddling the horses, they grabbed the towels hanging on hooks and rubbed the mounts

down. Because her parents still occasionally used the cabin, Jake wasn't surprised to find some feed and water for the exhausted animals stored nearby.

Once they were assured the horses were taken care of, the couple walked the short distance to the cabin and opened the door.

The sight that greeted them stopped them in their tracks, unable to believe what they were seeing. On the small sofa was one sleeping little boy, dry as a bone and snoring contently.

Their united whoop startled the child awake. Randy wasn't able to focus his eyes yet as he was grabbed and crushed between two people whose relief was so great they felt faint with it. They were too exuberant to care that they were dripping wet and soaking him before they thought about removing their slickers and tossing them onto a nearby chair.

"Oh, Randy, how could you do this?!" Donna scolded, but simultaneously laughed with pure joy. She grabbed a few towels kept in the hall closet and used them to dry the child, who was now wet from their initial hug. As she did so, she checked him thoroughly for signs of injury and was relieved to find none.

"I want to know how he made it this far," Jake said, ruffling the child's hair.

Randy looked from one adult to the other, and when he realized his hero was there, sitting next to him, he gave a garbled cry and threw his small arms around Jake. "Ake!"

Jake buried his face in Randy's neck, nuzzling him to hide his tears of relief. Donna had no such qualms; her tears flowed freely down her cheeks, unchecked.

They would probably never know how Randy made it this far from the ranch, especially wearing leg braces. But one thing they knew for certain: no one would ever be able to convince them this child was handicapped when he'd accomplished something so miraculous.

Jake looked up at Donna. "We'll stay here until the rain stops."

"Fine by me," she smiled, moving to the small hearth on the opposite wall to build a fire . The warmth would help take the chill out of the air the rain had brought, and help their clothes to dry. Though the oil slickers kept most of the rain from soaking their clothing, they were still damp.

Once the fire was going, she rummaged through the cupboards, thankful her parents kept this cabin stocked with the basics, even if they only used it a few times a year. Discovering some pork 'n beans, canned mini-sausages, and one can of Spam, she grabbed them, turned around, and laughed, "Oh boy, are we going to feast!"

Jake looked up from the small table, where he'd helped Randy join him. Seeing Donna's offering, he grinned. "As hungry as I am, it looks like a feast for a king." Turning to Randy, he winked, "Bet you're starved." At the boy's garbled affirmative, Jake chuckled.

Not long after they finished the simple meal, Jake got down to business. Now that he'd calmed down and Randy was safe,

he gently scolded the child. "Whatever were you thinking, buddy?"

Donna looked at the child, seeing past the involuntary facial movements to the heart of the matter as his eyes looked down, and he whispered, "Ake oooh."

"Randy, I know it upset you when the sheriff arrested Jake," she said gently. "I told you everything would be all right; that Jake had done nothing wrong and that the sheriff made a mistake."

Jake couldn't help himself. He stared at her, and his heart swelled at hearing those words come out of her mouth. "Do you believe that?" he asked softly.

Donna looked at him, a small, genuine smile touching her lips. "Of course I do. Besides, I recall someone I love having told me not long ago that if I've given them my heart, I should trust them."

"You love me?" His face looked utterly awe-struck, and the radiant smile she gave him warmed him down to his toes.

Chapter Thirty-two

The rain didn't let up until sometime after midnight, and by then it was far too dark to make the trip back to the ranch. They had no choice but to remain at the cabin until morning. Not that any of the three were complaining; they were warm, safe, and together.

Fatigued as Donna was, despite having Randy squished between them on the cabin's queen-size bed, located in the largest of the two bedrooms, she fell asleep with a smile on her face the second her head hit the pillow.

Jake was worn out himself, but sleep eluded him. He lay on his back for hours, wondering at the depth of feeling he had for this child no one claimed as their own, and the woman in deep slumber on the opposite side of the bed.

Realistically, Randy would be leaving in five weeks, assuming Social Services didn't remove him sooner because of this misadventure. The boy would go back to a foster home and return to school for the next grade. The thought of Randy being gone for that long didn't sit well with Jake. He didn't want him to go. And although they could visit now and again, but that wasn't the same as having him around all the time.

Jake's thoughts turned to Donna. He slowly lifted his head off the pillow and turned to look at her. Enough moonlight was shining through a window for him to make her out. Her mouth was open; she was snoring. She'd probably be embarrassed to death to know how ridiculous she looked, but he found the sight charming. There was nothing false about her.

Her genuine caring for children with challenges was something he deeply admired.

He'd never considered working with that specific group of people. Not because he was prejudiced against them, the opportunity had simply never arisen. But when he began working on the F&L, he felt drawn to them. He probably got more from them than they did from him. Those children were so honest with their emotions. Loving, trusting, how could anyone despise them? Yet some did; ignorant people that they were.

He laid his head back on the pillow, thoughts turning to what was before him. Unless they cleared up this mistaken identity and the charges were dropped, he had another trial to face. An involuntary shudder passed through him. He didn't want to think about serving time again.

He closed his eyes finally, allowing sweet dreams of Donna to take away the anxieties. But no sooner had he fallen asleep than something woke him up. Cracking one eye open, surprised to see he'd slept a couple of hours at least, as the sunlight now coming through the window indicated, he looked up to find three people standing next to the bed.

"Ah, shoot," Hunter said, disappointed. "Yah found him."

Colten gave his son a chastising look. He knew he shouldn't have expected anything less from a sixteen-year-old who had more zeal for danger and adventure than anyone had the right to. He knew his son was glad Randy had been found, but knowing him as he did, he was probably disappointed he hadn't been the hero of the day.

Seeing the look directed his way from his father, Hunter quickly reiterated, "I mean… good, yah found him!"

Mason guffawed at his best friend's discomfort, earning him a glare from that same friend that should have knocked him down from its intensity, but only made him laugh harder.

The other two occupants of the bed came awake. How could they not with so much noise? Looking up from the bed, Donna smiled at her dad. "Morning."

"Morning," he answered back, then looked at Randy. "Well, young man, you sure managed to add more gray hair to my head."

Randy looked down, properly chastised, again.

"Well, come on," Hunter said, heading for the door. "It's the Fourth of July, we're expecting guests, and I can hardly wait to shoot off the big one." He was referring to tonight's finale to the planned fireworks display.

Donna's eyes widened. The anxieties she had over Randy's disappearance had caused her to forget the date. She jumped off the bed, ready to follow her brother like an enthusiastic child on Christmas morning, but remembered where she was and who she spent the night with, and stopped. Turning to the bed, she gave Jake and Randy a bright smile. "Come on, you two! I want real food, a shower, and a change of clothes before the Lafayettes arrive."

She glanced at Mason and lowered her voice. She asked, "How are you feeling, Mason?"

He smiled. "I have mizzed my parentz."

SPITFIRE

He had said "parents," plural, and Donna gave him a gentle hug. Obviously, he was ready to accept the fact that Charles was his father in the truest sense of the word.

Almost eight hours later, a small twin-engine plane circled the sky above the ranch, making its final approach. Jake watched, curious as a cat. Sure, he had known for months that Mason's parents were due to arrive. However, with the security around here having been almost tripled seemingly overnight, he couldn't help but wonder just exactly who these people were.

He glanced at Donna; her face was aglow as she watched the plane expectantly. He had to know. "Okay, so I'll bite. Why is there so much security for the Lafayettes?"

Donna looked at him, puzzlement on her face. "You don't know who they are?"

"Other than Mason's folks?" He shook his head. "Nope, don't have a clue, so why all the security?"

"To keep the paparazzi out. We never know if one has found out where they are and will try to sneak a picture or two."

"Oh, well, that explains it," his sarcasm was thick; he was more baffled than before.

"They're landing!" she cried, cutting off whatever he would have asked next.

The excitement and joy coursing through each member of the Fisher clan was palpable. Jake watched the private aircraft as it landed and taxied to a stop on the ranch's small airfield.

A flash of yellow caught Jake's attention: it was Travis's Trans-Am coming up the road to the airstrip. The fact that

J.R. Zimmer

Travis seemed to feel comfortable enough to be here reminded Jake that Donna had not officially broken up with him yet.

There was going to be a confrontation, and for Donna's sake, he hoped Travis would give her up without raising too much argument.

For the time being, Jake dismissed the guy. Nothing could be done at the moment. The guests were exiting the plane. The first one out, after the pilot, was a five-year-old girl whose raven black hair was the longest Jake had ever seen on one so young; it was past her knees. The petite child raced from the plane and straight into Mason's arms, all the while crying and saying, "Frère, frère!" which Jake would learn later meant brother.

The next person out, Jake assumed, was Charles Lafayette. Nothing about the man jogged Jake's mind for a reason for the hush-hush operation going on here today. As he watched, Mason set the small child down and looked at the man. There seemed to be a moment of hesitance in both of them, but when the older man opened his arms, Mason cried out and rushed into the embrace.

They both appeared to be crying.

Jake felt a lump form in his throat. He was sure this was Mason's father and had a quick moment to wish his own father had loved him enough to shelter him from Clair. But he would put his past behind him. Somehow or other, he knew that by having found this ranch, he had found his salvation.

Then, Rosalinda Lafayette descended from the plane, aided by her husband, and Jake felt his mouth drop open. He now

knew exactly what Donna meant about paparazzi lurking in the bushes.

He could only stare, knowing it was rude, but he couldn't help himself. He didn't know the woman personally, but he was familiar with who she was only because he watched movies. This woman was hailed as one of the best actresses France offered the world. To that nation's people, she was royalty, and breathtakingly beautiful.

"Stop your drooling, Harper," Hunter's tone as he came up beside him was teasing.

Jake snapped his mouth shut. "I wasn't drooling, just surprised to find out exactly who the mystery guest was."

Hunter chuckled. "Hey, I know how you feel about my sister. I just couldn't resist." Then he caught sight of Travis walking toward them, and his smile disappeared. Under his breath, he mumbled, "Figured he'd show up eventually."

Jake watched in fascination as Hunter's entire demeanor changed before him, and the younger man gushed, "Hi buddy!"

"Hi yourself, sport." Travis glanced at Jake, startled to see him there. "Harper." His tone was curt and tense.

"Carlson." Jake's reply was just as brusque.

Hunter found the sight of the two rivals sizing each other up funnier than any comedy. This day was turning into the best one of his life, and when Donna came into the group, it was all he could do not to split a gut laughing. His sister looked profoundly uncomfortable, and he couldn't wait for these fireworks to begin.

Travis looked at Donna, giving her a lazy smile. "Hey, baby. Sorry I've been absent. I was kind of tied up." He gave Jake one last glare before stepping toward Donna, intent on giving her a kiss, but she smoothly took a step to the side, positioning herself closer to Jake.

"Travis," she told him softly, "we need to talk."

His eyes narrowed. "About what?" he snapped, already suspecting the worst, his body tensing with the knowledge.

Jake reached out and pulled Donna close, possessively. "Travis, Donna isn't interested in you anymore, and you can get lost."

Donna groaned internally. As accurate as the statement was, she had not expected the explanation to be quite so blunt.

Travis's face turned livid; curses spat from his mouth. "You son-of-a-bitch!" He pulled his arm back, intent on punching Jake in the face, but his fist was caught before he had launched it halfway.

His eyes widened in surprise, looking at Hunter, who held onto his fist, preventing it from going farther. The kid had been quick; faster than Travis would have thought.

"Ah, ah, ah," Hunter grinned, grasping the fist in a hold that felt like a vise. "I can't let you do that, buddy. You know, seeing how you're a black belt and all, and Harper isn't, it just wouldn't be a fair fight." He released his grip. "Besides, I like Harper. You? You're a dick."

"Now, just one minute!" Travis all but screamed, shocked beyond belief, not only by Hunter's sudden about-face but also by the fact Donna would dare throw him over for someone else. Sure, he had known there was something going on

between them, but had he honestly expected she would dump him? Girls just didn't do that to him!

"She's my girlfriend! You think I'm going to just walk away and tell him," he jerked his finger toward Jake, "'Hey, congratulations, the best man won!'"

Hunter shrugged easily. "Works for me."

Jake chuckled, enjoying the kid's style.

Donna finally found her voice. "Travis, I'm sorry if I hurt you…"

"You. Have. No. Idea!" The shock and disbelief in his eyes might have torn at her heart had he not dug the hole deeper for himself by adding, "He's supposed to be in jail!"

Out of the group standing there, two people gasped at that revelation. But Hunter smiled and said, "You're such a dork. I figured you would have held out for at least ten minutes instead of five." This brought the attention of the other two back to him, and the look on their faces was dumbfoundedness.

By now, a small crowd had gathered, wondering what was transpiring.

"Travis," Colten was thrilled beyond measure to say, "I think it's time you leave."

"The hell I will! This is the biggest joke! I've had Donna for months, then Mister Cowboy rides in, and then bang, I'm not good enough!" He looked around, spotted Rosalinda, remembered the other reason he was there, and a mental image of a million dollars going up in flames flashed through his mind, making him angrier, if that were possible.

"Damn it!"

Jacqueline figured it was time to take the guests to the house. "Perhaps we should head to the ranch." She looked at Rosalinda, who had a faint, amused smile on her face.

"Oui," Rosalinda agreed, "although deez eez entertaining." But she picked up her petite five-year-old daughter, Daniela, while Jacqueline grabbed the hands of Wyatt and Rebecca, with Melisa following behind them as they headed toward the vehicle they would use to drive back to the ranch.

Colten, Cadman, Hunter, Mason, and Charles remained behind, and it was Colten who got back to the statement Travis made earlier. "How do you know Jake was in jail?"

All eyes swung to Travis. Hunter seemed expectant as he jumped in, "Yeah, buddy. Why don't you tell us why you thought Jake would be in jail? It hasn't been in the papers, though perhaps a friend of yours, who just happens to have a truck like Jake's, might be able to tell us. But since he's now the one in jail…"

Donna gasped, staggered by the implication that Travis set Jake up. She'd never suspected he was capable of such underhandedness.

"Travis, is that true!?"

Backed into the corner as he was, Travis was not about to say another word. "Ah, hell," he mumbled, turning around and began heading for his car.

Hunter was seeing all his weeks of pretending to like the guy go down the drain. "Hey, wait!" He ran after him. "You promised me you'd spar with me one day."

Travis stopped walking when he reached his car. "Are you kidding? As mad as I am, I'd likely pulverize you."

"You can certainly try. I'll even give you the first punch."

Travis sighed dramatically, unable to believe the kid was that suicidal.

Just to egg him on, Hunter said, "Unless you're not so good yourself."

"Damn it, kid. I hold a second-degree dan."

Hunter's eyes widened with enthusiasm. "Seriously?!" If it were true... Oh, joy! Perhaps an actual competition for a change! Lord knew he didn't bother with the local tournaments because they lacked the skill level he possessed.

Travis made a frustrated snort. He had never seen the like. "Forget it, kid." He opened his car door, but found Hunter blocking his way.

"Hey, I'll tell you what," Hunter bargained, "If you're too afraid you might get hurt, we can do some other competition. If I win, the sheriff gets to arrest you, and you won't put up a fuss." He jerked his head to the left, and Travis followed the move, which allowed him to witness the sheriff just now stepping out of the cruiser.

Travis gritted his teeth. "And if I win, I get to go free?"

Hunter hooted. "Yeah, right. As if." He looked to Mason, who was close at hand because the others had followed them to Travis's car. "The envelope, please." Mason reached into his back pocket for an envelope that looked suspiciously like the one belonging to Travis, containing the photos and negatives he had been planning to sell to his uncle.

Travis's eyes widened, and Hunter explained. "If you win, you can keep a couple of these, although Mason gets to choose which ones, seeing how they're photographs of him

in certain stages of, ah, well…" He cleared his throat. "Anyway, you know what they are. And as I was saying, if you win, you can sell a few of these, although you won't be spending the money until you're out of jail."

"What are you talking about, Hunter? Exactly what are those?" Donna asked, feeling sick inside.

Hunter glanced at Mason, who only shrugged. He wasn't ashamed of what those photos revealed. Everyone around here knew he liked sex.

"Well, sister dear," Hunter explained, "Nude photos is a good enough explanation. I just want to go on record by saying, if you didn't already have Jake there, and if not for the fact we all like him, I'd tell you to pick your boyfriends more carefully in the future."

"What's that supposed to mean?"

"I did some investigating while I was in Bismarck. While Uncle Cadman was talking to the local police about Carlson, I searched Travis's apartment…"

"You were in my apartment?!" Travis screeched. "That's against the law!"

Hunter held up the photos, the implication clear. Taking pictures of people through windows while they were unaware bordered on the criminal side. "As I was saying," he took a breath, "Uncle Cadman was able to find out that Travis has an uncle who would love to get his hands on these shots of Mason with some of the girls who've worked here this summer. And not because the guy has a thing for porn. It's only because his uncle happens to be Ralph Alcott."

Charles Lafayette was wide-eyed. "Mon Dieu! But that is the man who hounds my family continuously!"

Donna was stricken by shock. "You used me!" Her accusing eyes turned on Travis. "You son-of-a-bitch!"

"No!" Travis tried to plead. "Baby, it wasn't like that! When we met, I had no idea you knew these people! This is North Dakota; the odds are so astronomical they're mind-boggling."

"But you weren't going to pass up the opportunity to make a quick buck!" she snapped, vibrating with anger.

He'd already lost everything. "Why not?" he admitted, and shrugged.

"Oh!" Donna turned around, taking long strides toward the vehicle, she had arrived in. She was utterly done with looking at the swine. Over her shoulder, she tossed, "Hunter, deck him. I've had enough."

The grin on Hunter's face, and the gleam in his eye, told everyone he just received the present he'd been anticipating for a considerable amount of time.

But before Hunter could carry through with his sister's request, Jake took advantage of Travis's distraction and let his fist fly. The punch was solid; a direct hit to the jaw. It threw Travis backward, and he landed unconscious on the ground.

Chapter Thirty-three

The North Dakota night sky illuminated with the explosion of yet another sonic boom. Lights flickered across the Badlands as assorted colors flowered out high in the air, and with the mixed colors, "oohs" and "aahs" reverberated throughout the two families, tourists, and summer help enjoying the show. The firework display was one of the best the Fishers had ever held. Jake was inclined to think it was the best presentation given anywhere in the United States that night.

Glancing over at Randy, sitting on a blanket next to the one Donna and he shared, Jake smiled at the boy's open mouth as he took in the sights. The child had to be exhausted, it was half-past one in the morning, but he appeared bright-eyed and bushy-tailed. What Jake wouldn't give for the energy of youth right now, because he was ready to find his bed and call it a night. However, he wasn't looking forward to spending the night alone, thinking Donna would probably go with her parents to the main house when the time came. The thought made him pull her tighter to him, circling his arms around her chest and drawing her back against his side.

She laid her head back, and he rested his chin on the top of her head. "Are you getting tired?" he asked, nuzzling her neck for a moment.

"Yes," she sighed, placing her arms on top of his, feeling goosebumps as the warmth of his breath touched her neck.

SPITFIRE

"Do you think anyone will miss us if we sneak out of here?" His tongue touched her ear, causing her to groan, feeling desire rock through her despite her weary state.

"Randy," she was finally able to get out once Jake's assault to her ear ceased. "Randy will definitely miss you leaving him here. He's stuck to you like glue since his little adventure." She moved her head back a notch, eyes locking with Jake's. "He's wholly devoted to you, you know."

He leaned forward, touching his mouth to hers. "I know. I've been running some things in my head about the little scamp."

Donna's forehead furrowed in puzzlement. "Yeah, what sort of things?"

Another boom vibrated the earth.

Jake chuckled. "This isn't a good place to talk about it, and besides," he shrugged, "I want to check things out before I say anything more."

Another boom, and Jake sighed. "Isn't your brother and Mason ever going to quit?"

Donna giggled. "They'll run out of ammo, eventually."

"Suppose we could convince Randy to leave now?"

Donna's giggle turned into full laughter. "Jake, even if you could do that, if you leave now, before Hunter's through, he will hate you more than he does already."

Grimacing, Jake had to concede. He sincerely did not want to piss Hunter off any more than he already had. But how was he supposed to have known Hunter spent weeks setting Travis up; pretending not to be good at martial arts? When Jake punched Travis, it had been a mere reaction. The guy had

tried to set him up after all; he had been a victim of the creep's scheme. He almost faced another trial for a crime he had not committed. Travis using Donna as a means to get rich tipped the iceberg and had him seeing red. So, he'd sucker-punched him. Not especially sporting, he admitted that, but he hadn't thought about it at the time. He'd only reacted to Donna's distress.

He would never forget the look on Hunter's face when Travis lay there on the ground. The kid had stood there stupefied, staring at Travis as though he couldn't comprehend what happened. And then slowly, oh so slowly, Jake even now felt the twinges of fear running up his spine, Hunter's eyes moved to him. The look on Hunter's face should have turned him to stone.

The sound that escaped Hunter's mouth had been a gurgle. He was so enraged for having his only opportunity to show Travis just how good he was at martial arts taken away in the blink of an eye. Distinguishable words were impossible for him to form. Then he walked away, stomped actually, looking for something to vent his wrath on. The side of Travis's Trans-Am was the first to have felt his fury. With one punch, he shattered the driver's window, and a right kick dented the door.

Mason went into a fit of laughter, almost falling to the ground from the intensity of his amusement. In between fits of chortling, he tried to explain what set Hunter off.

Colten had sighed, saying, "No one goes near him for a week."

Fortunately, Hunter calmed down by dusk; at least to everyone else, he managed a civil tone. As for Jake, Hunter hadn't spoken to him since, though he mumbled something under his breath about wanting to shove one of the bottle rockets in a place of anatomy Jake had no intention of letting him near.

"Finally," Donna declared, bringing Jake back to the here and now. "We can all head to bed." She took one look at Randy and smiled. The child was about to fall asleep sitting up.

"I'll carry him to the house," Jake stood, scooped Randy up while Donna gathered the blankets, and headed for that direction along with the others doing the same. Within a short time, he helped Donna dress Randy in his Teenage Mutant Ninja Turtles pajamas and tuck him into bed. The child was sound asleep before they finished placing the covers around him.

They watched him for a time. Donna stole a glance at Jake, and the love she saw on his face, directed at this boy who held a special place in her own heart, was staggering and warmed her to her toes. "He's a special boy," she whispered, once again scanning Randy's little face.

"Yes," Jake's voice was soft, full of choking emotion. Then he turned to her, reached out his arm, and placed it around her waist, winding her into his side as he moved toward the door. "So, Miss Donna," he drawled, "Shall I tuck you in?"

Her laugh was interrupted by a yawn. "Not tonight, cowboy."

He smiled, kissed her gently, then went down the stairs and out the door. He wasn't disappointed with her refusal; he was

ready to drop from exhaustion himself. Besides, if things worked out the way he envisioned, he would have a lifetime of tucking her in. Who would have thought he would come to love the little Spitfire so much? But he did; there was no denying that.

As he passed through the hall, he heard goodnights spoken to him from Jacqueline and Rosalinda. He raised his hand, giving an acknowledging wave, and headed out the door. Just as he reached the bunkhouse, he saw Hunter and Mason on their way to the main house. It was Hunter's haunting, "Pleasant dreams," as they passed each other, that caused the hairs on the back of Jake's neck to rise and kept him awake until dawn.

Chapter Thirty-four

Watching the antics of Melissa, Wyatt, Rebecca, as well as Mason's sister, Daniela, splashing in the pool, Jacqueline and Rosalinda laughed, enjoying the warm day and the deep friendship that had lasted since they themselves were small children.

"They do get along well," Jacqueline said, easily slipping into her native French.

Rosalinda reached for the glass of lemonade resting on the small poolside table and took a sip before agreeing. "Perhaps our children will remain good friends when they are adults," She smiled warmly at Jacqueline. "It is my hope."

"Mine too." Jacqueline reached across the small space, squeezing Rosalinda's hand, broaching the subject they hadn't talked about in the past year. "Mason seems to have come to terms with his parentage."

A slight look of pain crossed Rosalinda's delicate features briefly, then it was gone. "If there had been any way to keep the truth from Mason, I would have. He has such a good heart; I knew he would be devastated. But there was not any choice. Not when Mason resembles Pierre so much; he is becoming a mirror image of that vile man."

She shook her head, squeezed her eyes shut, and thanked her goddess that at least Mason's hair was black and he had inherited her green eyes. If not for that, she was loath to admit to herself, almost every time she saw him, she was in danger of slipping back and reliving the nightmare she had endured. But her love for Mason was undeniable.

"It was only a matter of time before people began to talk, if they hadn't done so already. And so, I came forward with what was done to me, although I did not share details. They are not necessary. But perhaps by coming forward with the truth, someone else who has been violated will find strength in my story."

Jacqueline reached over, squeezed her friend's hand. "You are the strongest woman I know," she whispered.

Because Rosalinda was behind the privacy fence, safe from prying eyes, and comfortable with only this family seeing the scars that riddled her arms and legs, she had chosen to wear a one-piece bathing suit today while the children played and the women soaked up the sun.

The scar on her face, a 'C' pattern that went from the corner of her left eye, traced along her jaw, and ended at the chin, was no longer as noticeable as it had first been. Now, void of make-up, people could only see it if they were looking hard enough.

In public, Rosalinda never went anywhere without make-up, and only dressed in shirts with long sleeves, and wore slacks or long skirts to hide the imperfections on her legs. When she was in front of a camera, filming one of her husband's movies, the creative director was able to use lighting to shadow what his wife wanted to hide.

One trusted make-up artist was allowed to help Rosalinda use specialized products to cover the scars on her arms whenever necessary. The woman was in the process of developing a product that would give better coverage. Perhaps one day,

SPITFIRE

the starlet would be able to wear shorter sleeves in public for a change.

"How are things in France? You were afraid this would ruin your career."

Rosalinda chuckled and shrugged. "My fans hail me a saint! Such courage, they say, for coming forward. They all look forward to Mason's return so they can embrace him. You know the people have always thought of my children as their personal property, and now they wish to shower him with more attention than ever before." She sighed dramatically. Mason needed more attention like he needed a hole in his head.

Rosalinda felt moisture form behind her eyes. "I have missed him so much this past year, and Charles's heart was broken. He was the one who encouraged me to give birth when it was discovered I was pregnant. He loves Mason with every beat of his heart."

Jacqueline squeezed her hand once more, letting her know she hoped Mason would accept Charles once again as his father.

"Well, we're going to miss him around here. He's been a big help to the ranch. He's even helped Donna with Horse Adventures."

"It is good he has learned to work hard."

They fell into a companionable silence, once again placing their attention on the children. It wasn't long before they were joined by their husbands; both men were in their swimming suits, and neither one of them hesitated to jump in the pool.

They did so with terrific splashes, bringing squeals of delight from the youngsters.

Daniela screeched and jumped at Wyatt. It appeared as though she was about to wring his neck. "Looks as though your daughter didn't get her way in something," Jacqueline observed, not with condemnation, but with amusement. Daniela Lafayette reminded Jacqueline so much of what Hunter had been like as a child that it brought forth the giggles. Rosalinda had always expressed exasperation back then at Hunter's temper, but she wasn't laughing now; the shoe was on the other foot.

Rosalinda sighed; she deserved that dig. She honestly did, which was why she didn't take offense. It was time to take Daniela into the house anyway. After last night, the child needed a nap, no matter the fact that the girl would protest. Tomorrow, all of them would be going on a two-day campout. Rosalinda wanted to make sure her daughter rested up before adding more lack of sleep to the already cranky child.

Chapter Thirty-four

One month later

Jake baited the hook with what Donna assumed was some tasty bribe for a fish, placed the pole in Randy's hand, and helped him pull back and cast forward. The hook landed with a plunk, one foot away.

"Let's try again," Jake chuckled, reeling the line back in and repeating the process. Six more tries, and they'd conquered ground; two more feet. But Jake didn't give up until he was satisfied the bait managed to get out an adequate amount. He then helped Randy settle into the folding chair to watch the bobber, while he joined Donna on the blanket spread far enough away, but still close enough in case Randy somehow managed to lure a fish.

Donna handed Jake a sandwich as he sat down. "Nice cast," she grinned.

Jake returned the grin around a mouth full of sandwich. "We thought so." He swallowed the bite he had taken and said, "The kid needs more practice, that's all."

"Sure, he does," she agreed wholeheartedly. "Unfortunately, none of the foster homes he's been in have taken him on a fishing excursion."

He nodded, took another bite, and studied Randy as he finished chewing. "Yeah, I've been thinkin' about that. What he needs is a dad."

Donna froze for a heartbeat, wondering... "There aren't many guys lining up for that job."

He looked at her, a twinkle in his eye. "I figure that. And it's why I shouldn't have any trouble gettin' to the front of the line."

Her eyes widened. "You mean… You want to… Do you think? Oh, my God!" She threw her arms around him. "Do you think the courts will let you adopt him?"

Jake laughed. "I don't know why not. Your uncle Cadman tells me the time I spent in prison has been removed from my record, which I should never have had in the first place. The recent stay in jail isn't going to amount to anything either, since that too was a farce. I'm clean, and I'm planning on finding a lawyer who will help me get the adoption through quickly. Might as well use some of that money that became mine when I turned eighteen. I want to adopt the little squirt before someone else discovers what a great kid he is."

She couldn't help herself; she kissed him long and hard.

He wrapped his arms around her, smiling that lazy smile of his and said, "I should have told you that a long time ago." Then he braved the next thing on his mind and told her, "I was also thinkin' he needs a mom."

She stared at him for the longest time. Her mind hadn't quite grasped the implication of that statement, and she frowned, wondering what that was supposed to mean.

Jake smiled at her confusion. "You got a fish on that hook yet, squirt?" he called over his shoulder.

Randy managed to look their way. "Ooow?" he asked.

Jake chuckled. "Yep, now."

Randy squealed and made a big show. "Eees! I ave a iish ooon my hoooook."

SPITFIRE

Donna shook her head. "He can't possibly have a fish on his line already."

Jake removed his hat, stretched out on his back, and placed the head covering over his face. "Why don't you go find out if he does or not while I take a nap?"

With a sigh of resignation, Donna stood up and walked the short distance to where Randy sat. Eyeing the bobber, she called out, "Well, if there was a fish, it's not there now."

"I'd still check the line. It could just be playin' possum." Jake's voice was muffled through the hat.

"I doubt that."

"Just check it anyway!" he growled.

With a deep sigh, Donna took the pole from Randy and reeled it in. "Nope, no fish. See?" She was just moving her hand down to grasp the end of the line when the sun reflected off something on the string where the hook and bait would have been. Gasping, she took it in her hand and looked up, eyes wide.

"Airy us!" Randy exclaimed.

Her eyes flew to the child. "What!?" Surely, she hadn't understood. Randy had difficulty speaking, after all.

"He said," Jake was there now, reaching for her and touching her mouth with a whisper-soft kiss, "Marry us."

She stared, stunned.

Jake chuckled. "You want me to do this the hard way, eh? And here I thought tying that ring to the fishing line was sort of romantic. But alright, you asked for it." He moved down to one knee before her. "Would you marry me, Miss Donna?"

"Nnnd me!" Randy chimed in.

Oh yeah, and Randy too. He'll be wanting a mom, you know."

Donna screeched, did a jig, and literally threw herself at Jake, knocking him back. He landed hard, the air almost knocked from his lungs, and he found breathing difficult since Donna was now lying on top of him, pressing against his chest. "Is—this—a—yes?" he managed to gasp out.

She was too choked up to speak. Her head bobbed up and down.

Jake shifted her weight just enough so he could breathe again and looked at Randy. "Hot damn, squirt, I do believe she said yes."

Determined not to be left out of this entertaining display, Randy got himself off the chair and took three steps before he was on the ground with them, laughing with joy.

* * * *

Almost a year later, to the exact day of Jake's proposal, they were married on a Sunday evening on the front lawn of the Château de Mores in Medora, North Dakota.

They obtained special permission from the State of North Dakota, who had been in possession of the building since the de Mores family donated it in 1936. Because of the Fisher family's connection to the de Mores's, and along with a sizable donation, the state was willing to oblige them their special day.

SPITFIRE

Security was tighter than usual as many prominent persons from the area were invited to the wedding, as were the Lafayettes.

Donna wore a tea-length white western-style dress with white cowboy boots. Her white cowboy hat had a veil attached to it. Jake sported black Levi jeans, a short-sleeved white button-down shirt under a black frock coat, and a black Stetson topped his head. Randy, as the best man, was dressed almost identically to his new father.

The reception was held at the F&L. Guests danced to the music provided by the live country band, and because it was a famous band, no one was anxious to leave the free concert they had been given, staying until the musicians themselves deemed it time to rest.

The wedding couple left the party long before the festivities were through. Randy would stay with his new grandparents, and Jacqueline and Colten were pleased to have him while the newlyweds flew to Hawaii for their honeymoon.

On their first night in their hotel, in bed and snuggling close, Donna rested her head on Jake's chest, stroking her hand lazily through his chest hair. She smiled to herself as a memory returned. "Jake, do you remember that night I pounded on your door when you'd been in the middle of a shower?"

His chest vibrated with his chuckle. "Oh yeah." He would never forget that moment.

"Well…" she leaned up to look at him. "There's something I've always wanted to know." At his raised brow, she asked, "Had you been wearing a towel, or not?"

He grinned up at her. "Spitfire, I'm going to keep that to myself until our fiftieth wedding anniversary. It will keep you guessing. But I can tell you this," he reached for her, rolled her onto her back and moved on top of her. He kissed her lazily, then nuzzled her neck. "I'm not wearing one now."

Fisher/Lafayette Saga

If There Hadn't Been You

Now and Forever

Someone Like You

Spitfire

Something Magical

Coming Home(This is a free Ebook when signing up for my newsletter at www.jrzimmer.com. Not available anywhere else.)

The Dreamer

Eagle's Wolf

Keep reading for a sneak peek of Something Magical!

You can find J.R. Zimmer at:

Web site: www.jrzimmer.com

Email: jrzimmer17@yahoo.com

https://www.facebook.com/jrzimmer.author

Something Magical

by J.R. Zimmer

Chapter one

)⊗(

July 1986

Early Monday morning Tabitha Turner all but stormed into her clinic's waiting room and past the reception desk.

The office manager looked up from the computer she was imputing information into, saw the look on Tabitha's face, and winced. In her six years with this veterinarian clinic, she had faced plenty of angry animals, but she got the feeling she would rather face a Rottweiler with rabies than the clinic's owner and valued veterinarian at this moment.

Tabitha had never shown a temper before, but something had brought it out.

"Umm," Grace was hesitant to say more as she watched Tabitha move behind the desk. Watched as she grabbed the chart with the list of morning appointments, then slam the clipboard back down without looking at it. "May I ask what's wrong?"

"I am so angry!"

Duh, Grace thought, but would not say it out loud. "Forgive me for saying this, Tabitha, but I understood that from your growl when you opened the front door."

Tabitha stared at her for a moment. "I'm sorry, Grace." She took a long breath, blew it out. "I'm not being very professional, am I? It has nothing to do with this place."

"I cannot imagine your adorable little girl caused your upset."

1

"No, she's happy as a clam because it's Monday, and she gets to spend the day with both of my parents, not just my mom. Who knows what they'll do today to spoil her?" she chuckled because she knew her parents enjoyed doting on their only grandchild.

"Then what's up? Unless you want me to bug off and tell me it's none of my business?"

With a sigh, Tabitha sat down in the chair next to Grace. "You know that empty land on the north side of town I want to buy?"

"The one you have been holding fundraisers for and want to turn into a dog sanctuary?"

Tabitha nodded. "I went to the bank this morning. I have raised enough funds over the past two years for them to take me seriously when I ask for the loan I want, so I could purchase those twenty acres. But guess what? Suddenly some development company called Badlander Builders bought it! That land has been sitting there for years! No one's made any noise about wanting it and now, poof," she snapped her fingers, "some damn construction company buys it."

"What are they going to put there?"

"The bank said the company has no intent on developing it yet, but they sure as hell had the money to squander on it." She took another deep breath, blew it out. "I just want to kick something."

Grace held up her hands. "Aim your foot away from me if you decide to follow through with that desire."

Tabitha blinked. Then a slight smile tugged at the corners of her mouth. "I'll be sure to find a wall that can withstand the impact. And thanks. I needed that small amount of humor."

"I wasn't joking. I don't like pain."

The statement caused both women to laugh.

After a moment, Grace told her, "I'm sorry that happened, Tabitha. I know what that project means to you. And I am not making light of things when I say, you'll find another area."

"Maybe. But I've had my eyes set on that land for so long it's hard to imagine any place else." Her shoulders slumped. "With the way my luck is going today, I'll probably get a call from Mason Lafayette's agency, and they will deny my request to have him be part of this year's fundraiser. You know darn well girls from miles away would have purchased tickets for the chance to have a date with that twenty-one-year-old model."

Grace shook her head as she chuckled. "I can't believe you reached out to his agency. The odds of them saying yes is astronomical, but if by some miracle you do get him here, I will probably buy more than my fair share of tickets too so I'll have a chance to go out to dinner with him."

Tabitha blinked. "You're fifty-five years old! Good lord, you could be his mother!"

"Well, I'm not his mother. And I have seen those ads for Touch My Bod Jeans." She used a hand as though it were a fan as she let out a dreamy sigh. "That boy is mighty delicious."

"I cannot believe you said that."

"And you cannot tell me you don't think he's to die for. Why else would you have even considered trying to get him for your fundraiser?"

"He's attractive, women swoon over him, and I would have probably raised more money this year than I have in the past two combined. That is the only reason I was trying to arrange for him to participate. I certainly do not think of him in any way that involves a bed."

Grace clucked her tongue. "I said nothing about trying to entice the boy into my bed."

Tabitha sighed. "It doesn't matter. I know it was a long shot. I'll just have to come up with some other scheme."

"His agency hasn't answered your request yet. Don't give up hope before the battle begins."

"I know. But after hearing the bank tell me the land I wanted is no longer available kind of gave my optimism a setback." She leaned back in the chair, feeling defeated. "I have wanted to do this for Owen for so long it almost feels as though my heart is breaking all over again."

Reaching for Tabitha's hand, Grace gave it a light squeeze. "I know, honey. I know what it means to you. I admire you so much for all you have accomplished since Owen died. You are the strongest woman I know."

Tabitha shook her head, tried not to allow the tears forming behind her eyes to surface. She no longer grieved over Owen's death, though he would always hold a special place in her heart. She was finally moving forward with her life, but the tears were from frustration. Building that shelter in honor of Owen's memory meant the world to her.

"I sometimes don't feel all that strong." She grabbed a tissue from the box sitting on Grace's desk, dabbed at her eyes to remove any traces of moisture that may have slipped past her lashes. "If it weren't for you and Greta, I would have lost this place. You will never know how deeply I appreciate everything the two of you accomplished that first year, and the ones after that. And my parents, for giving up their life to move here and help me out. They sold everything, including their diner in Clarion, Pennsylvania, because they love me that much. I know I would have been more of a mess than I was if it hadn't been for all of you banning together. You guys helped me make it through. That is the only strength I have."

Grace reached out, patted Tabitha's knee. "You know, Greta and I had no choice. Our jobs were at stake, and we happen to like it here." She grinned.

Tabitha's lips twitched. Greta and Grace, having applied for jobs here all those years ago, was a blessing from the goddess she could never repay.

"And your parents are amazing," Grace continued. "Your dad has some honest to God skills in the kitchen. It was great he got hired at Robbie's Family Diner right away when they moved here. That place sure as hell needed your dad's talent. I'm surprised your dad didn't want to open his own place here."

"Dad's fifty-one and not interested in trying to start over. But thank you for the compliment, I'll pass it along to him when I see him tonight."

Squaring her shoulders, knowing she needed to focus on the here and now and not the past, she stood back up. "Okay, I need to get my head into today's game. Who's my first patient?" Tabitha reached for the clipboard she had carelessly slammed down earlier.

"Bubbles McGillicuddy."

Pinching the bridge of her nose, Tabitha shook her head. "Of course, it would be Mrs. McGillicuddy and Bubbles. After discovering my dream was pulled out from underneath me, I shouldn't have expected anything easy." She looked at Grace, chuckled as she said, "Remember the first time that woman brought Bubbles in?"

Grace nodded. "It's hard to forget when an owner makes a frantic call to say they found lumps on their cat's belly, and they need an emergency appointment."

"It wasn't easy not to laugh when I explained to her that those lumps were the cat's nipples. Seriously, how can you be a pet owner and not know animals have nipples?"

"You've been a veterinarian for almost six years, four of which you have practiced at this clinic, and you are just now coming to the conclusion that a lot of pet owners are clueless?"

"Oh, no. I've known that since I was a little girl and collected strays. Each time I brought an animal home, I'm sure my mom and dad wanted to wring my neck." She grinned, knowing her parents never laid a finger on her in frustration because of their only child's habit of stuffing their garage full of animals she wanted to care for. "And knowing people are idiots was the reason I wanted to build a dog sanctuary. I know I can't save them all, but damn it. I wanted to do what I could for those poor things whose worthless owners dump them off somewhere when they don't want them anymore."

She ran her hands through her shoulder-length blond highlighted brunette hair. "Who in their right mind would name their company Badlander Builders? The name implies they build bad land. Why would anyone want to hire them?"

Grace blinked, though not surprised Tabitha had brought the land back up again. "They must be new to the area. I have never heard of them."

"Well, I would sure like to give them a piece of my mind for having stolen that land from me!"

"Umm, technically, they didn't steal it."

Tabitha narrowed her eyes. "Whose side are you on?"

Shaking her head, Grace turned her attention back to the computer at her desk and began working on a few bills owed to the clinic. "I was only pointing out the fact the land was for sale. I'm sorry they beat you to it, but they purchased it fair and square."

"Boy, you sure are playing the devil's advocate."

Grace finished with the invoice she was working on, began another. "Speaking of which, do you have a sitter for Wednesday night?"

"Fortunately, Greg and Kathy are in town for a few days and want to spend time with their granddaughter. In fact, they're having a sleepover Wednesday night, and they will drop Abby off at my parents on their way out-of-town Thursday sometime."

"Oh boy, Greg and Kathy want to spend time with Abby for a change. I cannot believe you allow them the privilege, especially because of the way they treat you."

Tabitha shrugged. "It's for one night. Who knows when they'll decide to come back? Abby is their granddaughter, and I will not deny her the little bit of time they want to give her."

Grace harrumphed. "You're a lot more forgiving than I am. After the hell they put you through when Owen died-"

Raising a hand, Tabitha cut her off. "Again, I no longer care what they think about me. It is unfortunate they have chosen to have little to nothing to do with Abby, but she can never say I didn't let her see them when she is older. She will know it was narrowmindedness on their part just because of their actions."

"Then, you're going to *Mindy's Over Yonder* with us since you, for a change, will not have mommy duty."

The bell over the door rang, signaling someone entered the lobby.

"Good morning, Mrs. McGillicuddy," Grace greeted the older woman. "You're a bit early…."

"Bubbles is pregnant!" the woman announced, setting the cat carrier onto the counter with a bang.

Tabitha shook her head. "Mrs. McGillicuddy, Bubbles cannot possibly be pregnant. She's spayed. We did that last year. Remember?"

"She sure looks pregnant."

Motioning for the woman to follow her, Tabitha led Mrs. McGillicuddy towards an examining room. "We'll do some blood tests and labs to be on the safe side, but I assure you, Bubbles is not pregnant."

"She had better not be! You charged me plenty for that procedure!"

Tabitha glanced over the woman's shoulder, met Grace's eyes, which conveyed the message, here we go again.

"Mrs. McGillicuddy, I did the procedure myself. Bubbles in no way can be pregnant." Tabitha opened the door to the examining room.

The older woman placed the cat carrier onto the examination table and opened the front grate to allow the cat out. Not that Bubbles had any desire to exit the container willingly. She was already hissing at the prospects of this visit.

Tabitha wished her assistant were here because this cat would not come out of that crate without the use of gloves or getting it wrapped in a towel to prevent it from scratching and biting. But Tabitha tried a soothing voice, regardless of knowing it would not do any good. "Come on out, Bubbles, so I can take a look at you."

Hiss.

Sigh.

"Have you allowed Bubbles outside recently?" Tabitha asked the pet's owner.

"Certainly not! I would never allow my Bubbles out of the house! She could get hurt!"

"Did you get another cat? A male, to be precise."

"What?" Mrs. McGillicuddy looked into the carrier, cooed, "Bubbles is the best cat in the world. I would never think of causing her stress. She might become jealous if another cat were in the house."

"Then, how in the world could she possibly be pregnant?"

Mrs. McGillicuddy stared at her. "How should I know?! You're the doctor!"

Tabitha looked up at the ceiling, counted to ten. The woman was beyond ridiculous.

"One moment," Tabitha told her. "I'm going to see if Greta has arrived yet so she can assist me with Bubbles." She stepped out of the room before Mrs. McGillicuddy could answer.

Grace looked up from the computer when she saw Tabitha heading her way. "How's the patient?"

"I'm sure Bubble's is fine. Her owner, on the other hand, always leaves me speechless. My patience left me about three minutes ago. Please tell me Greta's here."

Grace pointed over her shoulder toward the back of the clinic. "She came in the moment you closed the door to the exam room. I believe she's hiding as I told her who was with you in the room."

"I don't blame her one bit, but I need her. Please tell her to bring the gloves so we can look at Bubbles. That cat will not cooperate, and I need to examine her regardless of suspecting it's a phantom pregnancy."

"You're a saint, Tabitha," Grace told her, pushing away from the desk and standing up. "I don't know how you maintain your cool with that woman."

Tabitha grinned. "Trust me, Grace. In my head, I've kicked her in the knee several times."

Laughing, Grace moved toward the back room to tell Greta to prepare for battle while Tabitha walked back to the examination room.

Fisher/Lafayette Saga

If There Hadn't Been You

Now and Forever

Someone Like You

Spitfire

Something Magical

Coming Home (Free Ebook when signing up for my newsletter at www.jrzimmer.com. Not available anywhere else.)

The Dreamer

Eagle's Wolf